# THE PATRIOT OATH

LLOYD LOFTHOUSE

THREE CLOVER PRESS

Published in the United States of America

Cover, editing and launch promotion
by Imbue Editing
https://imbueediting.com/

Three Clover Press
Pittsburg, California 94565

*This novel is dedicated to everyone that has taken the Oath to defend the U.S. Constitution and meant it.*

*On April 30, 1789, when George Washington became the first president of the United States, after being received by Congress, he stepped from the chamber onto the balcony, where he was followed by the Senators and Representatives. Before the assembled crowd of spectators, Robert Livingston, Chancellor of the State of New York, administered the oath of office prescribed by the Constitution: "I do solemnly swear that I will faithfully execute the office of President of the United States, and will, to the best of my ability, preserve, protect, and defend the Constitution of the United States."*

*Later, George Washington wrote James Madison, "As the first of every thing, in our situation will serve to establish a Precedent, it is devoutly wished on my part, that these precedents may be fixed on true principles."*

*Since George Washington took that oath, every new Federal employee, including the President, is required by law to take an oath to support and defend the Constitution. The Oath of Office is administered on their first day of employment. Today, this is the oath officers in the U.S. military take: "I ___, do solemnly swear (or affirm) that I will support and defend the Constitution of the United States against all enemies, foreign and domestic; that I will bear true faith and allegiance to the same; that I take this obligation freely, without any mental reservation or purpose of evasion; and that I will well and faithfully discharge the duties of the office on which I am about to enter. So help me God."*

# CHAPTER 1

THE LAST TIME Josh Kavanagh saw his little sister, Susan, was in 1994, and she was three years old. Now it was the summer of 2018, and she was 27—and a rape victim.

When he'd left home for the Marine Corps Recruit Depot in San Diego, she'd thrown a tantrum, demanding he stay. The only image he remembered of that day was her tears, red eyes, and swollen face. She had repeated the same two words in her childish voice that followed him through the years like a dark shadow. "Don't die!" she'd said.

Well, he hadn't died. He'd come damn close, though, more than once.

Susan hadn't made it easy for him to leave, but growing up on his family's ranch had been hard, and he'd resented it. The day before he left, his parents had ordered him to stay. Since he defied them, Josh suspected they had banished his name from the dinner table. He wouldn't be surprised if his only sister forgot she had an older, third brother.

Now, he was returning home to Montana for the first time in twenty-four years.

A few months earlier, Josh had learned through a trusted friend that his little sister had been raped. The attacker's family was wealthy and had used their power to corrupt justice. Josh decided it was time to return home, retiring early. Susan needed her family more than ever, and he was her brother.

Without a car, he'd spent hours sprawled on the back seat of a Greyhound bus from Denver, Colorado, to Billings, Montana. From there, he'd hitched a ride with an eighteen-wheeler that dropped him at Great Falls. With his duffle bag slung over his shoulder, he'd then hitchhiked along Route 87 and caught rides that carried him to Stanford, where his brother Samuel waited to give him a ride home.

When he climbed down from the eighteen-wheeler's cab, he spotted his grandfather's familiar 1942, faded-blue Chevy pick-up parked on the far side of the gravel lot. Josh expected that it still ran like a Swiss watch.

"How is she, Sammy?" Josh asked his middle brother, who was leaning on the pickup's hood, watching him approach. As kids, Samuel had always preferred to be called Sam or Sammy.

Sammy was all smiles as he tapped the hood with the tip of an index finger. "This old, sexy Chevy keeps on running.I've been rebuilding it, and it's as dependable as the Energizer Bunny. Grandpa would be proud if he was alive."

"I'm not talking about the fucking pickup," Josh said. With one arm, he easily tossed his eighty-pound duffel in the open bed of the truck and slid onto the cab's worn passenger seat.

"I'm hungry," Sammy said. "Let's eat at Dauna's Deli before the drive home."

Sammy had a Rueben. Josh ordered a French dip, and every bite of the sandwich dredged up buried memories from his youth. He'd been so bitter when he'd left that he'd forgotten there had been good times, too.

After eating and small talk, they left the deli. Reaching the

Chevy, Sammy slid behind the steering wheel and said, "We never leave Suki alone. Today, my wife is with her. Wednesday, Cousin Betty will come from Eddie's Corner and stay for a few days."

"Who's Suki?" Josh asked.

Sammy stared at him for a moment before he answered. "Right, you weren't around when Susan decided that was her new name."

"When did that happen?"

"When she was fourteen, after reading Dead Until Dark."

"Huh?" Josh said.

"The main character in the novel is a small-town waitress turned paranormal sleuth, and her name is Sookie Stackhouse. But Susan spelled her new name in her own way. She thought the original spelling would tempt the mean kids at school to use it like they were calling pigs to eat."

"Tell me what you know about the guy that raped her," Josh said.

Sammy's voice was louder when he replied, "He's an asshole, and his father is worse! The old bastard hired a gaggle of crooked, hot-shot lawyers. The way they treated Suki during the trial was a crime."

Since his question had triggered his brother's rage, Josh changed the subject to calm things down. "How are the local farmers doing?"

Sammy looked confused while his train of thought switched gears before he replied, "Not so good. Too many of them have lost everything, or they were forced to grow Frankenfoods."

Josh hadn't heard this before. He knew times were tough for small farmers thanks to Trump's tariffs, but he'd never heard of Frankenfoods. "How were they forced?" he asked.

The answer poured out of his brother in a hot rush. "Seeds showed up from nowhere and blew onto farmland all over the county. When they sprouted, the corporation took them to court, claiming the farmers stole their genetically modified intellectual property. The court costs broke every farmer who fought back.

"To keep their farms, they had to agree to become wage slaves. Once a farmer signs the contract, the only way to escape is to die. We've been lucky because of what Mom earns from her western novels, and the area where we grow crops on the ranch is isolated."

Josh closed his tired eyes and rubbed them with the heels of his hands. "Is there any good news?" He blinked his eyes to moisten them.

Sammy glanced at his brother's craggy features. "You look older than your years, and you never wrote about what you did in the military."

"That's because I didn't write home," Josh said. "Most of what I did is classified. If I wrote or talked about any of it, the government would throw my ass in prison."

"What do you mean? Everyone knows about your Purple Hearts, the Navy Cross, and the other medals. But we don't know the details."

"Like I said, those are classified." Josh was chewing on a wooden toothpick from the deli.

"Can you at least tell me what you did in the Marines?"

"Once I graduated from boot camp, I became a Scout Sniper. A few years later, I left the Marines to become a Navy SEAL. After I was Special Forces-qualified, I moved around and tried other stuff too." He stopped talking, and the silence filled the cab like gritty sand.

"That's all you're going to say?" Sammy asked.

"Yep. What happened to Susan is more important than what I did for the last twenty-four years."

"She prefers Suki. Don't forget that." Sammy glanced at Josh and saw the sour look on his face. "Jesus," he said. "You don't enjoy talking, do you?"

Josh grunted. "I got better things to do." He switched the toothpick to the other side of his mouth.

It was quiet for the next few miles as Josh shredded the toothpick before Sammy asked, "What're you planning to do now that you're back?" He kept his eyes on the road, with worry lines creasing the spot between them. "Dad and Mom don't want any trouble with that billionaire and his son. They talked it over and decided we should forget about what happened."

Josh spit the mangled toothpick out the open window. "Sounds like nothing changed. Well, I will not forget."

"What does that mean?"

"You don't need to know, little brother."

"You're planning something," Sammy said with a shaky voice. "You can't leave me out of it. They crippled Mel after they drugged and gang-raped Suki. The way those trash-talking lawyers crucified our sister in court made her condition worse. It was like she was on trial instead of the thugs who abused her." Mel was Suki's fraternal twin.

"Sounds like you might disagree with Mom and Dad that we should make-believe the rape never happened."

"If you're going for some payback," Sammy said, "I want in on it too."

"You don't have the training or experience for what's coming," Josh said.

"Fuck that!" Sammy slammed on the brakes and brought the Chevy to a screeching, shuddering halt on the loose gravel by the side of the narrow, worn, two-lane road. His face had bloomed with anger.

Josh sighed. "I will not argue."

"You can't do this alone!"

"I'm not alone." His voice was crisp. "My Semper Fi brothers are already in the hills on the ranch waiting for me. We've done stuff like this before in too many countries to count. When we're done, that billionaire and his family will tuck their tails between their legs and leave Montana for good. We're going to teach them a lesson they'll never forget. Trust me. You don't want that hell-fire in your head when you try to sleep at night."

"You're underestimating Charles Tweet. He's a fucking brutal monster that thrives on getting even with anyone that crosses him. What if you make things worse for Mel and Suki?"

"I have a counselor from a Vet Center in California willing to use some of her vacation time to come to Montana and help them rebuild and manage their lives. Dr. Tate is an expert in dealing with this kind of trauma." Josh turned to stare at his brother. "As for Charles Tweet and his evil heart, he doesn't know what's coming. We have something special planned for his precious son."

"What do you mean by that?" Sammy asked.

"No more details." Josh's eyes were full of hard ice. "I've already told you too much. It's been a long trip, and I want to see the ranch before the sun goes down. I'm back, and I plan to have a home in Montana, even if I have to buy my own place. Our family and neighbors need me more than the US of A does, and I'm not alone. Some of my friends also grew up on farms, and I convinced a few of them to buy some of the smaller local spreads when they retire."

Then Josh smiled as he shifted his gaze back to look at the horizon in front of the truck. "Tell me, little brother, is it true that Rachel hasn't changed much, and she divorced Lazy Luke? I still can't believe she married that jerk."

"The night she kicked him out," Sammy replied, "she had the locks changed, and her dad and brothers were there when he came home drunk, as usual. A week later, he kicked in the door, but she was ready with a baseball bat and broke his right shoulder and a couple of ribs. The next day, she took out a restraining order on him."

Josh pressed his lips together as he thought for a moment. "Good for her. Rachel would have made a great Marine. When we were kids, she was a better shot than me." Then he lifted his butt off the seat and stretched his torso. With two fingers, he fished a quarter out of the tight watch pocket of his faded denim jeans. "Heads, I take the coward's way out—write a letter and mail it. Tails, I show up at her place unannounced, knock on the door, and hope she blows her lid."

Sammy glanced at him like he was crazy. "What are you talking about?"

Josh flipped the coin and grinned when he saw the results.

"What is it?" Sammy asked.

"Tails," Josh replied. "I'm going to enjoy getting my ass kicked. I hope she tries, at least. It'll mean she still loves me."

"What did the Marines and the Navy SEALS do to you?" Sammy asked. "Who in their right mind wants to get his ass kicked by his old high school sweetheart? That was a long time ago. Why do you want to poke that hornet's nest?"

Josh's eyes sparkled. He pinched a thumb and index finger together and pretended to zip his mouth shut.

"Damn it," Sammy said. "You were a blabbermouth when we were kids."

"It wasn't just the Marines and Navy SEALS," Josh said. "I had a girlfriend. When I asked her to marry me, she said no."

For a time, there was an empty silence before Sammy asked, "Do you know why?"

"Maybe because she's from Haiti and lives in France." He sighed, and his eyes looked sad. "That's the end of our conversation. No more nosy questions." He opened the glove box to discover a batch of cassette tapes. "You do know that CDs have replaced these things."

"Don't see any reason to change what still works," Sammy said as he indicated the cassette player below the dash. "Besides, I'd have to buy my favorite music all over again."

Selecting one cassette, Josh read the label: Johnny Cash, A Thing Called Love. "Perfect," he said. "With help from Johnny, maybe I'll get in the mood."

"The mood for what?"

Josh slipped the cassette into the player and turned up the volume as "Kate," the first song on the album, played. A wide grin spread across his face as he listened.

Sammy glanced from the road to his brother and said, "What?"

"You gotta love Johnny," Josh replied.

# CHAPTER 2

SOON AFTER JOSH flipped the quarter, the two front tires blew out, causing the pickup to jerk first to the right, then swiftly to the left. With the metal rims spewing sparks, Sammy brought the truck to a thudding but safe stop.

With his heart in his throat pounding like a drum, he said, "Sorry about that. Good thing I kept the speed down. I should've replaced those tires a long time ago. It isn't like we don't have the money. Mom doesn't say no to necessities, only luxuries. You know, she always says, 'need's more important than want.'" He turned to Josh, but his older brother wasn't there, and the passenger door stood open.

"What the hell!" Sammy looked out all the windows, but there was no sign of Josh. How could anyone vanish like that?

He howled in shock when the driver's door flew open, and two hands plucked him out of the truck to the ground. Sammy flailed about in a panic, but the iron hands held him down.

"Don't move," Josh hissed in his ear. "Someone shot out the tires."

"That's crazy," Sammy said. "I didn't hear no gunfire."

Josh shook his head. "It came from a suppressed sniper rifle." His eyes froze, then storm clouds replaced the ice. He jumped to his feet and gave one of the distant hills an obscene one-finger salute. "Fucking asshole! Always trying to prove you're the better shot!"

Sammy moved to his knees and peered over the truck's hood. Only his eyes and the top of his head were visible.

Josh walked around the pickup and stared at the closest hilltop. "He's up there." He pointed west. "If I was the shooter, that's where I'd be. An easy shot from 800 yards."

"Do you know who it is?" Sammy asked.

"Popsicle Dick," Josh growled. "And I see him."

"Who's that? I don't see anyone," Sammy said, sounding confused. "I think we're alone out here."

Josh turned to face in the opposite direction. "I expect some of them are over there." He walked from the pickup and crossed the road toward a thick stand of aspen.

Sammy saw some bushes and smaller trees move as if they had legs. He rubbed his eyes and looked again. Yep, he wasn't hallucinating. The trees were walking. He took a few steps backward until the Chevy got in the way and stopped his retreat. That's when one tree started talking with a raspy voice. "We decided on a creative welcome, Colonel."

Another voice said, "I was against this loony tunes crap from the start, but you have to fucking admit that truck needed new tires. That's why we agreed to help the captain get rid of the old ones in a dramatic display of marksmanship."

"What did LG say about this?" Josh asked.

Another voice answered. "The general left it up to us. Said he was confident we wouldn't hurt anyone. That we knew what we were doing. Said it would be good to get out in the field and scrape off some of the rust growing between our ears in that 'damn' valley."

*Did I just hear someone call my brother a colonel?* Sammy

thought. And who is this general? Then he was distracted by the sound of humming tires. Looking over his shoulder, he saw a tan-colored vehicle that looked like a tubular cage with large, multi-terrain tires. It stopped behind his pickup.

"Hey, Josh," Sammy called, "who is that, and what're they driving?" He hoped it wasn't trouble. There were two men in the rolling cage, and they were getting out. Once they were in the open, the blood drained out of Sammy's head, and he was dizzy for a moment.

They looked like terrorists, with balaclavas hiding all but their eyes, dressed in camouflage military clothing, including bullet-resistant vests. He saw pistols in holsters, big-ass knives strapped to legs, and submachine guns. *Holy shit!* Sammy thought, and his bowels almost let go.

"That's one of our GMVs," his brother said in a calm tone. "It's a ground mobility vehicle. A CH-47 delivered two of them to our location on the ranch." The two men started unloading tires and rims from the back of the vehicle.

Sammy relaxed. "What's a CH-47?"

"A heavy-lift helicopter," Josh replied.

"Where did you get all this military stuff?"

"If you think we borrowed or stole this shit, you'd be wrong. We're out of the military, but we didn't leave that life. We formed our own employee-owned LLC and do contract work. The weapons, the GMVs, and the Chinooks belong to us."

"What kind of contract work uses that stuff?"

"We're not plumbers or carpenters, if that's what you're thinking. Just watch and learn something and stay out of the way." With that, Josh finished crossing the road to join the camouflaged men who looked like walking shrubbery.

"I don't want to leave the truck out here tonight," Sammy said to his brother's back. "When morning comes, there's a good chance it'll be stripped clean."

"We know about the night riders causing trouble around here," Josh said. "No reason to worry, little brother. Your old Chevy's going to be safe. We dealt with those thugs last night."

An alarm went off in Sammy's head. "What do you mean you 'dealt' with them?" His voice sounded shrill, and his heart was thudding again.

"No need to tie your panties in knots. We didn't waste them. Just taught them a crap-your-pants lesson they'll never forget."

Sammy's face grew hot. *This is bullshit,* he thought. When he heard a metallic noise behind him, he turned to see more camouflaged men replacing the Chevy's tires. Where had they all come from? He'd seen no one work with such focus and efficiency. He couldn't take his eyes off them. They soon finished, left the road, and melted into the brush and trees like a cube of butter in a hot skillet.

Then another man appeared on the front passenger side of the pickup. He was carrying a big-ass, scoped rifle, and green and black streaks of paint hid his facial features. Was he the one Josh had called "Popsicle Dick"? He didn't look like a popsicle. He looked more like a rhino—and the rifle he carried was impressive.

Josh glared at the Popsicle Rhino, who grinned back and said in a loud voice, "I made that shot with one round?"

"Yes, you did, Captain. You got two-for-one, but you did it inside 800 yards." Josh pressed his lips into a thin line, erasing any hint of a smile. "I've made similar shots from a distance just inside two miles, and once I bagged three-for-one at 3,000 meters."

"What kind of rifle is that?" Sammy asked.

"An M21 with a sound suppressor," the Rhino replied. His voice had lost its bluster.

"I've never seen one like that before." Sammy couldn't take his eyes off the weapon. He didn't know the scope was a One-

Shot system developed by DARPA, and this prototype was worth $85,000. The scope used lasers to sense the wind up to two km from the shooter and automatically adjusted the crosshairs to help the sniper hit the target.

A moment later, the others left, and the Rhino followed them into the trees.

When an engine fired up behind him, Sammy spun around. The two who had arrived in the GMV turned the vehicle around and left the way they had come.

Acting like nothing had happened, Josh slipped into the Chevy on the passenger side. He said, "I'm going to tell Rachel that if I could do it all over again, I'd have returned every year. I'd have written to her regularly. We would have made it work."

Sammy stood in the middle of the road and turned in a full circle. There was no sign that anyone else had ever been there. And his truck didn't have two new tires. It had four with fancy rims that must have cost hundreds of dollars each. He was starting to understand how the last twenty-four years had changed his brother. He also had a long list of new questions that Josh would not answer, but he'd learned one thing: his brother had not been exaggerating when he said he wasn't alone. A chill raced through him, and he wondered what Josh had meant when he said he bagged three with one round. Three of what?

"Time's not standing still," Josh said.

"Those tires and rims look expensive."

"Don't worry about it. Chump change."

Sammy opened his mouth to ask a question, then shut it with a snap. Shaking his head and grumbling, he slid behind the steering wheel. They drove in silence for a few minutes before he cleared his throat and asked, "Why'd you hitchhike home if you got a CH-47 and a couple of GMVs?"

"No one remembers a man hitchhiking who looks like he's down on his luck. Imagine what they'd think if I came home leading what looks like a military convoy? I also didn't want a parade to welcome the fucking war hero back. I'm not a hero. I was just doing my job."

Sammy knew what would get a rise out of his iceberg-calm brother. "Josh, I'm not supposed to tell you this, but Rachel's at the house and doesn't know you're coming home. We tricked her. She thinks she's there for Suki. You better figure out what you're going to say to her before we arrive."

After a moment, Josh asked, "Whose idea was it to do that?"

"Me and Mel," Sammy replied.

"Why?"

"Because when we were kids, we didn't have any say when Mom agreed to do what Rachel wanted. Dad didn't like it, but... well, you know, Mom always gets her way. When you called and said you were coming home, we talked and decided it was time for you and Rachel to meet again."

"So, you and Mel played matchmaker?"

"That wasn't the reason. It was her two kids."

"What do they have to do with Rachel and me?"

Sammy avoided eye contact. "Her son's in the Marines and her daughter's attending the Montana State University in Bozeman."

Josh studied Sammy's flushed face. "How old are they?" His voice was soothing, inquisitive.

Sammy remembered Josh had only raised his voice when he'd flipped off that hill where the Rhino must have been when he took the shot. The rest of the time, his voice had been calm, almost magnetic. When he talked, you listened.

"Let's talk about Mom and Dad," Sam said. "Things are not good between them."

"Nothing new there," Josh said. "When I left, they were sleeping in separate bedrooms already. Don't change the subject. Answer my question."

"Rachel's children are both in their early twenties." His face turned a darker shade of red, and Sammy was convinced Josh translated that, too.

"When did she marry the jerk?"

"A few years after they were born." Sammy's voice sounded strained.

A moment of silence slipped by before Josh said, "Shit! She never told me. No one did. I hate secrets like that."

Sammy heard the tension in his brother's voice and struggled to suppress a smile. *Got you,* he thought. After all these years, Josh's weak spot was still Rachel. For all of his toughness, she was his Achilles' heel.

# CHAPTER 3

JOSH STOOD by the passenger side of the truck, staring at the house he'd been born in. His mother had the place painted every five years, and it was still an untarnished eggshell, white with gray trim. The covered porch surrounding the single-story house was like a wraparound shawl, and the trees shading the roof were silent sentries. An ornamental cherry tree on the northwest side of the place captured his attention. As he stared at it, his body grew still, but only for a little while before he started walking rapidly toward it, away from the front door.

"Hey, where are you going?" Sammy asked from the driver's side of the Chevy. "Our family is waiting." Shaking his head and rolling his eyes, he followed.

When Josh reached the tree, he found the heart carved deep in the smooth grey-brown bark. Inside were the initials JK & RC, with 4EVER right below.

"I didn't know you were the sentimental type," Sammy said from behind him.

"I'm surprised this tree's still alive. It must be forty feet tall now. It was half that back then." Josh reached out with one hand

and caressed the deep letters with his fingertips. "I never stopped loving Rachel. In boot camp, every morning when reveille sounded, I thought about her. I missed her something bad. It took a lot of years for my achy-breaky heart to heal. Even with other women, I often imagined I was with her."

"Then why did you leave like you did?" Sammy asked.

Josh wasn't ready to talk about that, so he changed the subject. "The first time I saw her was in second grade, and that's when I knew she was special."

Unbeknownst to the brothers, they were being watched. "Asshole!" Rachel growled. "We were in high school the first time you sang that 'Achy Breaky' Billy Ray Cyrus song to me. Back then, I thought it was cute. I was stupid to trust you."

Hearing her voice caused Josh's heart to stampede. While reeling in his ticker, he took his time turning around. "When I used those words just now, I wasn't thinking about the song, Rachel." It was a struggle to stay calm. He wanted to wrap his arms around her and discover her lips all over again.

She stood a few feet behind Sammy, who had jumped out of the way like a startled jackrabbit ready to run. His eyes were bouncing back and forth from her to his brother.

For Josh, she was an eye magnet. His gaze left her face and crept down her body, loving every inch of her five-foot-three-inch frame. Her only sign of age was the weathered tone of her skin and the beginning of fine worry lines around her eyes. She looked better than he remembered; she was still slim and her hips had filled out, making for a damn sweet feast. It was apparent that the years had treated her kinder than they had treated him.

"What do you think I am," she said, "a filly on the auction block?" From the look on her face, he knew he'd made a mistake checking her out like that. "Or maybe you think I'm a broodmare. I should poke your eyeballs out."

He never imagined they'd be reunited on this spot. They'd been sixteen when they carved that heart in the tree and swore it was the symbol of their undying love. That was also the first of many times he said he'd never leave her.

"Yea, you broke that promise, too, dickhead." The harsh tone of her voice stung.

"You always could read my mind," he said.

"What shitbucket full of bunk are you going to dump on me now? Fool me once, shame on you. Fool me twice, shame on me. I want to know about the other women." Her lips became a tight line, and her eyes flashed what he hoped was jealousy.

"What I did between boot camp in 1994 and today is history. It's none of your business, just like what you did with your life isn't mine." He didn't need to mention Luke, the abusive alcoholic gambler she'd married. She knew—no need to rub it in.

A moment of silence followed before she stabbed him with more words. "You broke my heart when you left."

He squirmed, trying to look pitiful. "I can't go back and fix it." He didn't know what else to say, so for the first time in twenty-four years, he let the words flow without controlling them. "Before I left on that bus to MCRD, I called your house and recorded a message on the answering machine."

"You're dumb as a rock," she replied. "You knew that machine was broken."

Jolted, he stammered. "I...forgot." The embarrassment was stuck between his teeth. Then he thought about something that happened in second grade. He was sitting behind her and leaned forward to whisper that he loved her. Without turning around, she had stabbed him with a sharp pencil and broke the graphite off under his skin, leaving a dark spot below his right knee that was still there.

"I think we should go inside." Sammy sounded nervous.

"Shut up!" Rachel turned her blazing eyes on him. "You and

the rest of your family tricked me. I'll take care of you all later." She walked forward until she was inches from Josh, who was getting ready to take whatever beating she was going to dish out. He hoped it'd be with her fists instead of more words.

He stared into her angry green eyes. "Until today," he said, "I didn't know I was the father of your children."

"You never wrote one fucking letter to anyone after you left, twit!"

He wondered if calling him a "twit" meant she was forgiving him. It didn't sound as bad as "asshole" and "dickhead."

"Jesus, Rachel," he said. "I was eighteen and naturally stupid. I made mistakes like most kids at that age. You could've found out through the Marines how to get in touch with me to let me know. I deserved that much. I would've come home the first chance I got."

"I was also eighteen, or did you forget that, too? Why was I the one who was supposed to be rational and do the right thing? Do you think it was a mistake that I didn't have an abortion?" Her face had turned into a frigid, emotionless mask. That she hadn't tried to break his nose or jaw worried him. Maybe she was moving in for the kill. Even in grade school, she had carried a folding Buck knife with a four-inch blade. He felt his abs tightening as if she were going to stick him with it. He'd let her do it once, before he stopped her from turning him into a pincushion. It would be worth it if she felt guilty afterward. He had so many battle scars; one more wasn't a big deal...as long as he didn't let her hit anything vital. When she was like this, it always turned him on. After they made up, the sex had been off the charts. Not even Mia could match her there, and his French sweetheart had also been exceptional, just different.

"What are our children's names?" he asked.

"Wyatt and Morgan," she replied.

For a moment, he couldn't respond. Instead, he stared at her, thinking, *You named our son after Wyatt, the famous gambler and lawman, and our daughter after his wife.* Then he said, "I hope our son doesn't have Earp as his middle name."

The look in her eyes answered for him.

"How could you?" he said. As a child, Josh had been obsessed with Wyatt Earp and talked endlessly about his hero. Rachel had listened without complaint. By high school, he had moved on to Audie Murphy, one of the most decorated American soldiers in World War II.

"Blame it on anger," she replied.

"Why didn't you want them to know about me?"

"When you're eighteen, you do stupid things," she replied, throwing his earlier words back at him.

"I'd never change anything that happened between us since the first time I saw you," he said. "For me, it was love from the start, and it just grew bigger as the years went by. I made a horrible mistake leaving like I did."

"You never give up, do you? If that so-called love wasn't big enough to keep you with me back then, why should I believe you now?"

This wasn't looking good. Desperate, he said, "I want to make it right and marry you."

Her mask shattered. There were tears, too, and he hoped they'd put out the angry flames. He wondered if their secret love nest was still in that old barn loft.

"I don't need to hear this," Sammy said, and covered his ears with both hands, but he was rooted to the spot and couldn't stop watching.

Josh had never known another woman like Rachel. Since leaving home, he had been with other women all over the world. Most of them had been prostitutes and one-night stands. Only Mia had turned out to be a serious contender for his heart.

He had to get Rachel talking again. "I will not give up," he said. "I'm going to win you back." Josh struggled to not crack a smile. It wasn't easy maintaining a sorrowful expression when he didn't feel that way. Seeing her again had filled his head with love songs.

Clouds covered the sun, and in the sudden shadows, he couldn't read her expression. Then a brief, chilly breeze agitated the trees, raising goosebumps on his bare arms.

Her voice went soft. "We'll have to wait and see, won't we?" She moved closer until he felt the warmth of her breath on his face and smelled her familiar, sweet Big Sky Country scent.

Bewitched, he couldn't take his eyes off her lips. Just as he was reaching up to stroke her bluish-black, shoulder-length hair and kiss her, she kneed him hard in the groin, and he went down with a grunt.

Looking satisfied, she spun around and headed toward the front of the house.

As far as he was concerned, that blow had been a signal that she still loved him. He snorted laughter and had an urge to sing "Somebody Like You" by Keith Urban, but he was still in agony and struggling to get his breath back.

A moment later, he asked, "Sammy, after she turned her back on me, did you notice if she was grinning?"

# CHAPTER 4

STILL LYING ON THE GROUND, Josh listened to the trees gossiping about what they had witnessed.

"Are you going to be okay?" Sammy asked.

Through watery eyes, Josh saw his brother struggling to look concerned. It was easy to see that a bucket of laughter was threatening to burst the fragile dam holding it back.

"I want to be alone," he said.

Looking disappointed, Sammy stared at him for a moment before he left.

Satisfied, Josh rolled over until he was on his back with his arms splayed, forming the shape of a cross. During his years in the military, he had suffered from too many injuries to count. To avoid becoming addicted to pain pills, he taught himself how to use exercise and meditation to deal with the discomfort.

If Rachel was watching, he couldn't exercise, so he closed his eyes, relaxed his muscles, and concentrated on deep breathing. The sound of the breeze through the trees replaced the music he usually listened to while meditating like this. Moments later, the pain had receded to a distant irritation.

Winning Rachel's love had been complicated. After he fell in love with her in second grade, he kept asking her out. She kept saying no. By the time they were twelve, she had challenged him to a shooting contest. If he hit the bull's eye more than she did at 800 yards, she'd go out with him. If he lost, he'd stop asking her out. If given a choice, he would have walked across hot coals instead. Before he became a Scout Sniper in the Marines, she had been the better shot.

"We're going to use the same rifle," she'd said. "And we each get ten rounds."

"What if we both hit the bull's eye the same number of times?" he'd asked.

Rachel chewed on her lip in thought before answering. "If that happens, I'll let you flip one of my quarters. Heads, I win, and you promise to stop asking me out."

"I think you should shoot first," he said.

"Are you scared?"

He shook his head. "No way. It's only polite to let a woman go first. What rifle are we going to use?"

"One of mine," she'd said.

"That's not fair. We should borrow a rifle we haven't used before."

She mulled it over before nodding.

They ended up using the bolt-action rifle that Josh's grandfather had carried in France during World War I, known as the American Enfield. It did not have a scope, and it hadn't been fired since that war ended in 1918. They cleaned the rifle together right before the match.

That competition had been a draw, but her shots had been tighter together inside the bull's eye. When he flipped her quarter, it came up tails. He'd won, but Rachel picked the day, time, and place for their first date. It turned out to be torture at a hot, dusty, local summer rodeo, and they sat in the stands sweating with hundreds of people. She didn't let him hold her hand, and there was no end-of-date kiss, something he'd fantasized about for five years since second grade.

Retreating from those memories, he stared up at the trees and said, "The Good Lord knows that love is both bliss and agony. What do you think about that?" He didn't expect a reply. Groaning, he rolled over and levered himself to a sitting position, where he stayed for a moment, with his head hanging between his shoulders.

There were several windows on each side of the house, and Josh was sure Rachel was watching from one of them. The pain had subsided, but if he was going to win this game, he had to play it better than her.

Reaching for the cherry tree, he used it to climb to his feet and ended up staring at the heart again. Thinking it would be a nice touch, he gently kissed the initials RC before fake-limping toward the front door. *She better be watching*, he thought, and a voice in his head reminded him not to overdo it.

Their first date didn't end with a kiss, but he'd seen the look in her eyes as she glanced back before closing the door. It was apparent she had been feeling something. He never found out what.

Then, out of the corner of his left eye, he saw the curtains of one bedroom window ripple. He reminded himself not to smile. While she could read him like a book, he had learned how to predict her behavior.

When he climbed the five steps leading to the front door, he turned right and went straight to one of the hanging porch swings and sat. He pushed off with both feet and started rocking. The chains leading to ceiling joists creaked against the metal hooks. From there, he could see the hills in front of the house, where there were the shadowy shapes of cattle bunched together, grazing. He searched for the Anatolian Shepherds on guard and spotted three of them lying in the grass, watching. It was the dog breed his dad preferred to watch over their cattle.

Closing his eyes, he recalled the touch of Rachel's brown, smooth skin under his exploring hands the night she surrendered her virginity on this swing.

It was a little after midnight, and their families were inside playing cards at the dining room table. Muted laughter had drifted through the windows, reminding the lovers they weren't alone. But she let him slip his fingers under the waistband of her tight jeans, anyway. Thinking she'd curb him like she'd done so many times before, he pulled his hand out. She shocked him dumb when she said in a high-pitched, breathy voice, "Don't stop!"

Aroused by that recollection, it tempted Josh to comfort himself. "I will not do that," he muttered. Besides, the real thing was so much better. Wasn't patience a virtue? He imagined his mother reciting one of her favorite verses from the Bible: "But if we hope for what we do not see, we wait for it with patience."

With his eyes still closed, he cracked a smutty smile. This wasn't the only time Rachel had aroused him. After their first lousy date, she became an expert at driving him crazy. In high school, he feared someone would notice his hard-ons until he figured out he could hide them by not tucking in his shirts.

A barely noticeable creaking sound alerted him he wasn't alone. Then he smelled the sweet scent of perfume. *Oh shit,* he thought. *If it was Rachel, she'd know what he was thinking.*

Seeing Rachel again had lit his fire. If there was such a thing as a slave to one woman, he was that person, and Rachel was his master. It hadn't been that way with Mia. Even though his French lover was a strong woman, he'd been the one in charge. That was probably because she fell in love with him first. He resisted as long as he could, and it took several years before he fell off that cliff, too.

Thinking about Mia caused him to have a twinge of regret. Yes, she had turned him down when he asked her to marry him, but they were still in business together and were friends. That would never change. They were linked in ways most people could never know.

Then he remembered Rachel hadn't been wearing perfume when she'd been standing in front of him by the cherry tree.

*Oh crap!* He almost leaped off the swing to stand at attention. There was one woman more dangerous than Rachel, and that was his mother. He wasn't ready to face her yet. Dreading that conversation, he opened his eyes to discover who was there.

# CHAPTER 5

WHEN JOSH SAW his Grandmother Clay standing there, he was glad he hadn't broken his rule to only have solo sex alone and behind a locked door. When he'd been in the SEALs, Doc Milo, the medic, said jerking off was a natural way to improve the immune system, release tension, and help fight depression. Josh and the other four SEALs had listened and nodded. They waited until Milo left before logging on to the internet to discover that he wasn't messing with them. It seemed to be true.

Milo's advice helped dispel the constant, low-level sense of guilt Josh's mother had planted in him about masturbation when he was a teen.

"Why are you here, Grandma Clay?" he asked. Thinking the rest of the country wasn't safe for a lesbian, she never strayed far from San Francisco.

"Why do you think I'm here, Joshua?" His mother had named him after one of the twelve spies sent by Moses to explore the land of Canaan.

"For Suki, your only granddaughter."

She sat beside him and patted him on the knee. "What are

you going to do about the psycho that turned her life into hell? During the trial, she suffered more than he did. That wasn't right."

"Rape cases are almost always a 'he said, she said' thing," Josh replied. "There isn't much the victim can do."

"How are we ever going to get justice for that sweet child?"

"Don't worry, Grandma. Mom always said whoever sows injustice will reap calamity."

"One of Judith's quotes from the Bible doesn't answer my question," Clay replied. "What are you planning to do about it?"

As a young man, Josh's father had left the ranch to earn a BS in Forestry and Natural Resources at UC Berkeley. That's where he met Josh's mother, who was majoring in English. She accidentally collided with him in the crowded student union, shattering his ceramic coffee mug. He mentioned it had been in his family for more than a century. She rescued the pieces, glued the cup back together, and presented it to him a few days later. They fell in love in record time. Months later, she learned that dozens of coffee mugs just like that one were on the ranch, and all of them had been in the family for more than a hundred years.

His mother's dream had been to become a writer and publish bestsellers. His father wanted to escape ranching and get a job with the United States Fish and Wildlife Service. They lived together in Berkeley in a studio apartment over a small, two-car garage. Josh's mother was already three months pregnant with him when they got married.

Judith's father had been a sperm donor, and she didn't know who he was. Grandma Clay's real name was Hazel, and she was a liberal Democrat. Her partner, and his other grandmother, was christened Catwoman by her hippy parents, and she'd grown up to become a Reagan Republican. Josh heard Grandma Clay ask more than once, "What sane parent names their child that?"

"Did Cat stay home?" Josh continued to rock the swing. He thought Grandma Clay looked years younger than her seventy-two.

She stared into the distance, watching dusk give way to night. "Do you remember that incident in Mississippi when Cat was nineteen and beat the shit out of three rednecks? When she returned to San Francisco, she swore she'd never leave again. That's also the reason we had that safe room built in the basement of our Victorian. Cat had it built like a bank vault, so we'd even survive a big earthquake."

Josh couldn't help but smile. To make it easy and fast to reach that fourteen-by-fourteen-foot fortified panic room, his grandmothers had a fireman's pole installed from the third floor to the basement. When he'd been a child and visited them during the Christmas and Easter school vacations, he'd slid down that pole too many times to count. His trips to San Francisco also meant hearing reruns of the same old stories, and he was about to hear one of them again.

Clay continued. "By the time Cat graduated from high school, she had black belts in Brazilian Jiu-Jitsu and Muay Thai. To make her escape from Mississippi, she took a Harley from one of the three rednecks and fled. Reaching San Francisco, she dismantled the bike and shipped it back to its owner in pieces, one box at a time, all mailed to the same rural post office near where he lived.

Josh craned his neck and stretched his back muscles. "I've heard that story a thousand times. Do you have a new one?"

"Do not avoid my question with another question." His grandmother turned her eyes on him. "I want to know what you're thinking. You didn't return home just to comfort a sister you haven't seen since she was three."

"It would be better if you didn't know," he replied. If Catwoman had stayed home, he wondered who came with Clay.

This was her first trip to the Bible Belt. She thought rainbow people like her were considered a biblical abomination here. She wouldn't have come alone. He guessed one of her gay male friends came with her.

"Are you planning something illegal?" she asked. "Because I don't want my grandson in prison or on the run."

Josh felt his face growing hot. In the military, he had no problem hiding what he was thinking, but not from those he loved. "Grandma, I know how to be stealthy."

She nodded and clicked her tongue. "I thought so," she said. "You spent too much time with Cat when you visited us each year. She might be a vegan, but she'd geld the bastard, slice his Rocky Mountain oysters thin, fry them in garlic oil, and force him to eat them. Are you going to do something like that?"

"Grandmother!" he protested.

"Well, it's true." She slapped him on the knee hard enough to sting. Her face broke into a brilliant smile. She winked and said, "You have my blessing; just don't get caught."

During his years in the military, he'd spend some of his annual leave every year with his mother's mommies.

"Seriously," Clay said, "it's good you're home. Go inside and give Judith a hug and a kiss. Make things right between you two."

"I've read all of her westerns," he said, wanting to change the subject. He dreaded the inevitable conversation loaded with guilt-inducing Bible verses that would follow a hug with his mother.

"I guess you're expecting the worst. Well, let me tell you, twenty-four years can change a person. She'll be pleased to know you read her books. You should have written letters. Every time Suki found another story about you being wounded in combat or getting another medal, your mother cried."

His mother had published twenty-nine bestselling westerns

set in the nineteenth century that combined had sold over 300 million copies in thirty-one countries. Her pen name was Cat Clay, and she used a clean-shaven headshot of his dad when he was in his early twenties for the dust jacket copy above the fake author's bio. Opposite the copyright page was a black-and-white image of the patched coffee mug that brought them together.

"Does Dad still have a beard and mustache?"

"You got eyes," she replied. "Go in and find out."

"You know what I want right now?" he said.

"A toasted cheese, avocado, sauerkraut, and tomato sandwich with mustard," she said. "After your never-ending talk about how much you missed those homemade sandwiches, I had to have one. I understand your obsession now. If I stay here much longer, I'm going to gain a hundred pounds. There's nothing else to do but eat."

*There's a lot more to do than that on a working ranch,* Josh thought, but he couldn't imagine this grandma repairing barbed wire fences or rounding up cattle on horseback. Cat maybe, but not her.

Clay studied him for a moment. "You're worried about how you're going to be treated. At least you weren't a prodigal son. We're all proud of what you accomplished in the military and are thankful you didn't get yourself killed."

"After Rachel's greeting, I think my concern is justified."

"When she returned to the table after seeing you, she looked mighty satisfied. Didn't look mad at all. What did she do?"

Josh burst out laughing.

# CHAPTER 6

STILL THINKING ABOUT THE SANDWICH, Josh said, "A few years back, I added grilled onions. But no matter what I did, it was never good enough without Mom's homemade bread."

"You're making me hungry," Grandma Clay replied. "Let's join the others." She left the swing, but stopped at the front door to ask, "You coming?"

Josh's feet had become 30,000-pound anchors.

"Oh, honey," Grandma said. It must have been his forlorn expression. She returned and sat beside him again.

"I left home angry and feeling sorry for myself," he said. "Then, over time, I realized I was being selfish and didn't know how to fix it."

She slipped an arm across the back of his shoulders and pulled him closer. "Sounds like you're feeling embarrassed and anxious."

He wanted to start over and be a child again, but with a different mother, one who wasn't obsessed with scripture. "Why does she have to consult the Bible for every decision she makes?" he asked.

"Well, that's Cat's fault," she replied, "but it has been twenty-four years. People change."

Was she talking about Cat, him, or his mother? Special Forces had transformed him and became his substitute family. Maybe it was time to attempt mending the wounds with his biological one. "What if they won't forgive me for never calling or writing?"

Grandma Clay nodded as if she agreed, but said nothing. Avoiding the warm, comforting pools that were her eyes, he shifted his focus to his feet.

"Don't let your boots decide for you." She slipped off the swing. With the sound of the front door closing, he was alone again. His mouth had turned dry, and he wanted an ice-cold beer. God, he hoped his parents had changed, too.

Josh remembered Romans 12:18: "Do all that you can to live in peace with everyone." After boot camp, he had turned his back on religion but hadn't forgotten what his mother had taught him from the Bible. How could he? When he was almost four, she started using a wire coat hanger as a motivation to pay attention and memorize the passages.

He rubbed his tired eyes with both fists. If he stayed on the swing much longer, the night was going to swallow him like it did when he was in the field on risky missions.

Forcing himself to stand, he dragged his anchors into the house and was greeted by a deserted living room. He'd been gone for over two decades, and it hadn't changed. Was that an omen? He hoped not.

When he walked into the dining room, he saw one empty chair at the table. It was between his mother and Rachel. His first thought was to retreat and find a place in one of the barns, where he could be alone.

Then he saw Suki on the other side of the table across from that godawful uninhabited chair. Even after all these years, Josh recognized her because of her smoky hazel-brown eyes. No one else in the family had eyes like that, but Mia did. His sister was sitting between a couple closer to her age. He focused on her and paid little attention to them. She noticed him, and her dull expression was transformed. Getting up, she hurried around the table and rescued him.

Once she was in his arms, he heard his voice say, "I'm sorry I wasn't here to protect you, Suki. I'm back, and I'm going to help make everything better." Why the hell had he made a promise like that? He should've treated this coming home thing like another military operation. Then he'd have planned everything he did and said.

He stared at the top of her curly, silver-streaked, dyed pink, shoulder-length hair, and couldn't remember the actual color. Then he noticed the clatter and chatter around the table had ceased.

Everyone was watching, and he felt the sphincters guarding his arse tighten. The next few seconds stretched like hours.

His dad's gravelly voice got the second hand moving again. "She hasn't moved that fast or hugged anyone since..." With a stunned expression, his mouth came to an abrupt stop.

"Actually, Dad," Sammy said, "she hasn't done much at all except lose weight and worry us. She's going to turn to dust and blow away."

His dad had shaved off his beard, but still had the waxed handlebar mustache. Then Josh sensed his sister watching him. He tilted his face down because she was a foot shorter than him.

Seeing her striking eyes up close triggered memories of his lost lover Mia and caused an empty pit to sprout in his chest. It had been several weeks since he'd been with Mia, and Rachel was the only other woman he'd loved with an epic passion. He figured once he and Rachel were together again, he'd mend.

"I'm glad you came home," his sister said in a frail voice, with undertones of hope. Her eyes were swimming in tears, triggering a lump in his throat. When she didn't let go, Mia's image faded and slipped out of his head.

Then Grandma Clay wrapped her arms around both of them and whispered in his ear, "She only talks to Mel, and she looks like she's in a trance when he isn't around. The first time I helped feed her, it took me an hour to get her to finish a bowl of vegetable broth."

Josh spotted three pies on the table and said, "Suki, no one makes apple pie better than Mom. I've dreamed about them, but I will not eat any unless you do, too."

"Since my misfortune happened," she said, "I prayed every night that you'd come home." Her lower lip trembled, and her face looked like it was ready to collapse.

Josh felt a rush of anger, but hid it. Is that what their mother had told her, that being raped was a misfortune? The Bible didn't treat women kindly. According to Ephesians, a rape victim had to be stoned to death if the young woman didn't cry for help. *But,* Josh thought, *what if she was drugged or there was no one to hear her?*

Then there was a shuffling sound around the table, and Josh discovered that Suki's chair had been moved next to the one meant for him. With an arm around his brittle sister's waist, he guided her to it. As soon as they were sitting next to each other, the chatter started up again, and they dished apple pie slices out. It was apparent that everyone was doing their best not to stare anymore.

Suki folded her hands on her lap and looked at her slice like it was a mound of mold.

Josh leaned closer and said, "We fight better when we aren't hungry."

Suki hesitantly picked up her fork, sliced off the tip of her apple pie wedge, and lifted it to her lips where it lingered.

"It has to go in your mouth to get to your stomach," he said.

Her lips twitched, struggling to form a grin, then she took the bite and chewed. A moment later, she swallowed and said, "It's good."

Rachel was sitting on Josh's left. His mother was on the other side of his sister, and she glanced his way and mouthed a silent, "Thank you."

His first thought: *Please, Mother, do not quote scripture.* Keeping his face expressionless, he replied with a nod.

Then Rachel's warm breath caressed his left ear, and he stiffened. Her voice was so low that no one else could hear what she said. "All Suki knows is what she's read about you. To her, you're bigger than life, like Odysseus. In her room, you will discover one wall is a shrine. She must have a copy of every newspaper and magazine piece ever published that mentions you. She subscribes to Army Times, Navy Times, and Soldier Magazine. There're others, but I don't remember 'em all. The two she honors the most was about you being awarded the Navy Cross when you were with the SEALS and the Distinguished Service Cross when you were in the Green Beret."

He replied, "I'm not Odysseus."

With a teasing smile, she said, "Don't tell Suki that. By the way, are you still feeling pain down there?" Her eyes glanced briefly toward his lap and she winked, then turned back to her slice of pie.

By the time Josh took his first bite, Suki's plate was half empty. "I want seconds," he said. "How about you?"

His sister nodded.

"I'm planning a midnight raid after everyone has gone to bed," he whispered. "Do you want to join me in the kitchen for an avocado, tomato, and cheese grilled sandwich made with slices of Mom's homemade bread?"

"I don't like mustard," she said in a barely audible voice.

"How about if I make a batch of Thousand Island dressing? Our sandwiches will be messy with it."

Her eyes glowed, and this time, she smiled. Josh looked past her and saw a tear slip from his mother's left eye and slide down her cheek.

# CHAPTER 7

WHILE EATING his second slice of pie, Josh noticed his sister pacing her bites with his. If he sliced off a forkful, she did, too. Her fork went to her mouth in sync with his. She also chewed at the same pace. Why was she acting like a child? She was twenty-six.

Then he revised his thinking. Maybe Suki was managing her trauma by being a kid again and pretending to be his shadow. To her, the time had been dialed back twenty-four years. She was three. He was eighteen. In her imagination, the hero had stayed on the ranch, and she followed him around while he did his chores.

Maybe she thought that if he hadn't joined the Marines, she would have never been raped. Was she aware of the contradiction? If he had stayed, he would have never become who he is today. Instead, he would've been a bitter, worn-out cowboy like their dad.

Josh didn't see himself as a hero. They had trained him to become an efficient killing machine and became an expert at it. He was like a junkie who hated being hooked on drugs but couldn't stay away from what he craved.

As they polished off their second slice, Suki made an unmistakable sound of contentment. Then she leaned her head on his shoulder and seemed to fall asleep in an instant, as a child would. He made a mental note to call Doctor Tate and tell her how his sister was dealing with the trauma.

Since he'd been sitting at the table, his focus had been on Suki. With her out like a light, he scanned the faces around the table. There were his father and mother, and his two brothers: Mel in his wheelchair, and Sammy with his wife and three kids. Good God, he didn't even know their names. He'd have to fix that.

An older man Josh didn't recognize was sitting next to Grandma Clay. Maybe he was her escort. At least, he thought it was a man. With Clay, you never knew.

Across from Josh were the two twenty-somethings whom Suki had been sitting between before he arrived. When he focused on their faces, an intense shock ran through him, and it was all he could do to keep his mouth from dropping open.

The young man had a high-and-tight Marine Corps haircut and looked a lot like Josh when he was the same age. The girl had Rachel's cheekbones, but she had inherited his nose. Thank God he didn't have a big beak.

Josh couldn't take his eyes off them, and it was apparent he was making them nervous. He almost bounced when Rachel pinched his inner thigh close to his nuts.

When he looked over, her lips formed a sly smile, but her eyes told another story. "Josh," she said. "Meet Wyatt and Morgan, our son and daughter. They're as shocked as you are since they didn't know who their real dad was until just a little while ago, when I told them after we reunited in front of that hacked heart." She paused for a moment before asking, "And whose idea was it to invite us here for dinner so they'd meet Josh and find out?" Her tone was bitter.

Wyatt said, "Drop it, Mom."

"Yea," Morgan chimed in. "We're glad we finally know who our real father is."

Controlling his breathing and heartbeat, Josh leaned across the table and offered a hand to his son, and they shook. "Wyatt, what did your mother say when you learned I was your dad?"

"That I was hot-headed like you, sir." He was sitting at attention and looked like he was ready to salute. "In boot camp, the drill instructors talked about you, but I didn't make the connection because they referred to you as The Badger. Sorry, I'm babbling. I'm a bit dazed right now, sir. Until today, I didn't know The Badger was my father."

Josh hated being called The Badger, the moniker he'd earned for his fierceness in combat and the risks he took. "Please do not call me sir or The Badger. Relax, Wyatt. I'm not in the military anymore." He watched the stiffness bleed out of his son's body.

Josh switched his attention to Morgan. When she offered a hand to shake, he took it between both of his and held it in a warm embrace. "In the last twenty-four years, I've never seen or met a woman more beautiful than your mother. Now I have, and she is the daughter I didn't know I had until today."

"You're still full of bullshit," Rachel breathed in his left ear.

Ignoring her, Josh turned back to his son and asked, "Do you prefer being called Wyatt or Cooper?"

"Cooper is just fine, sir." Wyatt stuttered. "I mean, Josh." Since they printed last names over the left breast pocket of field uniforms in the Marines, that was the standard way to refer to someone else.

"If you don't mind, I'll call you Wyatt. There are other Coopers here, and it will get confusing." His eyes went back to his daughter. "And you, young lady?"

"I prefer Josie," she said.

"Josie?"

"That's the short version of Josephine, my middle name."

Josh wanted to roll his eyes but didn't. "I have a lot to learn." He turned to Rachel again and raised his eyebrows. She winked back. Josephine had been Wyatt Earp's common-law wife of forty-six years until he died.

Josh swept the table with his eyes and returned to the faces of his children. "I'm sorry for leaving home like I did and not keeping in touch. I hope everyone at this table will forgive me."

"Sir." Wyatt's face flushed. "I mean, Josh. You served your country with honor. There is nothing to forgive."

"Speak for yourself, Wyatt," Josie said. "I want to know why Mom never told us." There was a touch of anger in her voice. She was staring at Rachel now.

Had she inherited her mother's temper? Josh hoped not. "Josie, it isn't your mother's fault. I think it would be best if we agreed to bury the past."

"Josh is right, Morgan," Wyatt said. "Listen to him."

"Oh look, my brother, the Marine, is standing up for another buzz cut." But this time, Josie's voice was lighthearted.

Self-conscious, Josh ran a hand through his hair. He hadn't had a buzz cut in years.

Josie noticed and blushed. "Sorry, I'm used to seeing Wyatt's friends with haircuts like him. Why don't you have one, Josh?"

"Because Special Forces need to blend in and may have beards and long hair," Wyatt replied. "How cool is that, Sis?"

Josie glared at her brother and stuck her tongue out at him.

Josh felt Suki's warm breath on his ear when she whispered, "I'll make sure they forgive you and Rachel if you teach me how to be a killer like you."

It was apparent she hadn't been sleeping. When he shifted his attention to her, their noses almost touched, and she didn't budge. She was so close, he could sense her personal magnetic field. "Dear little sister, Suki," he whispered back, "that will not happen. Don't take this the wrong way, but I wouldn't wish that curse on anyone."

"I don't care. I want you to teach me, anyway."

"What I learned took years of training, and it wasn't easy. If you want to learn hand-to-hand combat, why not ask Wyatt to teach you the basics?"

Her answer was to keep her eyes glued to his, and he read the message in them that said: As far as she was concerned, he didn't have a choice. She wanted revenge, and she knew he was more lethal than Wyatt.

"Excuse me." He turned back to Rachel. "How did my sister turn out to be as stubborn as you?"

"Didn't you know? My kids and I are her best buddies. Imagine that, when Suki was six, our children were three, and she was their aunt, but they didn't know. Look at what you missed." She kicked him under the table, and he pretended not to feel the pain. When was she going to stop treating him like they were still kids?

# CHAPTER 8

WITH SUPPER OVER, the older women moved to the kitchen. The men headed to the living room. To avoid his dad, Josh retreated to the veranda and Suki, Wyatt, and Josie followed him. His son and daughter disappeared around the nearest corner, searching for something to sit on.

After his sister lit several citronella candles and turned on a couple of electric insect killers, she joined him on the memorable swinging bench. A moment later, she fell asleep on him again, his shoulder acting as her pillow. He wondered how much time she spent sleeping each day.

Josh leaned back and tried to relax. It wasn't easy. He'd expected muted voices from the living room, but heard a sports program blaring from the only flat-screen TV in the house. His mother never watched TV, but his dad was a sports addict. After supper, he sat in his overstuffed recliner with a six-pack of beer and fell asleep with a game playing.

The loud announcer's voice made it impossible to hear the subtle sounds around the house. That put Josh on edge. No one talked when on a mission, instead communicating mostly with hand signs. Hearing every noise was essential to survival.

Josh had forgotten that porch sitting was a popular pastime here, and Friday night dates often meant going to the local high school football game. The slower lifestyle, clean air, and open space also meant less stress, but winter weather could be brutal if you weren't prepared. He had no intention of returning to that life full time.

Then Wyatt and Josie returned, dragging heavy-duty, wood-slat Amish rocking chairs behind them. Josh stared beyond the railing, looking for anything suspicious, but all he saw were the dark shapes of the barns and bunkhouses. This was why he didn't enjoy spending much time with civilians. They took their safety for granted.

Wyatt got the conversation going. "How many times have you been deployed?"

Josh knew the number but decided on evasive tactics. "I don't know. Hundreds of times in too many countries."

"Wyatt, I'm not interested in war talk," Josie said. "Save that subject for a man cave. I want to know why Mom never told us about our father and why he never came home to find out about us." Her eyes shifted to Josh, and he'd heard the challenge in her voice.

"It wasn't his fault," Wyatt said. "Mom admitted she kept him a secret from us."

"She didn't tell us her reason for doing it," Josie said. "I want him to explain that!"

Josh held his hands up in a sign of surrender. "Blame me for what happened if you have to," he said. "When I joined the Marines, I wanted to escape the ranch and Montana. Why I left had nothing to do with your mother." He paused for a moment before adding in a sober tone, "I planned to come back for her once I was established in the Marines, but that didn't work out."

"What stopped you?" The dark clouds hadn't left Josie's eyes.

"Soon after boot camp in '93," Josh replied, "they sent me to Marine Corps Base Quantico, Virginia, to train as a Scout Sniper. In '94, they assigned us to the 2nd Marines, and we ended up in Cap-Haïtien, Haiti, as part of Operation Uphold Democracy. Once we arrived, my partner, Cheéte, and I mostly conducted reconnaissance missions. Then we were sent to Bosnia. Before I came home to get your mother, they ordered us to join the NATO-led international peacekeeping force in Kosovo. Then there was 9/11, followed by the Afghan invasion. After Cheéte retired, I found out Rachel got married. That's when I became a Navy SEAL, and they assigned my first team to the USS Nassau, a Tarawa-class amphibious assault ship."

From the look in her eyes, Josh thought her anger had cooled until she said, "You must have done something that made Mom angry. What was it?"

"I will not second guess what she was thinking," he replied. "She should explain that."

"Then I'll go get her," Josie said.

She stood, but before she took a step, Wyatt said, "Sit down, Josie. Leave Mom out of this for now. Instead of rehashing their history, I want to know more about him."

She looked deflated and dropped back into her rocking chair. "Maybe you're right, but I still want to know what he did to Mom?"

Josh took that as his cue. "You have nothing to worry about, Josie," he continued. "And there won't be much war talk because most of my deployments were classified. If I blabbed, I'd end up in federal prison."

Josie looked stunned, and Wyatt raised a hand like he was in a classroom. Josh nodded for him to go ahead.

"Mom said you joined right after high school like I did," Wyatt said. "How did you become an officer without a college education? You can talk about that, right?"

Josh asked, "Are you planning to make a career out of the military?"

"Maybe. My four-year active-duty contract is almost up. They've offered me a reenlistment bonus and the rank of E-6 if I make a lateral move to counterintelligence for six years. Should I accept?"

"That's your decision," Josh said. "I don't want to influence you." He suspected he saw movement near one of the older barns, and studied the shadowy areas.

"What are you looking at?" Josie asked.

"Thought I saw something out there," Josh replied.

"I don't see anything," she said as she stared in the same direction.

"He's just alert," Wyatt added. "If you had been to Iraq like me, you'd understand." His face brightened. "How did you reach the rank of O-5 without a college education?"

"I earned a college education while I was on deployments."

"How did you do that?"

"Does it matter?" his sister asked. "He earned a college degree, just like Mom. Now you don't have an excuse, Wyatt." She turned back to Josh and continued, "He hated school."

"I didn't hate it," Wyatt replied. "It was boring."

"My favorite part of school was your mother," Josh said. "If it hadn't been for her, I would've been the classroom slacker. To impress her, I worked my ass off to learn stuff."

Josie jumped on that with what sounded like an accusation. "If she was that important, why did you leave like you did?"

"Because I was blind with anger that had nothing to do with her," Josh blurted out with little thought, regretting saying something that had reignited her fuse.

"What made you so mad?" she asked.

"I don't want to talk about that," he replied, and her eyes smoldered again. Not wanting to give her an excuse to ask another question, he focused on Wyatt. "After experiencing combat, I changed my mind about college. For almost a decade, I carried a laptop and earned three degrees online from reputable public universities in the States. Once I had my first degree, I went to Officer Candidate School." He shifted his focus to Josie. "You wanted to know what I did when I wasn't on duty. Well, I was usually studying or sleeping. I was still a SEAL when I finished OCS in 2007 and was commissioned an Ensign."

"Oh snap," Wyatt said. "Is that all it took?"

"Really," Josie said, sounding irritated, "were you even listening? It took him more than a decade to earn those college degrees. It wasn't easy."

"She's right, Wyatt. SEAL training was far more rigorous and demanding than the Marines. The dropout rate is about 80 percent compared to 11 percent for Marine recruits that fail to finish boot camp."

Josie was nodding with satisfaction as she continued to stare at her brother. To get her attention, Josh leaned forward and touched the back of her hand. Startled, she jerked around to face him.

"There's more," he said in a soothing voice, designed to relax her as he studied her eyes to determine what she was thinking. "I had encouragement from an Army O-6 in Special Operations. When he moved up to flag rank a few years later, I transferred to the Green Beret to be under his command. By the time Delta recruited me, I was an O-3."

"Who was the O-6?" Wyatt asked.

Josie cut in. "My turn. It's only fair."

Wyatt sighed and leaned back. "Okay."

Josie turned to Josh. "You said you carried your laptop everywhere you went." She looked skeptical. "What if it got destroyed by a bullet or one of those roadside bombs? Replacements could get expensive."

Josh hoped her question was proof he'd distracted her from the resentment she'd expressed earlier. "When we were in the field," he said, "the laptop stayed behind on the ship or a base camp."

Before she asked another question, Josh added, "Let me make this clear. I don't want this conversation to be all about me. We'll take turns, and I'll go first. I understand you're in college, Josie. What are you majoring in?"

"Computer and information sciences," she said.

"Where?" he asked.

"The University of Montana in Missoula. I'm in my third year."

"Why that major?"

"Because I didn't want to be a teacher like Mom."

That surprised him. "Rachel's a teacher?" He realized there was a lot he didn't know about her now that twenty-four years had passed. They'd been eighteen when he left and were now forty-two.

"It's a crappy job," Wyatt added. "It doesn't pay enough for the way teachers are treated and all the hours she works at school and at home."

Josie said, "It was almost like we didn't have a mother. Even when she was home, she was busy planning lessons, calling parents, and correcting her students' work. To earn money during the summers, she had another job that also took her away from home for long hours."

"Where was that?" Josh asked.

"A Walmart in Great Falls," Wyatt said. "The pay was worse than teaching with few benefits. If you had been our dad, growing up would've been better." This time he sounded irritated, and Josie nodded as if she agreed with him.

*Not if I'd stayed in Special Forces,* Josh thought. "Come on, guys," he said. "We can talk about what happened back then, when your mother is part of the conversation."

Josie reluctantly nodded, and Josh focused on her. "Your turn," he said.

"Since you've been all over the world, what were your favorite countries?" she asked. "I want to see the world, too, but as a tourist. I'll never join the military."

"You'd like Thailand. I've been there several times."

She leaned forward and said, "Tell us more."

He talked about the opulent royal palaces, the ornate Buddhist temples, Chiang Mai in the north, and Phuket Island in the south. He left out the thriving prostitution industry in Bangkok.

During his trips to Thailand, he'd stayed away from the red-light districts and bordellos that offered younger girls whom Cheéte said were probably sex slaves. His partner said to go to wine bars and find more mature, part-time girlfriends. They'd appreciate any financial help Josh offered to make their lives easier. Over time, Josh had compiled a list of women in different countries and cities to call when he was on leave.

After he and Cheéte had rescued Mia from sex traffickers in Haiti, his partner found an older couple in France to adopt her. She stayed in touch with Josh through social media, and a decade later, they became lovers. By then, Mia had been twenty-four, and he was twenty-eight. After he deleted the part-time girlfriend list from his laptop, he started spending most of his vacation time in France with her. Just thinking about her now caused a sense of depression that weighed him down.

Sometime later, Josh glanced at his wristwatch and discovered it was 0300. "Look at that." He held his wrist out, so they saw the time, too. "When you're enjoying yourself, the time has a way of retreating underground. This conversation will have to be put on hold. I haven't slept for a couple of days, and I have plans for tomorrow."

Wyatt looked disappointed. "I have to return to base, or I'd join you."

Josh thought that was a good thing. He didn't want to introduce Wyatt to his dangerous world. Special Operations Forces had much higher casualty rates than the conventional military, and he had the scars to prove it. "Where are you stationed?" Josh asked.

"The Mountain Warfare Training Center in Bridgeport, California. My unit is getting ready to deploy to Afghanistan."

"Then I suggest you accept the move to counterintelligence."

"I thought you were against giving me advice," Wyatt said.

"Do that and I'll reserve a few weekends for Josie and a couple of weekdays to spend with you." He didn't mention that it would also keep Wyatt out of danger for a while.

"I'd like that," Wyatt said. "But my unit will train during the week."

"Not to worry. Your commanding officer is a friend. You know that once your unit finds out I'm your father, they'll treat you differently, and it won't always be a good thing."

That sobered Wyatt. Then his son stood at attention, saluted, and almost shouted, "Oorah!" He shot out a hand, and they shook.

"You don't have to be so gung ho around me. In Special Forces, military etiquette is relaxed."

"Really?" Wyatt's eyes glowed with excitement. "Maybe I should try out for the SEALS, then."

Josh fought back laughter and kept his expression sober. "Now I'm worried I've planted the wrong seed in your head."

Josie left her rocking chair and stepped past her brother to hug Josh. "Can I call you Dad?" she asked.

A lump appeared in his throat. "It's okay with me, but I'm not sure I've earned that title yet. And don't blame your mother for what happened. We were both eighteen and had it rough growing up. It was complicated. When we have more time and all four of us are together, we'll talk about it."

"Mom never talks about what it was like growing up," Josie said. "It's like she burned that book."

"If your mother forgives me, I think she'll be able to talk about that life again," he said. "When we were together, we shared everything, but it has to be up to her to want to go there. I won't attempt to force her to do it."

There were tears in Josie's eyes as she grabbed her brother's hand. "Come on, dummy, can't you see our dad wants to get some rest." She pulled Wyatt toward the front door. Before they slipped inside, she glanced over her shoulder and flashed a brief smile, perhaps a temporary gesture of forgiveness.

Once they were gone, it took time to wake Suki. It was as if she were drugged.

"I want to grab some sleep, Suki. At 0700, I'm saddling a horse and taking a ride."

"What time is 0700?" she asked, sounding dopey.

"Seven in the morning."

"What do you call seven PM?"

"That's 1900."

The cobwebs in her voice vanished, and she said, "I'm going too. Since we have less than four hours, why not stay here?" She went to a chest against the wall and pulled out two folded wool blankets. Josh smelled the familiar scent of cedar when she opened the storage container.

She covered his legs with one blanket and wrapped the second one around her before sitting and resting her head on his shoulder again. "I'm sure you've slept in worse places." In no time, it seemed, her breathing signaled she was asleep.

*What the hell am I going to do now?* he thought. He'd been

planning to meet with LG and their teams to work on their plans for this operation. Maybe he could introduce her to Audie. Meeting LG's service dog might be good for her, and the canine would keep her company. Resting his head on top of Suki's, he catnapped but was always alert.

When a sizeable, four-legged furry beast appeared out of the dark and climbed the steps to the veranda, Josh thought it was a bear at first. He almost reached for the 9mm Glock 43 in his ankle holster, but as soon as he recognized the big dog as one of his dad's Anatolian Shepherds, he relaxed.

Then he remembered this guy wouldn't know him. All the dogs that had been here when he left were long dead. This one had to weigh at least 140 pounds, and it took up a bold stance and stared at him. Josh tensed up, ready for a fight. His dad trained the dogs to be aggressive, not friendly. If this one attacked, it would move fast, but Josh was fast, too.

There were several things he could do if it attacked. One would be to jam a hand in its mouth and grab its tongue with a death grip or cram his fist and forearm down its throat. He could use other maneuvers, like quickly slipping out of his windbreaker as the dog was leaping for his chest and wrap it around its head. He could also use a fist like a spear and strike its nose hard.

The beast sniffed the air, and its intelligent eyes found Suki. Relaxing, the dog turned in the other direction and went out of sight along the veranda.

With a sigh, Josh felt at ease for the first time in days. He'd forgotten that his dad always trained two or three of the Anatolians to guard the house, barns, and corrals at night. They were no threat to the family and regular ranch hands, but that wasn't the case with unexpected strangers. Resting his head on top of Suki's, he catnapped and trusted the dogs to warn him if there were any threats.

# CHAPTER 9

SOON AFTER 0700, Suki was following Josh as they hoofed it into the hills. At first, she thought he didn't know where he was going. Then she remembered he grew up working on this ranch like her other brothers and probably knew it better than she did. While the boys were out repairing fences and doing other ranch work, she grew up helping her mother with the household chores.

Lost in thought, Suki jerked when a woman's harsh, wobbly voice stopped them. "What you doin' on my land?"

Suki recognized who it was, but they had ridden their horses into a natural depression, and the voice was bouncing off the rough terrain around them. Even so, she saw Josh trying to spot her location.

"I've got my Winchester," Gracie called. "Get off my farm. No one is taking it from me."

"Do you know who that is?" Josh asked.

"It's Crazy Gracie. Don't mind her. She's part deaf, a little blind, and mostly hot air."

Josh twisted around in the saddle to stare at Suki. "Are you talking about Gracie Stuart? She was old when I left."

"She's in her nineties now but doesn't know it." Suki looked past him and shouted, "If you fire that old Winchester, Gracie, it will probably blow up in your face. I suspect it hasn't been cleaned properly for decades. And for your information, this isn't your land. It's ours. You have strayed from your place."

Montana was home to over 28,000 farm and ranch operations.

"I have not," the old woman replied as she appeared from behind a boulder about thirty yards from them. She carried a lever-action rifle. Around her feet swarmed what looked like a flock of tabby cats. "I was making my morning rounds, making sure those sneaky, genital-manipulating varmints weren't about."

"Gracie," Suki said, "you mean genetically manipulated seeds, not someone's privates, and I'll bet that Winchester is empty."

The old woman pressed her lips together in a thin line and shook her head. Then she added, "It isn't empty, and I'll shoot their stones off, too, if I catch them sneaking around here. I can still hit a coyote's eyeball at 300 yards."

"When's the last time you shot a coyote?" Suki asked.

Gracie was holding the rifle, so it wasn't pointing at anyone. "Don't remember."

"How much you want to bet that the last time you hit anything at that distance was in the 1950s?"

"You are a sassy little thing, Suki Kavanagh." The scrawny old woman's snowy white hair looked like a silvery rat's nest exploding from under a sweat-stained, soiled Stetson.

"Those greedy Frankenfood people must have you all riled up," Suki said.

"Those scoundrels have been threatenin' to take me to court because some of their demon seeds sprouted on my land. I ain't responsible for the wind. I sprayed their sprouts with Roundup." She cackled. "Wait 'till they get me in court, and I show the judge photos of what I did. Those piss-ants treated me like a thief."

Gracie had stopped about a dozen feet from them. Josh swung out of the saddle, and Suki copied him. Once she was on her feet, she watched her brother stretch his back like it was stiff. It must have been a long time since he'd been on a horse.

"Do you remember me, Ms. Stuart?" Josh asked in a loud voice.

"Tone it down," Suki said. "She's not that deaf. You'll rile her up again."

Gracie cocked her head to one side, squinted, and studied Josh. "Don't know if I do," she replied.

"It's my older brother Josh," Suki said.

"The one who ran off to the Marines?" Gracie's cats were swirling around her legs, purring, and rubbing against her ankles. "He should've stayed and married Rachel. She's a fine school teacher. One of my great-grandchildren was in her class last year."

"Well, he's come home to marry her if she says yes," Suki replied. She noticed Josh had snapped his head around to stare at her. She met his eyes and added, "That's what Rachel said after you two met outside."

"I thought Sammy told you," he said.

"Sammy never said a thing about what happened out there."

Josh pointed at Gracie's rifle. "Is that the Winchester Model 50, with the 10-round box magazine?"

"Yep, before I was born, my long-dead daddy bought this .35 caliber for forty-three dollars in 1905."

"I was a kid the first time you let me fire that rifle at a half-dozen empty bean cans," he said.

"I remember," she replied, "and you didn't miss once."

"If you ever want to sell it, think of me first. I'd love to add it to my collection."

A chime sounded, and Gracie looked at a pink Fitbit on her wrist. "Pardon me. My doctor said I have to eat six to eight snacks a day instead of two big meals. But no candy and no meat." She took a handful of raw garlic cloves and a small onion from a pocket, popping three of the cloves in her mouth before taking a bite of the onion. After a moment of chewing, the old woman stepped closer to Suki and gently touched her face. "I heard what happened to you, sugar. You going to be okay?" Her voice turned crusty. "That bastard is going to get what's coming to him."

Suki's eyes filled with tears from the old woman's garlic-and-onion-infused breath and body odor. Seeing the tears, Gracie's face filled with compassion. "If you want me to bushwhack that mongrel, I will!" She wrapped her arms around Suki and hugged her tighter.

"Thank you, Ms. Stuart," Suki replied, her voice muffled against the old woman's doughy breasts, "but my brother came home to teach me how to defend myself." She wondered how long she could hold her breath.

When the old woman let go, Suki took a step back and glanced at Josh to see his reaction. His expression offered no clues. She wanted to be tough like him.

"I better be gettin' home," Grace said in a rush. "My clowder of cats will scold me if I don't feed them soon." She pulled another handful of raw garlic cloves out of a different pocket and held them out. "You want some? They're good for what ails you."

"Thank you, but no," Suki said. "We already had breakfast."

"I've got wild mushrooms too. They'll protect you from gettin' old." She cackled again and started poking her free hand in different pockets, searching for them.

"Don't bother," Suki replied. "We ain't hungry yet."

After Gracie left, Suki said, "She seriously needs to brush her teeth, take a long bath soaking in Epsom salts, and wash her clothes with white vinegar." She shuddered. "I feel itchy."

"I always liked her," Josh said, "but let's get this mission back on course."

"I didn't know we were on a mission. I thought we were just out for a ride so you could see the ranch again."

"Sweet little sister, you are the mission."

"What do you mean?"

"You'll see."

"Why do you have to be so cryptic?" she asked.

"Blame it on the military," he replied. Back on the saddle, she followed him through the hills until they found a dry streambed that led toward a gash in a hillside where Josh dismounted and said, "We walk from here."

Suki thought something was watching them and kept glancing over her shoulder to see if it was a wolf, coyote, mountain lion, or grizzly.

"What is it?" he asked.

She took a jittery breath. "I think something is stalking us."

"The only eyes watching us are the friendly kind." He cupped his mouth and called out. "Nick, give us a hoot."

When a hoot owl replied, she was stunned. "Really," she said, "you have an owl named Nick? That is just plum strange."

Josh laughed. "Nick is not an owl. He keeps watch on this gap to make sure where we're going stays a secret. Come on." They walked their horses along the narrow, dry streambed. It didn't take long for Suki to discover why it was safer to lead the horses than to ride them.

Thick stands of trees clung to the steep slopes on both sides of the streambed. The evergreen branches hung low over their heads, blocking out most of the sun and making it gloomy. Suki shivered. Looking down, she studied the ground, searching for tracks, and saw no sign that anyone or anything had ever been here before. That wasn't right. There was always wild animal scat and tracks to be found in places like this. "I don't like it here," she said. "It's spooky."

"My ghosts will not hurt you," Josh said.

"Yea, right," she replied. "There's no such thing as ghosts."

"They're not the dead kind."

She gave him a glance that said she suspected he was full of shit. "Are you joking?"

"No way! I'm as serious as the fifth act of a tragedy."

Rounding a corner in the narrowing, water-carved channel, they were confronted by a ten-foot-tall clay-and-rock dam. She saw a small, boxy-shaped iron sluice gate near the bottom. "Looks like a dead end."

"Not yet," he replied.

It surprised Suki when Josh led his horse up the slope to the left until they were out of sight. She heard his boots and the horse's shoes slipping on the steep, rocky surface. Then she was surrounded by silence and thought he'd abandoned her. She hadn't been left alone like this since the rape. That made her nervous, and her heart thudded.

A moment later, there was the clatter of iron horseshoes on stone above her, and she looked up.

"Are you coming?" Josh was in his saddle, watching her from the top of the dam.

"When's the last time you rode a horse across that dam?"

"Twenty-four years ago," he replied. Then she watched him get his horse moving. When he was almost to the other side, she started up. When she reached the top, he was gone. It was a narrow surface, and she doubted it was safe, but she had just witnessed her brother cross it on his horse. If she hadn't seen that, she would've never attempted to do the same thing.

A moment later, she joined him, where he was waiting in the dry watercourse on the other side of the dam.

"That was not okay," she said with ice in her voice.

A toothpick had materialized in Josh's mouth. The visible tip jiggled as he chewed on the other end. "We can ride from here. The overhanging branches have been cut higher."

"What about our tracks?" she asked.

"My ghost owl will take care of those, at least the ones on the other side of the dam. If a stranger gets that far, Nick will warn us with the screech of a red-tailed hawk."

"Do you use bird and animal sounds as a code?" she asked.

"Yep," he replied.

"You should think about adding some animal tracks and scat," she said. "They don't clean up after themselves."

"We know," Josh replied. "We keep it that way for another reason."

When he didn't explain what that was, she said, "Don't leave me alone like that again."

His body grew still, and he fixed his eyes on her face. A moment later, he nodded.

She didn't know what to make of her older brother. He hadn't said a word, but it was apparent from his expression that he understood what she'd been thinking.

After a long time in the narrow, twisting streambed, they entered a meadow surrounded by steep, forested slopes that climbed skyward. The hidden valley was at least a thousand yards and a hundred wide.

"I want to know if you can spot our encampment," Josh said.

"There's a campground in here?" The sun was hovering just above the mountains at the far end of the meadow, blinding her and making her eyes water. Suki shaded her eyes and scanned the pocket valley. A moment later, she said, "I don't see anything."

"That's the way it should be with ghosts."

She frowned and shook her head. He popped a grin, turned

his mount to the left, and rode parallel to the tree line toward the far end of the basin. She'd expected her brother to be more talkative. Over the years, Sammy had shared stories about Josh before he'd joined the Marines, and most of them included the fact that he had been a blabbermouth as a kid and couldn't keep a secret. Well, he wasn't that way anymore, and she wondered what had changed him.

Suki's horse stopped when Josh reined his in. He pointed at the open space to their right. "When it rains, that area floods, and the winter snowmelt keeps feeding it until summer. That meadow is higher than the creek. The water runs out, and this cozy little valley becomes dry again...that is, if the sluice gate is open. Closed, this area becomes a shallow lake that breeds mosquitos. Between May and August, they swarm, starved for blood. I even heard one of 'em say, 'So, should we eat him here or drag him back into the brush and eat him?' After the first mosquito asked that question, the others said, 'We'd better eat him here. If we drag him back into the brush, the really big ones will get him.'"

"You did not hear a mosquito say that," she said, trying to hide her smile.

"True, but I read it in the Billings Gazette. I found this spot one summer when I was twelve and kept it a secret. Now it's your secret, too. Don't tell Sammy or anyone else."

"Rachel would love this place," she said. "Did you build the dam?"

"No, that was done by two of our ancestors, but I repaired it and got the sluice gate working again. That was a damned hard job too—for a twelve-year-old."

"It would be nice if there was a cozy cabin here," she said.

A toothy grin cracked his face.

"What?" she asked.

"Wait for it," he replied.

After they reached the far end, he stopped and faced her again. "Look for a loose, scattered pile of rocks at the base of one of the nearby trees," he said.

She stood in her stirrups and scanned the closest trees until she spotted the irregular pile of stones. She pointed at them.

"The slope isn't as steep to the right of that tree," he said. "On the other side, you'll find a trail. Follow the switchbacks for about a hundred yards, and you'll reach an enchanted cabin just perfect for ghosts. It's hidden up there on a deep ledge."

"Ghosts and supernatural cabins," she said. "You have an imagination." She glanced at the sky and noticed it was already late afternoon. "Our ride took longer than I expected. Are we staying the night?"

"That's the plan. I told our grandmother we'd be back tomorrow morning, so no one will panic." He urged his horse forward and led the way past the subtly marked tree and up the slope.

"We didn't bring any sleeping bags," she said, "and what about food? All we have are a couple of water bottles and a few energy bars."

"Not a problem," he replied.

A moment later, they reached a one-room cabin. Suki stopped and stared at it like it was an illusion. She hadn't expected to find a log cabin here that looked this good; it was clearly old, but in decent shape.

"This was a wreck the first time I saw it," Josh said. "It took me several summers to fix it up."

Dismounting, she tied her horse to a hitching rail and went exploring. What she discovered amazed her. Behind the cabin, there were tents, neat piles of gear, and camouflage netting in the trees, covering it all. There were also men dressed in military-style clothing that blended with the surroundings. It was apparent they were busy doing something.

She sensed Josh had followed her. "They must be your ghosts," she said. "How many are there?"

"Thirty-six."

"How did you get all this stuff in here and not get spotted doing it?"

"We have a couple of Chinooks that fly in at night. During the day, they're grounded in Idaho on a remote potato farm our outfit owns. It's about 300 miles from here."

"Why does your outfit have a potato farm in Idaho?"

"It's part of our contracting business."

When a large Golden Retriever slipped under her right hand, she gasped and glanced down. "You didn't warn me about the ghost dog," she said.

"His name is Audie Murphy. We call him Audie. He's a service dog and the friendliest guy you'll ever meet. He wants you to pet him because he loves everyone who isn't a threat to his human."

"He has a human?" Suki shook her head. After hearing that, she thought nothing else would surprise her. She was learning to expect the unexpected from Josh. "Why is he so friendly?" she asked. "Audie doesn't know me."

As if he understood what she'd said, the dog lifted his head into Suki's hand and nudged her until she petted him.

"Trust me," Josh said. "He already knows you better than you know yourself. PTSD haunts most of us, and Audie is our guardian angel. He's going to take care of you, too. Tap your cheek and ask him to give you a kiss."

*Might as well,* Suki thought. She knelt on one knee and tapped her cheek with a fingertip. "How about a kiss, Audie?"

The dog looked eager and wagged his tail. When his eyes were even with hers, he leaned forward and gently touched Suki's cheek with his nose. Then, looking pleased, he backed up a couple of steps and sat on his haunches.

Stunned, Suki watched Audie peel back his lips in a dog smile. That triggered a burst of giggles from her that quickly vanished when she turned to Josh. "That's the first time I've laughed since..." She covered her mouth, and her eyes misted over.

"I told you Audie was going to be your guardian angel."

Suki wrapped her arms around the dog's neck and buried her face in its soft fur. "I don't want to ever leave this magical place," she said.

# CHAPTER 10

THE NIGHT'S dull glow filtered through the trees and turned the area around the cabin into an enchanted realm. Suki wouldn't have been surprised if a band of Celtic druids appeared dancing a jig and playing "Road to Camelot."

She sat cross-legged on the ground with one hand resting on the back of Audie's neck. Occasionally, the dog took a deep breath and sighed, as if he sensed the same magic Suki did.

Soon after arriving, Josh had put Suki to work moving bags of trash from the campsite to the area where the helicopters were landing. She was no stranger to hard work, but now her muscles ached. All she wanted to do was crawl into a warm sleeping bag, but feared surrendering to the sleep she craved. Because she got a few blisters on the palms of her hands, Josh had sent her to see the medic.

Even with all the Special Forces troops around her, she didn't feel safe. She sensed these men differed from those who abused her, but she doubted her own judgment.

It was apparent that the dog's human was the oldest man in the camp. She guessed he was at least in his seventies. When

Josh had introduced her to LG, he'd nodded and hadn't said a word. Now he was sitting on the other side of her four-legged chaperone. When anyone talked to him, she heard the tone of reverence in their voices and wondered what he'd done to earn that level of respect. His responses were usually only one or two words, or just the same nod she'd received.

Everyone was sitting together, eating MREs warmed inside the flameless heater packets that came with each meal. Suki had a veggie burger with BBQ sauce. She missed the campfire but understood the need to do without. They had also given her a twenty-ounce plastic blender bottle and told her to shake it a lot to mix all the goodies added to "create a perfectly relaxing protein shake." The blend tasted sweet with lots of rich, dark chocolate and a hint of mint.

"Which meal do you have?" she asked LG before taking another sip of the tasty drink. There was enough light to make out his weathered face and close-cut salt-and-pepper hair. When she first met him, she'd noticed he didn't have an ounce of fat on him.

"Chili with beans," he replied in a raspy whisper. He leaned over Audie to study the packets in front of her. With a low, throaty rumble, he continued, "I'll trade my cherry-blueberry cobbler for your fudge brownie."

"Deal," Suki said, pleased she'd gotten more than two words out of him.

Another long silence crept by before Suki broke it again. "Why do they call you LG?"

It made her uncomfortable when he studied her for a moment. Then he said in a louder conversational tone that reminded her of Johnny Cash, "When I retired after serving thirty-nine years, I was a lieutenant general. LG is short for that."

Stunned, she thought, *What is a three-star general doing taking orders from my brother?*

LG grinned. The smile dropped years from his face. That's when she noticed his blue eyes and realized he could've been Daniel Craig's older brother. She was curious. Considering his profession, was he another James Bond type?

"Josh is in charge because it was his idea to start The Oath Group," LG said. "In Special Forces, he who has had the most combat experience usually calls the shots no matter what their rank is, and Josh is one of the best."

"My brother recruited you?"

"He did. When I retired, I was single and wasn't interested in rocking chairs, fishing, writing a book, or getting into politics. Truth be told, I didn't know what to do with my life until Josh showed up and made me the offer. I grabbed hold of it like it was a parachute."

"Have you ever been married?" She regretted the words the instant they slipped out. "I'm sorry." She was glad the gloom hid her bloom of embarrassment. "I shouldn't pry."

"No bother," he said. "By the time I graduated from West Point as a second lieutenant, I was already tethered to the Army. A few years later, I was so dedicated to my career that I didn't think to ask the woman I was living with to marry me. When I was gone again on another deployment, she found a civilian to fill her life, and he popped the question.

"The next time I fell in lust, I married that one. Number two lasted long enough for us to have a couple of kids. Because I was gone so much, she found someone else and ditched me, too."

"That was mean!" Suki blushed again. "I mean, you deserved better than that."

"It wasn't her fault," he said. "I was never around. During my decades in the Green Beret, I was married and divorced six times."

When he saw Suki's shock, he held up both hands as if he were surrendering and shrugged. "It's easy to confuse lust for love. I never could ignore a pretty face and a cute figure. Each marriage lasted long enough to produce a kid or two. But a marriage built on lust isn't strong enough to survive when she's going crazy, raising the kids alone, and feeling neglected.

"How did you get Audie Murphy?" she asked, wanting to change the subject.

"He's my third service dog. I got them when they were pups and trained them myself."

"You must have enjoyed being in the Green Beret to sacrifice so much. Why did you get out?"

"It wasn't my choice. All general officers have to retire the month after their sixty-fourth birthday. If it weren't for your brother, I don't think I'd be here today. He must've known what was going on in my head."

Suki thought she knew what he meant and wasn't about to bring up her own battles resisting suicide. "Will you teach me how to train my service dog?" she asked. "I want one like Audie. If you say yes, Josh will have to bring me with him every time he comes here. What about horses? I read they can also be trained."

LG chuckled. "Yea, horses can be trained. But a dog is better. In fact, you can train a pig or a bird too. You talking about that white horse you rode in on?"

She nodded. "She's been mine since she was foaled. We've been together for twenty years, and I trust her more than dogs and men. The only dogs around the ranch are humorless, like my dad."

"I understand, but the only service horses I've heard of are miniature ones, and they're trained to guide the blind and pull wheelchairs. Your horse is also too old to train. It's better when they're young. What's her name?"

"Pegasus," she replied. "I'll go with a dog, then."

"Think of it this way," he said. "You can't take a horse everywhere you can take a dog. You can still ride Pegasus. In fact, the dog you train will probably become best friends with your horse." He took another bite of the fudge brownie and gestured at its MRE pouch. "I'm cursed with a sweet tooth, and dentists have a love-hate relationship with me."

She heard the thrumming sound of helicopters in the distance, and they were growing louder.

"Eat up, Suki," LG said. "It's time to unload and reload those Chinooks before we turn in."

She couldn't believe it. She'd worked all afternoon until dusk, and now they were going to do it again. "Aren't you worried that noise will give away this location?"

"Do you remember the Alamo?"

She wondered where he was going with that and said, "Sort of."

"Well," LG continued, "we're all committed and willing to fight to the end for what we think is right. That's what they did at the Alamo. It's a better way to go than gettin' old and becoming useless."

Suki thought about what had happened at the Alamo and blurted out with a barely audible stammer, "Are you saying you'd die for me?"

"You're darn tootin', doll," he replied in a lighter tone. "We'd do it for any law-abiding citizen who was victimized, as you were." LG stood, dusted off his camouflage fatigues, cleaned up his space, and hurried off with the others toward the clearing.

She jumped when her brother spoke from behind her. "You don't have to do this, Suki."

"LG said he will die for me."

"We all are. We didn't start this outfit to fight for a gang of greedy billionaire extremists and the lying politicians they own. We did it so people like you can live free and safe, but achieving that goal is much harder than it sounds."

It was quiet for a moment before he continued. "I see you're having trouble wrapping your mind around that, so let me share with you the oath I took when I became a commissioned officer."

He held up his right hand. "I, Josh Kavanagh, do solemnly swear that I will support and defend the Constitution of the United States against all enemies, foreign and domestic; that I will bear true faith and allegiance to the same; that I take this obligation freely, without any mental reservation or purpose of evasion; and that I will well and faithfully discharge the duties of the office on which I am about to enter. So help me God."

He looked sincere when he added, "Chew on that, little sister. Now you know why we call our outfit The Oath Group."

"That oath must be something new," she said. "That's the first I've heard of it."

He shook his head. "Nope, congress approved it in 1789 and it applies to all commissioned officers, non-commissioned officers, and privates. George Washington was the first president to take it. Once you take that oath, there's no expiration date, even if you reach a hundred, and anyone that breaks it is a traitor."

"I'm tired," she replied, "but I will not let that stop me from working alongside your men. It's the least I can do."

Without warning, he leaned forward and kissed her lightly on her forehead.

"I thought LG was a man of few words," she said. "Why did he talk to me?"

"His sweet tooth includes pretty women," Josh said. "That's why he's been married so many times. Think of it this way: that he opened up to you is proof you're a head-turner."

Dazed and dizzy with mixed emotions, she replied, "I didn't think he was flirting with me."

Josh shook his head. "He might want to, but he knows the restrictions that come with age. He wouldn't do that to you, or any girl as young as you are."

"I'm not that young," she said in a defensive tone.

Josh laughed. "You're twenty-seven. To us, that's young. Come on, little sister. Let's get going."

She followed him toward the clearing where the others were already unloading the Chinooks. When the large helicopters flew back to the potato farm in Idaho, they'd take the trash she'd lugged down here with them.

That's when she realized Audie was still with her. "He's not my dog," she said. "Why isn't he with LG?"

Josh glanced at the dog and smiled with genuine affection. "Audie senses you need him more than the rest of us do right now." His body seemed to sag, and he sighed. "I'm tired, too. Haven't had much sleep the last few days, but that's nothing new. Let's get this task done, then we can catch some winks."

"What were your men doing all day? I never saw what they were up to, but they seemed busy."

"I'll reveal that secret another time," he replied.

---

Later, Josh led Gary, the team's medic, to where his sister was sleeping. Audie was beside her. The dog looked up as they approached and wagged his tail.

"Come here, Boss," LG said, and the dog went to its human and sat beside him to watch. LG draped an arm across Audie's shoulders.

Unzipping her sleeping bag to expose her left arm and hand, Josh knelt beside his sister, ready to assist. The medic checked her vital signs to make sure she was in a deep sleep.

"She's ready," Gary said.

Josh knew that meant her heart rate was below sixty beats per minute. They had timed everything from the moment she'd fallen asleep.

Special Forces medics trained for more than a year. Their skills included dive medicine, altitude physiology, large animal veterinary care, dental extraction, orthopedics, and advanced trauma life support.

Audie thumped his tail against the dirt, showing his worry, and moaned deep in his throat. LG made eye contact with the dog and said, "It's okay. We're doing this for her safety. Besides, you have one of those chips, too, just like we all do in case we hit a snag and what we're doing turns into a clusterfuck." He rubbed the dog's neck to reassure him.

To make sure Suki would fall asleep, freeze-dried Fiji kava powder had been added to the drink that came with the MRE ration she had for dinner.

A moment later, it was over. The medic had used a hypodermic with a large-bore needle to inject a DARPA microchip the size of a grain of rice under the fascia between her thumb and forefinger on her left hand. Everyone in The Oath Group had one. The chips monitored vital signs and location. They were heavily encrypted, and no one was going to hack into one without the proper program and code.

"This is the best spot to insert the chip," the medic said. "It'll be hidden under a blister. If she were awake, the injection would be no worse than a bee sting. I can remove it easily when she doesn't need it anymore."

Josh wanted to chip everyone in his family, but the layers of secrecy behind their primary operation in Montana and Idaho made that impossible. What they were doing for Suki was off the books. The Oath Group had voted to help Josh get justice for his sister, and the risks they were taking meant what she didn't know couldn't come back and bite them later.

They were here because the FBI had dropped the ball for monitoring organized hate groups in the United States. A handful of influential people in leadership positions in the CIA and

DOD had hired The Oath Group to do that. Although the CIA was focused on gathering intelligence from foreign nations, it also performed classified missions in the United States to achieve its goals. Another level of compartmentalized information was added to the Top Secret Op by hiring contractors like them.

There were six states with high concentrations of hate groups. Montana had the highest ratio, and Idaho, in fifth place, was next door. Organized hate was concentrated in areas that were poorer, less educated, less diverse, whiter, more religious, and more conservative.

# CHAPTER 11

SUKI AWOKE, thinking she was in her bedroom, but someone was shaking her. No one had done that before. She grumbled, "Go away!"

Then she heard a distant chorus of singing voices and what sounded like the rhythmic thumping of savage war drums. *What the hell,* she thought. Maybe this was a bad dream, but none of her nightmares came with music. With blurry vision, she stuck her head out of the sleeping bag to discover she wasn't at home—she was on the ground, and it was freezing cold outside.

She remembered where she was and said with a croaking voice, "I never get up when it's this dark." She retreated inside the toasty cocoon of the sleeping bag.

"Get out of that fart sack, Suki. It's time to chow down and get going."

"I'm not leaving this sleeping bag, Josh." The tone of her voice summoned Audie, who nudged her shoulder with his nose.

Like a turtle, her head emerged from the sleeping bag again, and she stared at the dog's muzzle, inches from her face. "Traitor," she said. The chanting voices sounded louder now. Maybe it hadn't been a dream.

She heard a booming lone voice belt out, "I don't know, but I've been told Eskimo pussy is mighty cold."

Then a chorus repeated the refrain.

The lone voice returned with, "Mmm, good."

The chorus repeated those two words.

"What's that?" The only a cappella she'd heard was in her mom's chapel on Sundays. She'd never heard jogging troops singing bawdy cadence. "Never mind," she said. "It sounds gross. I don't want to know." She rubbed her face to warm it up. The sound of the singing and synchronized thumping receded as it moved away.

"Nothing to be concerned about," LG said. "Our troops are doing their morning PT. Me and Audie would be with them, but we're joining you and Josh on the ride back to the ranch."

Suki squinted and blinked. She was still mired in sleep inertia and was groggy. "What?" Her voice was slurred. Had someone drugged again her? With that thought, she had a flash of panic, but Audie was there. She watched him lift his muzzle and bark in a mid-range pitch. "Ar-ruff." She imagined he meant, "Get up, lazy."

"Did I just hear that Army dog say I was lazy?" Suki slipped farther out of the sleeping bag and wrapped her slender arms around Audie's furry neck. Stunned, she realized the dog had distracted her and disarmed the panic attack.

"He was thinking about dragging you out," LG replied. "He's done it to me before when I've been too slow at reveille. Our retirement quarters are on a military base."

"Reveille?" she asked.

"When the troops hear a bugle in the morning, they know it's time to start a new day," LG replied.

"Cold water works better," Josh said. "That's what I do after I'm up."

"Josh doesn't like reveille, so he's always up before the bugle," LG said. "None of us know how he does it."

"I have a silent alarm in my head, and cold water works better than anything else to get the blood moving."

Suki glared at her brother. "You wouldn't?"

"Don't tempt me," he replied. "Back when I was a kid, I did it to our brothers to get them out of bed faster. All it took was twice for them to learn that lesson."

Suki let the dog go, stretched, and yawned. "What's for breakfast?"

Silently dancing on four paws and wagging his tail signaled Audie knew what the word "breakfast" meant.

"How long do they keep up that PT stuff?" she asked.

"We start at 0500, and it doesn't end for two hours," LG replied.

She remembered that meant five in the morning and groaned. "Damn, that's just way too early." Suki forced herself to crawl out of the sleeping bag into the cold. She'd slept in her clothing, but her boots had spent the night outside. Before slipping them on, she turned them upside down and gave them a shake to make sure nothing that stings had crawled inside.

An hour later, the sun was still reluctantly lurking below the horizon. When Josh led Suki, Audie, and LG out of the pocket valley, dawn, like a sheepdog, was slipping silently across the landscape, herding the night west.

"Suki, do Mom and Dad still debate politics and religion?" Josh asked as they rode in a single file, with LG bringing up the rear. Audie was well ahead of them, inspecting the trail. Occasionally, he glanced back to see if his humans were keeping up.

She shrugged. "They don't argue much, if that's what you want to know. They don't talk much either. They started sleeping in separate bedrooms when I was seven. He spends all day outside working somewhere on the ranch. She spends most weekdays away from home at her chapel. She has an office there, and that's where she writes her novels. She also has a bedroom in the chapel's basement and sometimes sleeps there."

"Eventually, I'm going to have to talk to them, and I want to know what the unwritten rules are."

"Well," she replied, "Dad is antiwar. Mom thinks like an Old Testament fire-and-brimstone preacher."

Josh nodded. "I remember her favorite Bible passage was 'Thou shalt love the Lord thy God with all thy heart, and with all thy soul, and with all thy mind.' "

"Still is," she said.

"Where do you stand, Suki?" LG asked from the rear.

Without thinking, she looked over her shoulder and flashed him a smile. Then, stunned, she erased it as her face heated with a blush. "I agree mostly with my dad," she said, avoiding eye contact.

"When Mom and Dad are in the same room, do they ever talk politics or religion?" Josh asked.

Suki shook her head, and her voice cracked when she said, "No, never!" She turned aside and spit to get rid of the awkward gunk that had appeared in her throat.

"Good. No shouting matches. That's the way it was after they agreed to stop trying to convince each other to change their views." Josh shifted his eyes to LG. "That means we avoid those same subjects when we're around them."

"Crystal clear," LG replied.

"When Dad and I are alone, we talk," Suki said. "I agree with him most of the time, so we get along."

"What about Sam and Mel?" Josh asked.

"Sam agrees with Mom, and Mel couldn't care less." She

glanced from LG to her brother. "Explain why you two are still playing soldier."

With a low-key voice, LG said, "We're chasing the thrill."

"I don't see it that way," Josh said.

Suki looked confused. "Explain, older brother."

"The thrill chases me like a shadow. I can't get rid of it."

"When we're on a mission, we're more alive," LG added.

"Wow, sort of like an obsession, right?"

"Change the subject, please," Josh said.

"Mom might be more of a warmonger than Dad, but she will not approve of someone who gambles with death." Suki twisted around to see LG again.

She saw a lot of character and mileage carved in his lean face. And, since he had trained Audie, a loving creature by any measure, LG must have had a very patient, kind heart. If she'd had a choice for a father, she'd have picked him. "What's your real name?" she asked.

LG looked uncomfortable.

"He doesn't like it," Josh said.

"The initials are the same," LG replied. "That's what counts."

Suki scrunched up her nose. "Now I'm really curious."

"His name is Linus Lamont Graves," Josh said.

"Shit!" LG hissed. "Why did you spill that?"

Suki couldn't help but grin. "I think that's a cute name. It reminds me of Linus Van Pelt in the Peanuts comic strip. Why do you hate it?"

"I don't," LG replied. "I just don't like it. Children should be allowed to rename themselves when they're old enough. If you grew up as a kid with that name, you'd understand."

"The troops talk about this when he's not around," Josh said. "The consensus is that he stayed in the Army until he had three stars so he could get away with using LG as his name. We all know he doesn't like his birth name, and it's a bad idea to kid him about it. And never ask him where his blanket is."

"Really?" She looked back at LG.

"It isn't funny," he replied.

The nearby crack of a rifle followed by fierce sounds of growling, hissing, and spitting broke the natural silence surrounding them.

Then they heard a man's harsh, guttural voice shout, "You old bitch! Get them off of me!"

Without hesitation, LG turned his horse up a hillside toward a thick stand of trees. "Let's take cover up there," he said, and made a clucking noise to summon Audie.

"Take my horse, Suki," Josh said as he dismounted and handed her the reins. He followed them on foot using a branch he broke off a smaller tree to brush away their tracks. He selected one from the high side of the tree, so the fresh scar wasn't noticeable from the trail they'd been following.

# CHAPTER 12

AFTER REACHING THE TREE LINE, LG stayed behind to keep watch. Josh and Suki led the horses deeper inside the grove to a more secluded area where they were tethered.

To stop the horses from being spooked by more gunshots, they used foam earplugs. To keep them from falling out, they used ear bonnets. They also filled feedbags with fodder and attached them to the horses' heads.

"Do you have any idea what's going on?" Suki asked.

Josh shrugged. "I don't know what's behind that shot and the shouting, but I'll find out."

Once they were satisfied the horses were secure and safe, Josh found a stick and started poking around through the nearby underbrush.

"Why are you doing that?" Suki asked.

"Making sure there are no rattlers near the horses," he replied.

"Then I want to help." She wasn't a big fan of snakes and found a much longer stick, hoping she wouldn't run into one. Since Montana's Prairie Rattlesnake blended into terrain like this, they were difficult to spot until it was often too late.

Once they returned to the tree line and joined LG, Josh asked, "What caliber rifle fired the shot we heard?"

Before he replied, LG thought for a moment, "Sounded like a .35 with a 180-grain bullet."

"If that was Gracie," Suki said, "she could be in trouble."

"That's what I was thinking," Josh said. "On our way to the pocket valley, Suki and I ran into her." He stood. "I'll go check. You two stay here. Safer that way."

"Take Audie with you," LG said.

"Good idea." He made a clucking sound to alert the dog, and Suki watched them go, taking her courage with them.

After they were out of sight, Suki drifted closer to LG. Without the dog by her side, every tree and shadow had become threatening—no telling what might be getting ready to pounce.

She wore an old-fashioned wristwatch with a yellow face. Watching the second-hand race around, sweeping away the minutes, she said, "They're taking too long."

"Not to worry," LG replied. "They know what they're doing. This is kid stuff."

About a half-hour crawled by before Josh and the dog returned, herding a bald, bearded man in front of them. Audie was nipping at the guy's heels to keep him moving in the right direction. His hands were tied behind his back. A tight strand of rope ran from his wrists through his crotch. From there, it crossed his chest and surrounded his neck in a closed loop. He was wearing a short-sleeved shirt, and his muscular arms were covered with black-ink tattoos. Recognizing him, Suki's stomach flip-flopped. It was all she could do not to vomit.

"Keep that fucking mutt away from me," the man growled in a familiar, rancid rumble.

Suki averted her eyes, struggling not to stare at the prisoner. She didn't want him to recognize her.

Once Josh was close enough, he said, "Gracie caught this fool following our trail and decided he was up to no good. When she confronted him, he threatened her. She fired a shot to warn him off, barely missing him. Then the brainless bozo charged her, and her cats attacked him."

Suki couldn't help but look. Wherever bare skin was exposed, she saw inflamed, crisscrossing scratch marks.

Josh continued, "She wanted to stay and help, but I told her to go home, that we'd handle this varmint. It turns out the only reason she fired one round was because she's running out of ammo for that rifle. She's saved the empty casings over the years, so I offered to reload them for her."

"She's a crazy bitch," the tattooed man cursed.

Audie snarled and lunged. The man's eyes flashed with fear, and he lost his balance, landing hard on his butt. Then his feet stirred up a cloud of dust as he scooted away from the gnashing canine teeth.

"From your expression," LG said to Suki, "it looks like you know him."

She stared at the ground. "I don't want to talk about it."

Josh shared a glance with LG. The older man slipped a comforting arm across Suki's shoulders. Her first reaction was to escape the embrace, but the gesture comforted and confused her at the same time. She didn't know what to think.

"Do you remember what we talked about last night?" LG asked.

She gave a slight nod but continued to avoid eye contact. Part of her wanted him to remove his arm while rival thoughts wanted it to stay.

"Suki," LG said, "we can't do our job unless we know all the facts, no matter how painful they are to talk about. Is this guy one of the rapists?"

She looked up, her lips trembling, and her eyes were swimming in tears. In a barely audible voice, she said, "No, he's the pastor of a small Protestant congregation between Stanford and Lewistown. He films his sermons and puts them on his Facebook page. During the trial, my friends said he preached I was a tree that would bear only rotten fruit." She used the back of one hand to wipe away the tears streaking her face.

The tattooed prisoner said, "You're that slut bitch!" He almost added something else, but Audie shut him up with a deep-throated growl, revealing his canines, as if he were ready to eat the man.

Josh turned and pointed an index finger at him. "Don't say another word. Don't move. That dog will happily rip a second mouth in your throat if you upset my sister like that again."

The guy protested, and Audie gnashed his teeth a fraction of an inch from the man's nose. When he attempted to roll away from the dog, the rope tightened around his neck, cutting off the air. His eyes bulged, and gagging, he struggled to breathe.

"What else did this fake dumbass say?" LG asked.

"He said that a diseased tree like me needed to be cut down and thrown into the fire. He said I was an adulterous sinner. Soon after he posted the first sermon about me on his Facebook page, the threatening phone calls started. Mom wouldn't let me answer. Only Dad did. When the calls kept coming, he had our landline disconnected, and Sammy flew to Billings to buy several prepaid mobile phones."

"Does this maggot have a name?"

This time, Suki heard the venom in LG's voice. "He calls himself the Prophet Abraham and claims God speaks through him."

"That's not his real name," Josh said.

"Did you see the 1488 prison tattoo on his right bicep?" LG asked.

"I did," Josh replied.

"What's that mean?" Suki asked.

"The 14 represents a quote from white supremacist leader David Lane," LG said. "It means they're dedicated to secure the future for whites and their children. The 88 represents the eighth letter of the alphabet twice, meaning Heil Hitler. Another tattoo on his other arm is for the Aryan Brotherhood."

"I want to know why he was following our day-old trail," Josh said.

"Me too," LG added. "Tell us everything you know about this scumbag, Suki."

"That penis flytrap is a liar," the man shouted before Audie was all over him in a cloud of dust. His screams were louder than the dog's growls.

"Don't let Audie kill him!" Suki protested.

"Unless he gets permission," LG said, "he won't. All he'll do is literally scare the crap out of him."

Gaining strength from the cold steel she heard in LG's voice, Suki continued, "He arrived in Montana about a decade ago. He has a small following of cultish fanatics. Mom says they cherry-pick the Bible and revise phrases to support their hate."

"I want to have his brain drained." LG removed his arm from across Suki's shoulders, tapped his left ear with a finger, and talked.

As soon as the arm was gone, Suki wanted it back. She couldn't make out what he was saying. "What's he doing, Josh?"

Her brother indicated an earbud in his right ear. LG had one too. She hadn't noticed them before.

"He's talking to our men back at camp," Josh said. "We're linked through a military-grade scrambled net. Without the proper chip and algorithm, there's no way to decipher the encrypted words. It's a stand-alone system, and we only use it when necessary."

"What's he telling them?"

"Keep your eyes on the sky." Josh pointed back the way they'd come. "We have a Killer Egg hidden in the pocket valley that you didn't see when you visited. It'll be arriving soon."

"What does this Killer Egg do?" Suki glanced at the prisoner, thinking he was going to be dead soon. *That would be nice,* she thought.

"It's a helicopter used by special operations troops," LG replied. "The cockpit is small, and it's sort of shaped like an egg."

When the chopper arrived, it came in fast, hugging the ground and weaving between trees. The cockpit only had room for two. Then, with a whoosh, it hovered before landing on the trail below their location. With the rotors still spinning, Suki saw half a dozen heavily armed men with balaclavas hiding their features. They were sitting on seats outside the cockpit, three on each side of the aircraft.

In no time, they scrambled up the hill, took possession of the prisoner, and returned to the Killer Egg without saying one word. They strapped the prisoner to one of the chopper's skids. Then the aircraft lifted straight up, spun around, and returned the way it had come.

"What are they going to do to him?" Suki asked. Even though the guy deserved it, she didn't want to be involved in a murder.

"He's going to get a sample of Old Testament justice," Josh said.

A voice whispered in her head that didn't sound right. "Are you going to torture him?" she asked, thrilled and shocked at the same time.

"We aren't barbarians, Suki," LG said. "Since torture is unreliable, we don't use it. We'll dress the men who question him as Islamic terrorists, and one of them will hold a long, curved, razor-sharp blade. When they aren't questioning him in heavily accented English, they will speak to each other in Farsi. There will be a camera on a tripod. We also have specialty drugs, thanks to friends of ours."

Josh picked up from there. "Believe me, before our men are done, he'll have diarrhea of the mouth. And thanks to those drugs, he won't be able to tell a lie. After he's questioned, he'll be dosed with something similar to a date-rape drug. When he wakes up tomorrow, he won't remember a thing that happened to him."

"That's all?" Her voice sounded disappointed, even to her, and that made her guilt grow worse.

"No," LG added. "He'll be depressed and suffer from a loss of coordination. When he attempts to move, he'll vomit his guts out."

"Does he have a family?" Josh asked.

After a moment, Suki replied, "A wife and eight kids. I saw her once. She was bone thin, and her back was bent like she was lugging around a thousand pounds."

"He could be abusing her," LG said. "These white nationalists are capable of emotionally and physically mistreating women because their false ideology says women are genetically and physically inferior to men."

"Eight kids." Josh shook his head in disgust. "Damn, too bad we don't have a pill to give them, so they grow up normal instead of brain-hacked racists and misogynists."

She looked from LG to her brother. "You've done this before." It wasn't a question.

"We're professionals," LG replied. "Not monsters. There will be no physical scars." LG took Suki's chin in one hand and gently turned her face toward him.

"Look at me, Suki."

She heard him, but refused to meet his eyes.

"Nod if you hear me," he added.

Tears were leaking from her closed eyes when she replied, "I don't want to be a bully and a killer like him."

LG's voice was gentle. "That will not happen. But if you tell anyone, even one person, what happened yesterday and today, we'll have to leave. That means the men who raped you and the monsters calling the house with death threats will continue to get away with the same abuse. How many others do you want them to victimize?"

"It's up to you, Sis. We'll release him and leave, if that's what you want."

Suki's thoughts swirled like gutter water going down a drain as she stared at her brother. When she finally spoke, her voice sounded timid, even to her. "I don't want anyone murdered, even if they deserve it. I couldn't live with myself."

"We're not vigilantes," Josh said.

LG cleared his throat. When she looked, his expression soothed her. "We have evidence related to your case that didn't reach the trial, and Dandy Darwin is guilty as hell."

"Dandy Darwin?" she asked, looking confused.

"It's what we call the walking cowpie who molested you," Josh said. "If you want to read the file, you may. You're not his first victim, and his father is worse."

Audie was sitting a few feet away, scratching an itch behind one ear. Suki turned to the service dog and asked, "What do you think?"

Looking solemn, he came over and rested his muzzle on her lap, making eye contact with her. Then he lifted a paw and put it on her left knee in a comforting gesture. A moment passed while Suki rubbed the back of the dog's neck.

"Okay," she said. "I won't tell anyone about that valley or what happened here."

## CHAPTER 13

AFTER WATCHING the Killer Egg fly off with the prisoner, Josh thought about telling Suki how he'd discovered the hidden valley. He'd been twelve. By the time he turned sixteen, he'd rebuilt the cabin and started working on the old gold mine that turned out to be worth a fortune.

They soon reached the top of a rise above the ranch house and its outbuildings. It was midafternoon by then, and he'd changed his mind. He wouldn't bring up the topic unless Suki reminded him. He hoped she'd forget his promise.

As they rode down the slope toward the buildings, there was a faint breeze. There was also an eerie stillness about the place, as if it had been abandoned.

In Josh's experience, a sense of calm like that could be deceiving. As his alert level went into overdrive and his body started producing more cortisol, his hand drifted toward the concealed Glock in its holster.

Because this wasn't a global hot spot, he distracted his PTSD by asking a question, "Is Mom working on another Esther Warren novel?" He'd learned from his Vet Center counselor, Dr.

Janet Tate, that starting a conversation was one method to avoid being triggered.

"Why the interest?" Suki gave him a sideways glance.

"I've read every book she's published," he replied.

She raised one eyebrow and lowered the other like she didn't believe him. "With your life, when did you find time to read?"

After a moment of thought, he said, "We measure most of the fighting in seconds and minutes. The downtime can stretch for days, weeks, or months."

Deciding to leave out the part about dive bars and the world's oldest profession, Josh fell silent. He suspected Suki wouldn't understand what it was like to be asked to risk your life for your country while being told it was against the rules to pay for sex. He agreed with General George Patton that if they don't fuck, they don't fight.

"It's not as bad as he makes it sound," LG said, filling the void. "We enjoy shooting and blowing up stuff, but there's never enough of that to satisfy our addictions."

"Speak for yourself, LG," Josh said. "I was never that eager." He pointed at his friend. "Suki, after he became a general, he went out with the troops every chance he got. Made the grunts babysitting him nervous as hell."

With raised eyebrows, Suki glanced over her shoulder at the older man behind her on his horse.

LG shrugged. "There were times I was tempted to start over as a lieutenant. As God is my witness, when they gave me the first star, it turned out to be a pain in the ass, and I mean that literally. I got assigned to the Pentagon, and if it hadn't been for my CMH, it would've been the end of my career. There were too many assholes in that place that outranked me who didn't deserve to be saluted."

"CMH?" Suki asked. "What does that mean? You guys throw out too much military slang that flies right over my head."

"He's talking about the Congressional Medal of Honor," Josh replied, "and he doesn't enjoy talking about it. Why don't you answer my question about Mom instead?"

"She's working on Esther Warren, number twenty-seven," Suki replied.

"When I left, there were only three books in the series, and she'd just signed her first foreign contract with a publisher in the UK."

The fictional Esther Warren belonged to a northern Methodist sect that allowed women to preach. She also roamed the West throughout the second half of the nineteenth century as a biblical feminist gunslinger caught between two worlds. She was too radical to be accepted by evangelicals and too conservative for women's rights activists. They sold the Esther Warren novels in every country where Christianity had a significant presence and they often hit bestseller lists.

"Mom named the newest one *Shameless for Christ*," Suki added.

"I enjoy the endings," Josh replied. "They always have an unexpected twist."

Suki's mouth fell open, and she rolled her eyes. "Are you joking? There's too much preaching in those stories." She turned to LG. "Have you read them too?"

"Guilty as charged," LG replied. "I like the action."

Talking about his mother reminded Josh that he wasn't eager to spend time with her or his father, not yet, and that was why he didn't want to sleep under the same roof. There were several barns, two bunkhouses, and some storage sheds. He could also sleep on the porch, but that was too close for comfort. "Does Mom still keep the same writing routine?" he asked.

"Nothing's changed," Suki replied. "Living on this ranch sometimes makes me think I'm an insect trapped in amber." She paused for a moment. "I guess I like Esther because she's tougher than the male characters."

"I thought you didn't like those stories," LG said.

"I didn't say that."

"What's your favorite part, then?" Josh asked.

"Where Esther saves the souls of prostitutes." Suki dismounted and started walking her horse toward the nearest barn.

Josh followed. When he glanced back, he saw LG was still sitting on his unmoving horse. Suki had also stopped and was watching.

Audie was off to the side, watching a squirrel sitting high in one tree. From the way the squirrel's tail was twitching, it was taunting the dog.

The retired general sighed. "I'm not looking forward to being reminded of my age."

"How can getting off of a horse do that?" Suki asked.

He slowly dismounted, placed both hands on his lower back, and stretched. It was apparent from his expression that he was in pain. When he noticed they were staring, he said, "Go on. Don't worry about me. If you live long enough, it'll happen to you, too."

"Except for those that died young," Josh said in a somber tone. He was thinking of the friends they'd lost in combat.

Suki slapped her horse on the rump to get it moving. It trotted off like it knew where to go. Walking back to LG, she held out a hand. "I'll take care of your ride," she said.

"Thanks, but no thanks," LG replied.

Her hand waited for the reins, and her posture told Josh she wasn't taking no for an answer.

"Look, I go through this every day," LG said. "I'm used to it. In fact, I welcome the pain because it reminds me I'm not dead yet. Just because it takes time for my damaged parts to wake up doesn't mean I'm ready to be turned out to pasture." He cracked a disarming grin. "You won't be doing me any favors. I got to do this." He guided his horse around her and headed toward the barn.

Shaking her head, Suki said to his retreating back, "After you take the saddle off, brush her down good and give her a carrot or two. You'll find them in a bucket just inside and to the left of the barn doors."

Without looking, LG nodded and tapped the brim of his hat briefly with two fingers, letting her know he'd heard.

Josh joined Suki and said, "Even with three stars, LG lets no one carry his gear. Out in the field, he wanted to be treated like any other grunt." He reached out and tugged on her shirtsleeve. "Sis, I have a question."

Looking at him, she cocked her head to one side and waited.

"How well do you know Rachel?" he asked.

"She's like an older sister. Mom took her in after she got pregnant. Her parents didn't approve of her having a child out of wedlock. They wanted her to marry a friend of the family twenty years older than her. When she refused, they kicked her out, and Rachel came here. Why are you asking?"

"Well...people change, and I've been gone a long time."

Suki rolled her eyes. "What did you do?"

"I had a gift delivered to her place this morning."

"Really? You're worried how she'll react to flowers or a box of chocolates?"

"It's a white convertible," he said. "When we were kids, it was Rachel's dream car."

"You bought her a toy, like a Matchbox car?"

"Where'd you get that idea? It's not a toy. It's a restored 1970 Ford Shelby GT500 convertible. You think she'll like it?"

"You idiot! Why didn't you deliver it yourself?"

"I dunno." Even to him, his voice sounded lame. Avoiding eye contact, he continued: "I had it delivered to her driveway at three this morning. We wrapped it in ribbons with a bow on the front windshield. I included a love note with the paperwork and keys." After a moment of silence, he added, "Well, what do you think?"

"Jeez." Suki turned her back on him and started toward the barn.

"Shit!" he said to his horse. "Sounds like I fucked up." He tugged on his horse's reins to get it moving. "Come on, you old nag."

The roar of a high-performance engine stopped him. He turned to see a virgin-white Shelby Mustang with the top down race into sight. Rachel was behind the wheel.

Josh was worried she was going to run over him. Knowing she wouldn't hit the horse, he stepped closer to it.

When she braked, the Shelby slewed sideways across the gravel before it came to a stop a few yards away. The driver's door flew open, and Rachel shot from the car and leaped into his arms, wrapping her legs around his waist.

"I guess that means you liked it," he said, looking at her mouth inches from his and imagining what it would be like to lock lips with her again. Just thinking about it turned him on, and she had to know, considering where she'd planted herself.

"Whoa, slow down," she said and leaned back to stare at him. "You're not out of the flea-infested dog house yet, but you earned a few points for not forgetting." She pushed away from him, landed on her feet, and stepped back, opening some space between them. "Don't get any ideas. You're going to have to do a lot more to earn my trust back."

"How many more points will I need for a kiss?" He couldn't take his eyes off her lips. "I want to take you out to dinner tonight," he said, moving closer. He liked her shade of lipstick and the scent of whatever lotion she was using—vanilla and coconut, he guessed.

She placed a hand against his chest to keep him at arm's length. "Not so fast, soldier boy. Wait until Saturday for our first double date, and on Sunday morning, we're going to church together." Her eyes swiveled to the car. "How did you come up with the money to buy something that expensive?"

"Investments," he replied. "What do you mean by a double date? Is this going to be another hot, dusty rodeo nightmare like the first one when we were kids?"

"Not this time. We're going out for dinner and dancing, and Suki is going to join us. It'll be good for her to get out. All she has to do is find a guy she trusts to be her escort."

"What if she doesn't want to go?" he asked.

"She'll go. She feels safe when you're around."

Unbidden, Josh thought about Mia. Unlike Rachel, she didn't care for flashy cars or lusty nightclubs. She preferred cuddling in front of a fireplace or campfire, just the two of them.

# CHAPTER 14

AFTER SUKI AGREED to go on the Saturday night double date with LG as her escort, Rachel drove home. Audie followed Suki to the main house while Josh and LG slept in the older bunkhouse. For the rest of the week, Suki hung out with them while Josh avoided the main house and their parents as much as possible.

On Friday, while having breakfast in the bunkhouse, Suki said, "Josh, I think you should sit down and have a conversation with Mom and Dad. It's time to forgive each other. On Sundays, I've heard Mom preach about kindness and forgiveness, as God in Christ forgives everyone.'"

"I'll think about it," he replied without looking up from his tin plate as he filled a fork with hash browns smothered in ketchup. "Let's not dwell on that. When the time is right, I'll know."

Late Saturday afternoon, Rachel arrived in her Shelby. She relegated Josh and LG to the cramped back seats. As Suki slipped into the front passenger seat, she expected a quiet dinner at the Waterhole Saloon in Stanford, just the four of them. This was Suki's first outing since the rape and trial.

"Where are we going?" Josh asked when they reached Route 87 and turned west.

"Great Falls," Rachel replied.

Suki avoided staring at her friend and bit her lower lip to keep from protesting. She should've known Rachel wasn't planning a quiet dinner. Her friend liked to party and often drank too much. She'd also been telling Suki it was time to live again.

It didn't help that Rachel drove like a lunatic. The top was down, and the wind chilled Suki to the bone. About an hour later, they reached the restaurant in the old downtown area of Great Falls, close to the Missouri River. The sun was balanced precariously on the horizon in a blaze of color.

Once parked, Suki slipped out of the car and waited on the sidewalk beside Rachel. Wearing high heels, they were both dressed in form-fitting one-piece outfits that revealed their figures. For warmth, Rachel wore a black-knit Merino wool shawl draped across her bare shoulders, and Suki had on a silk-lined, black leather jacket that wasn't warm enough.

Josh levered himself out of the back seat and popped out of the car. He leaned down and touched his toes several times. Then he stood and groaned while stretching his back. "It was like being a cork in a wine bottle in that back seat," he said.

LG looked like he was stuck. Holding out a hand to Suki, he said, "This old man needs someone to be his church key."

Grinning, Suki pulled until LG was free of the car.

Rachel glanced at her smartphone. "We're running late. They only hold reservations for fifteen minutes."

"How can we be late?" Josh asked. "You drove like the car was a Hellfire missile. Good Lord, I hope getting you that Shelby wasn't a mistake."

Rachel laughed.

LG eyed the entrance and the stairway leading down. "Can

we find a family-style restaurant above ground? I know a place just outside Malmstrom Air Force Base's main gate."

"But this is one of the nicest spots in town," Rachel said, pouting.

"Yea, we want to eat in style," Suki added to support her friend while wishing they were in Stanford and closer to the safety the ranch offered.

Rachel said, "Come on, soldier boy, let's get moving. There's fun planned for tonight." She hooked arms with Josh.

"I haven't been out dancing in decades," LG said. "I'm not sure my feet know how anymore, and my knees will not cooperate."

Having already decided not to spoil Rachel's date night with Josh, Suki took one of LG's hands. "Don't worry," she said. "I promise to go easy on you."

Josh rolled his eyes, and Rachel, who saw, elbowed him in the side. "Don't ruin the night. We have done nothing like this since..." Looking stunned, she stopped talking.

Suki saw Rachel look her way and pretended she hadn't heard. Being reminded of the rape caused her stomach to spasm.

"Me and LG don't do well in crowds or underground," Josh said. Both men wore walking shoes and relaxed blue jeans with polo-style long-sleeved shirts.

Rachel stared at him. "Seriously, you don't sound like the Josh I knew."

"That Josh escaped from his adolescent cocoon a couple of decades ago, about the same time he stopped partying."

Rachel pressed her lips together in a tight line and didn't look happy.

"This place is a classy restaurant," Suki said, wanting to lighten the mood.

"Okay, I'm in," LG said. "But be careful with Josh. He might be a lot younger than me, but he's been wounded more and has spent more time in hospitals and rehab."

Josh groaned. "You make me sound like a shipwreck. I'm not that bad."

Looking concerned, Rachel led the way down the stairs to the basement restaurant. Suki, Josh, and LG followed. A hostess guided them to a table in the center of the room.

LG indicated an isolated four-top far from the main entrance and said, "We'd like that one, please."

Suki glanced at Rachel, and their eyes met. Rachel shrugged, and Suki said, "It doesn't matter where we sit."

At the isolated corner table, LG and Josh stood behind the outer chairs and pulled them out for the girls to sit. Then they backed the two empty inner chairs against different walls. LG took the chair on the right and Josh the one on the left. Then Suki watched them scan the dining room. She glanced over her shoulder to see what they were looking at. Facing forward, she asked, "What's so interesting?"

"Nothing," LG said. "Remember when I told you about my PTSD? Well, there are specific situations that trigger us. This is one of them."

"Do you want to go someplace that feels safer?" Suki asked, concerned.

"Wait a minute," Rachel said. "Explain, so I'll understand. After all, I must be the only one here without PTSD."

A bleached-blond waitress with leathery skin appeared and asked, "Are you ready to order?" She had a raspy smoker's voice.

"We're still deciding," Josh said. "Give us a couple of minutes, please."

After the waitress left, LG said, "We don't have to leave, but please be patient. Did you notice how Josh and I took the chairs against the walls so we could monitor things?"

"Jesus!" Rachel said. "That's horrible. Isn't there a pill for that?"

"There is, but those drugs turn us into numb zombies," Josh said. "Instead, we focus on self-control through exercise and meditation and try to avoid environments and circumstances that trigger us."

"I understand," Suki said. She reached across the table and covered one of LG's hands. She hated it when a tear slipped out of one eye and slid down her cheek. Hoping no one noticed, she struggled not to cry.

Rachel pushed her chair back and stood. "I'm sorry. I didn't know. Let's go to the place LG suggested."

Josh moved behind Rachel and slid her chair back in, forcing her to sit. "After we eat, we can talk about what you want to do next. The waiters are going through a door close to us and coming out with food. That means the kitchen is on the other side and offers an escape route."

Rachel stared at him, her lips parted in concern. "Seriously... that's what life is like for you two?"

LG lifted a hand and waggled it back and forth. "Sort of. We're not basket cases. Just alert. For instance, in an urban setting, we scan the streets and buildings as far as we can see. We also check open windows for snipers. And when someone comes near us, we watch their eyes for warning signs."

"And we are always prepared," Josh said. He glanced at his ankle and pulled up a pant leg, revealing a holster with a pistol. "It's a good thing Montana has some of the most permissive firearm laws in the country."

Seeing the Glock helped untie the knot in Suki's stomach. For the first time since they'd arrived in Great Falls, she relaxed.

When the waitress returned, they ordered. There wasn't much small talk while they ate. Near the end of the meal, LG asked, "What's next?"

"Do you like karaoke?" Rachel asked.

Suki stiffened. The night she was drugged and raped had started in a karaoke bar. Rachel didn't know about that. Avoiding eye contact with the others, Suki did her best to hide her reaction. That night, she went out with a couple of flaky friends. If Rachel had been with her, it might have turned out different. She was great at giving flirty guys the cold shoulder.

"I'm not much of a singer," LG replied, "but I enjoy listening." He nodded at Josh. "Him, he sings in the shower, and I have to admit, he has a decent voice."

Rachel raised her eyebrows. "You guys shower together?"

"There isn't much privacy when you live in the barracks," Josh said.

When they left the restaurant, Rachel led the way to an aboveground karaoke bar. When Rachel wanted Suki to join her on stage, Suki shook her head. "I'm not ready for that," she said.

Without hesitation, Rachel turned to Josh. He held up both hands, palms out. "Don't look at me. If I go on that little stage, I'll think someone in the audience might shoot me."

Rachel looked disappointed, ordered another beer, and drank half of it before going on stage alone and belting out three songs.

The next stop was a crowded bar with live entertainment and dancing.

By then, Rachel was feeling no pain. Once inside, she dragged Josh straight to the packed dance floor.

Suki stayed close to LG and searched for a shadowy spot near the back wall where they could hide.

"Well, look what we got here," a familiar voice said as a man forced his way through the crowd and stopped in front of Suki. Close behind him were two heavily muscled and tattooed men wearing short-sleeved shirts.

Shocked, Suki couldn't speak or move. She just stared. It was Darwin Tweet, the man who raped her, and the two brutes behind him were his bodyguards, but not the ones who took turns with her that night. It was apparent Tweet was alcohol-sloshed and possibly using a drug that made him more aggressive than usual.

A girl wearing a skimpy dress pushed her way through the crowd and slipped in front of Darwin. It exposed more skin than covered. "Dar," she said in a whiny tone. "You promised me the next dance."

"Not now, Boobs," he said and used an arm to sweep her out of his way. She stumbled, and the bodyguard with the most tattoos saved her from falling. Darwin stepped closer to Suki, but LG filled the gap, putting her behind him.

"Back off," the retired Special Forces general said.

Darwin pointed an index finger at LG's nose. "Get out of my way, you mother-fucking geezer, before I swat you like a blowfly." His voice went up several octaves. "That whore behind you must have scraped you out of a trash can. If the bitch is picking up homeless farts, she must be desperate."

The next thing Suki saw was Darwin on his knees in pain because LG had plucked the offending finger out of the air and was bending it toward the back of his hand. Then she gasped when the two burly bodyguards moved to protect their client.

That's when she heard Josh's voice. "You are some ugly motherfuckers." When the brutes turned around, she saw her brother standing calmly in front of the mountains. Suki's first thought was how slight Josh looked compared to them. They were taller and bulkier, oak trees towering over a sapling. Josh stood a little over six feet, but these two had several inches on him and a lot more weight that was mostly muscle.

Ice water flooded her body.

Josh continued in a matter-of-fact voice, "How do you want to do this, one at a time or both at once?"

*How can he be so calm*? she thought.

Without warning, one bodyguard swung a ham-sized fist. Suki saw Josh smoothly avoid the blow by swaying around and below it like bamboo bending with the wind. He ended on one knee, pivoting on it to face the second bodyguard while delivering a back kick with his free leg into the first guy's groin. He followed that with a swift second blow to number one's left knee. There was a sharp crack as the bones shattered.

Time slowed for Suki as seconds stretched to minutes.

Before the first beefy bodyguard hit the floor, Josh came up like a gymnast to meet number two. At the same instant, his right elbow jabbed blindly behind him into the first man's throat. That one had doubled over from the first two blows. His neck had been in the right spot, as if Josh had planned it.

The brute's mouth opened wide in shock. When he hit the floor, his eyes rolled into his head, revealing only the whites. After that, he didn't move.

Suki gasped. Had her brother just killed someone? She placed both hands over her thundering heart. Then she saw that the man was still breathing.

Like an angry bull, the second man rushed Josh. Suki held her breath, expecting the worst. She couldn't see how Josh was going to escape the destruction headed toward him.

But in a blur of movement, Josh spun on his toes and twirled out of the way. For an instant, number two was disoriented.

Suki couldn't believe what she saw next. After the second brute found Josh and charged, Josh's arms flew up and back. He completed an amazing gymnastic 180-degree backflip and landed in a perfect crouch. In one fluid movement, he'd magically found a space between two startled dancers, putting several feet between him and number two. As that bodyguard continued forward, Josh dropped and rolled onto his back. Once down, his legs shot out like pistons meeting number two's armpits, lifting the man off the floor. The stunned gorilla flew and landed hard several feet away. Each move Josh had made appeared effortless, as if it had been choreographed. Suki had seen no one fight like that before in real life, only in movies.

The crowd had stopped dancing. Everyone was staring. Then someone started clapping, as if the fight had been entertainment. What she'd just witnessed had happened in a few seconds, not minutes.

The second bodyguard was dazed. He shook his head and struggled to stand on rubbery legs.

Josh said, "As you were, Marine! This beer garden isn't Iwo Jima."

That's when Suki saw the Marine Corps tattoo on number two's left forearm. The man's eyes met Josh's. Then his eyes widened—not in fear, but in what looked like glowing awe.

Josh gestured toward the unconscious thug sprawled on the floor behind him. "I went easy on you, but if you want to play tough, Semper Fi won't save you."

With a whistle of pent-up air, the Marine sagged and stayed down. Keeping his eyes on Josh, he said, "I know who you are, Colonel." There was nothing but respect in his voice. "I saw you once on TV. I think it was 2005 when you were still a SEAL. You were competing in mixed martial arts in Japan. You took what should have been a crippling blow. It didn't stop you. You won that match."

*I didn't know that,* Suki thought, and realized there was a lot she didn't know about her older brother. Over the years, her focus had been on the medals he'd earned in combat. She hadn't been interested in the rest of his life.

After a moment of silence, Josh continued, "How long have you worked for this shit-brick family?"

"A few weeks."

"My suggestion is you get off that floor and walk out. Do it now. Ignore the contract you signed. If you have to, change your name and go to another state. You cannot trust this toxic idiot and his father. They demand total loyalty, and once you have served them, they will dump you like you're a bucket of shit. You'll end up broken, in prison, or dead."

Rachel appeared behind Josh, and her alcohol-glazed eyes and gaping mouth revealed that she couldn't believe what she'd witnessed.

Suki heard LG mumbling. She turned and saw he was touching his left ear with his free hand. Remembering the earpiece he had used on the trail, she asked, "What?"

He winked at her and shifted his gaze to Josh. "Why did you get involved? I was handling it."

"I wasn't about to let you have all the fun." He nodded at LG's earbud. "Did you let the shadow crew know the rotten fruit is ready to harvest?"

LG nodded and let the pressure off of Darwin's index finger.

Suki wondered what that meant.

"Do you have any idea who I am?" the thirty-something said as he rubbed his injured finger. "When my father is done, you two will be lucky to still have your cocks."

LG grinned. "Be warned, big mouth, your poking days are numbered." With that, he turned to Suki. "I think it's time to leave. What do you think?"

She nodded as relief flooded her.

Josh said, "Good idea." He half-carried Rachel out of the bar and to the Mustang.

At the car, Josh waited for LG and Suki to squeeze into the back seat. Then he turned to Rachel and held a hand out for the keys. Once he had them, he swept her close and planted a long, passionate kiss on her lips. When he broke contact and leaned back to study her eyes, he said, "I decided not to wait like when we were kids."

Then Rachel's eyes opened wide in shock, her cheeks bulged, and she bent forward and vomited on their shoes.

LG glanced at Suki with a worried expression.

"Don't look at me," she said. "I only had one glass of wine. I lost count of the brews she drank. She's always been a heavy drinker."

With the top up and the heater on, Josh drove east on Route 87. Suki fell asleep with her head on LG's shoulder. Rachel was unconscious, with her head lolling against the passenger window and her foul-smelling mouth hanging open.

# CHAPTER 15

WHEN THEY REACHED Rachel's house, Josh lifted her out of the car's passenger seat, cradled her in his arms, and carried her inside. Once in her small house's living-room and kitchen space, he said, "It's too late to drive back to the ranch, so we're staying here tonight." He looked at Suki. "Which way to her bedroom?"

She pointed.

Without a word, Josh walked down the short hall to the open door at the end, entered that bedroom, and kicked the door shut behind him.

A moment passed as Suki waited for him to return. "What's he doing?" she asked as her body turned numb.

"I'm guessing he put her in bed and stayed with her," LG said.

Suki continued to stare at the closed door at the end of the short hallway, willing it to open. When that didn't happen, she imagined what Josh was doing to Rachel, and her face blossomed with heat. The last man Suki had sex with was Darwin when he'd drugged and raped her. That had been more than a year ago. Loneliness swept through her like an icy wind, causing her to tremble. She wanted someone to love who felt the same way about her.

"I don't know about you, but I'm ready to turn in and get some shut-eye," LG said from behind her. "I see three other doors down that hallway. Pick one, and that room's yours. I'll take what's left."

"Only one of those rooms is still a bedroom," Suki heard herself say while her thoughts went on a carnal rampage. "After Rachel's kids left, she turned one of the other two bedrooms into a home office with storage shelves along two walls. The third door is to the hall bathroom. There's barely enough room to stand in there, and the shower's the size of a wooden coffin."

"Then you get the guest bedroom. I'll sleep out here."

Suki didn't want to spend the night in that cold, cramped bedroom with its lonely twin bed. The mattress was so old there was a body-sized trench in its sagging center that threatened to swallow you whole. It was safer and more comfortable to sleep on the floor.

Remembering what LG had done at the nightclub to defend her, a ball of heat spread through her abdomen. Her heart also beat like a thundering kettledrum.

She sensed him standing close behind her. Turning, she took a half step forward and wrapped her arms around his waist, pressing her body tight to his. She felt his arms slip around her back, avoiding her waist and butt. He also wasn't holding her tightly, like a lover should. It was a friendly hug. A long moment passed as she waited for him to react like most of the men she'd known since she'd been ten. Over the years, she'd learned the hard way that all men wanted one thing from a girl: sex!

To avoid spending the night alone, she'd do it with LG. Besides, she reasoned, she liked him. She trusted him, too. In the nightclub, when he'd grabbed the bastard's finger and drove him to his knees in pain, she was thrilled.

She also knew from experience that after consensual sex, she slept better. After not having a good night's sleep for months, curious, she'd searched Google and found the answer from *Women's Health* magazine's website. From it, she learned that sex boosts oxytocin and lowers the stress-related hormone cortisol.

God, she'd give anything to have a good night's sleep, and who better than to do it with than this mature gentleman willing to fight for her honor.

Since she was pressed tight against his crotch, she didn't feel the erection she expected. Was something wrong with her? Her rush of arousal turned to hot shame. With her guts twisting into a Gordian knot, she stepped back. Her eyes filled with tears, and she couldn't look at him. Instead, she stared at the floor between their feet and said in a shaky voice, "I'm sorry. I don't know what's wrong with me. You must think I'm a horrible person."

---

The instant Suki looked down and started silently sobbing, LG's sense of compassion went into overdrive. He placed a hand behind one of her shoulders and guided her to the couch where she then sat, avoiding eye contact and continuing to cry.

At first, he considered sitting next to her to comfort her, but changed his mind. He'd had enough experience with women under his commands who were rape victims suffering from PTSD to know what was best in this situation. They did not train him to deal with this trauma, but he knew what to look for and recognize when it was triggered. The next step was getting the victim treatment from someone trained to deal with it.

While most combat vets suffering from PTSD were men, too many military women had gained their mental trauma from physical abuse. As a commanding officer who refused to ignore the rapes, he also knew that victims with PTSD who didn't get help soon after the trauma were unlikely to recover without treatment.

In three steps, he reached the small dining table between the kitchen space and the living room. It was really one large room divided into two areas. Grabbing a chair, he placed it in front of Suki and sat. "May I hold your hand?" he asked. He'd learned from his PTSD counselor, Dr. Janet Tate, that he shouldn't touch a woman suffering from the trauma Suki was dealing with. Ask permission first to avoid making the situation worse.

Suki calmed, but continued to avoid eye contact.

That was a good sign. She must have heard his request.

Without looking up, she held one hand out, and he took it between both of his. Tate had taught him not to hold too tightly.

"There is no rational reason for you to feel guilty about anything that just happened," he said. "It isn't your fault."

A moment of silence slipped by before she asked in a frail voice, "What isn't my fault?"

"When you hugged me and held on," he replied.

"I don't understand."

"What you did is an emotional reaction caused by your PTSD. It triggered you in that bar when Darwin Tweet confronted us." Now she was studying him. Tate told him when that happened, it was a good sign. Her eyes were red and swollen.

LG knew he was on thin ice here. He wasn't an expert. He had to walk softly and not trigger another breakdown. "Josh and I have a counselor who has helped us manage our PTSD and avoid being triggered. Her name is Janet Tate." LG thought it important that she know Tate is a woman.

"Dr. Tate served in the Air Force for twenty years before she retired," he continued. "She has a BS in Psychology and a master's. After she retired, she earned a Psychology Ph.D. in Trauma and Disaster Relief with a focus on therapy. We all suspect this interest was because she was a victim of physical abuse when she was still serving her country."

LG could see from Suki's expression that he had her attention now. It was time to let her think and respond before he said anything else.

A long moment crawled by before Suki asked, "Why did you mention this Dr. Tate?"

"Because she's good at what she does. She works for a Vet Center in the Bay Area near San Francisco and also has a private practice outside of the VA. She's especially great working with Special Forces vets like Josh and me but also works with women who have been traumatized like you. We've recommended all the members of The Oath Group who have PTSD to work with her, too." Once he sensed it was her turn to respond, he stopped talking again.

"You didn't really answer my question," she said, and this time there was a hint of a challenge in her tone.

"I apologize," he said, giving her hand a gentle squeeze at the same time. "I thought I should let you know more about Dr. Tate before I mentioned Josh has asked her to help you learn how to manage your trauma, like she helped us."

From her shifting expression, LG sensed he would not get much sleep, if any at all. He was in for a long conversation with this young lady.

Changing the subject, she said, "I wanted Josh to teach me how to fight like him. I asked, but he doesn't want to. How long did it take him to learn what I saw him do tonight?"

"Over twenty years," LG replied. "He started out earning advanced belts in Karate, taekwondo, judo, and aikido. Ten years into that, he made a few friends in the Mossad and got into Krav Maga. A couple of years later, he added Muay Thai, gymnastics, and ballet. He blended it all into something brutally effective that is uniquely his. He's still learning, and his moves are always changing."

# CHAPTER 16

THE CATTY LIGHT oozed around the dusty shades and pounced on Rachel's unconscious face, stabbing her eyes even through her closed lids. The morning-after hangover didn't help.

Groaning, she pulled a pillow over her head to escape the shards of pain. She was on her side, facing the window. Her left arm was trapped under her body, and she couldn't feel her fingers. To gain relief, she rolled over, then froze when she contacted another body.

Her breath caught in her throat. *Fuck,* she thought, and was afraid to find out who it was. The last and only time this had happened to her had been several years ago, soon after the divorce. She'd gone to Billings with colleagues from the grade school where she taught. It was a Friday night, and they helped her celebrate by buying her one boilermaker after another. She remembered nothing after she'd finished chugging the sixth tall glass of beer with a shot of whiskey added to each one. With that much alcohol in her blood, her brain had stopped forming fresh memories.

Later, she learned from her friends about the crazy stuff she'd done.

After that first alcohol-induced memory blackout, she'd avoided drinking that much until last night. Now, she'd done it again and didn't remember much of anything after they'd left the karaoke bar and reached the nightclub.

No telling where she was this morning. The first time this had happened, she woke up in a stranger's apartment. God, she hoped this wasn't a repeat.

Fearing what she'd discover, she cracked an eye open and was flooded with relief when she recognized her own bedroom—but she still wanted to know who the man in her bed was. She knew it was a man because she could feel his erection pressing against the small of her back.

She vaguely remembered last night out in Great Falls with Josh, Suki, and LG. Since she'd been with friends she trusted, she allowed herself to drink too much. There had been a fight, but she didn't remember much about it. What if Josh and his older friend lost, and one of those big, muscle-bound guys had claimed her as his consolation prize?

Without looking, she reached behind her and discovered the man was naked. Covering her mouth, she stifled a gasp. She hoped it was Josh, but what if it wasn't him? She was afraid of the answer.

Maybe some stranger had spiked one of her beers with a date-rape drug, like what happened to Suki.

Rachel imagined her unconscious body slung over some homeless guy's shoulder as he carried her out of the bar to his rusty ride. Once Rachel had been dumped inside his pickup, he'd rummaged through her purse to get her address and keys. Then the asshole drove her home and took advantage of her.

She slipped a hand between her thighs to check. There had

been no sex, but the body spooning with her had a massive erection.

She prayed this was a dream, a hallucination. That idea vanished when the man stirred, and one of his arms snaked possessively around her waist and pulled her closer until their naked flesh was joined. Trapped like a deer in a car's headlights, she couldn't move and stopped breathing. The fear made her hangover worse. She thought her head was going to explode.

She'd never get shit-faced again.

To her relief, he let go and said in a familiar voice, "Good morning, angel. I'm going to brew coffee and cook some grub. You take a shower. By the time you're done, I'll have food on the table. You'll feel better after you eat."

Rachel rolled over, and with the sheet and blanket pulled up to her chin, she saw Josh slipping into his blue jeans. When she discovered he wasn't wearing any underwear, it was all she could do not to stare at what she'd christened Lady Godiva's Horse when they had been teenagers. Remembering how much he'd hated that name, she almost laughed. Before he reached for his shirt, she saw the battle scars, and that rattled her. With a shaky voice, she asked, "What time is it?"

"Half-past noon." After tucking in his shirt, Josh pulled up the zipper on his trousers, and their eyes met. "I can see you want to know why I didn't take advantage of you," he said. "After all, it wouldn't have been our first rodeo, but when we have sex, you have to want it, too—and be sober."

She couldn't think of a reply. Instead, she stared at him. This was the guy she gave her virginity to. They'd been serious lovers for five years between the ages of thirteen and eighteen, and she still liked what she saw. Then she felt guilty because his scars made him seem hotter than he'd been before.

"I bet you also want to know why I was in your bed," he said.

That wasn't what she was thinking, but she nodded anyway.

He shrugged. "Well, I wanted to sleep with you because I've missed waking up with you cradled in my arms. We didn't get many mornings like that when we were kids, and the few we had are some of my fondest memories. Remember the time we made a love nest out of hay in one of the barn lofts?"

They had spent a lot of time in that loft one summer making lazy love. Remembering those good times, she wanted him back in her bed. "What are some of your other fond memories?" *Damn, why did I ask a stupid thing like that?* she thought.

"For better or worse," he continued, ignoring her question, "this happened decades later on the morning after our second first date." He pursed his lips together. Then he nodded and said, "Yep, being in bed with you is how I wanted our first date to end, but that didn't happen. The second time around, I made sure it did, even if we didn't fool around." Barefoot, he went to the door and paused briefly to look at her before leaving the room. His expression said he liked what he saw, and her stomach fluttered.

After he closed the door, she waited for it to open again. When he didn't return, she threw off the covers and sat up too fast, causing the room to spin around her. There was an intense throbbing behind her eyes, and she cradled her head in both hands. She heard the pipes knocking as the shower in the hall bath went on, signaling that someone else, probably Josh, was washing off last night. Staggering into the master bathroom, she turned on the water in the cramped shower stall.

She wanted to take a really long, hot shower, but with both bathrooms in use, the hot water wouldn't last long. She should've replaced the hot water heater years ago, but didn't have the money. Hell, she never had enough money.

Instead, she took a Navy shower, turning the lukewarm water on long enough to get wet. She hated the next step. With the water off, she shivered from the cold as she scrubbed her body with a soapy washcloth. Finished, she turned the water back on long enough to rinse off the suds. After hastily drying off, she went to the sink and brushed her teeth with cinnamon-flavored toothpaste.

While brushing, a cruel memory surfaced, reminding her of what happened the morning after her divorce celebration in Billings. Her heart raced, and she froze, staring at her image in the mirror. The foam-covered toothbrush she was holding hovered in front of her mouth.

The morning after the celebration, she awoke in a stranger's bed. Because of her drunken blackout, she didn't remember how she got there. Flustered, she'd slipped out of his bed to escape, and that's when she'd almost had a heart attack. She counted four women sitting on a couch and three more on chairs around the small kitchen table. Their eyes were wide open, their expressions frozen as if they were dead, and they were all staring at her.

When none of them moved, she thought a serial killer had abducted her, and these girls were his stuffed trophies. It took a moment to get enough courage to pad to the closest one and touch her, only to discover they weren't human. They were creepy, life-sized, high-quality dolls dressed in skimpy outfits. Even their cold skin seemed real. It took all of her willpower not to scream in hysteria or burst out laughing in relief.

When she'd reached the door, she'd looked over her shoulder. That's when she realized they hadn't been staring at her but at him, as if the guy wanted his silicone lovers to worship him.

Whoever the guy had been, it was apparent he had a boob fetish since all the dolls had Dolly Parton breasts. Since her boobs were smaller than average, she still wondered why he'd seduced her, maybe because that night she'd been the only game in town for a guy like him.

With a sigh of pent-up air, she'd slipped out of the cluttered studio apartment, never to return.

Back in the present moment, she took a calming breath, finished brushing her teeth, and rinsed with a mint-flavored mouthwash, hoping it would also wash away the memory of that long-ago morning she wanted to forget ever happened.

In the bedroom, she checked the calendar hanging from a nail on the wall to the left of the small, second-hand table she used as a desk. When she went to bed every night, the last thing she did was mark off the day that was ending. Saturday hadn't been crossed out, so she picked up a black Sharpie and did it. Then she leaned closer and squinted at a handwritten reminder scrawled inside the Sunday box.

"Oh my God!" Josh had promised to go to church with her, and there was only one service left. Because of her hangover and the alcohol-induced blackout, she'd forgotten.

The last service started at 2:00 p.m., followed by a picnic-style pot-luck supper behind the chapel. Her original plan had been to attend the first service at 8:00 a.m., so they could leave when it was over and spend the rest of the day together, just the two of them.

She hoped Josh wouldn't be angry when he found out who the pastor was. It wouldn't help that everyone in the congregation would expect her and Josh to sit at the pastor's table. Biting her lower lip, she stared at the cheap, body-length Walmart mirror fastened to the outside of her closet door. To see all of herself, she had to take a step back.

*Girl,* she thought to her naked reflection, *you might feel miserable, but you still look good, so everything will work out. Don't worry. Your man wants you back, and he's going to get what he wants as soon as we finish supper and return home. Whatever the consequences, I don't think he'll be mad enough to take off again. This Josh isn't the same kid who abandoned you when you were eighteen. This Josh is battle-hardened with the scars to prove it, and he's come home to you.* She pointed at her likeness in the glass.

She desperately wanted to believe what she'd just thought. Any man who did what he'd done while sharing the same bed... naked...had to love and respect the woman he was with, didn't he? Besides, they had a history together.

She placed a hand over her heart and said, "Dear God, I swear I'll never get that drunk again. That was really stupid." She paused for a moment before continuing, "Oh, and I almost forgot. Sorry about that. Thank you for keeping him alive and bringing him home to me in one piece."

# CHAPTER 17

AS RACHEL SHIMMIED into her one-piece, body-hugging, knee-length dress, she smelled onions, garlic, and bacon cooking. Then she heard the agonizing, high-pitched howl of the old blender she'd picked up for two dollars at a garage sale.

*What is Josh doing,* she thought, *cooking a feast?* The tantalizing smells caused her belly to mutiny, and she hurried to the toilet, just in case.

After her gut calmed, she returned to the bedroom and stared at her choice of shoes: high heels, flats, or running shoes. The high heels were the best match for her outfit and also made her legs look toned. Still feeling shaky, she slipped on the black running shoes.

On her way to the kitchen, she heard voices. The chatter stopped when she arrived, and three pairs of eyes turned to her.

"Since when did you dress like that for breakfast?" Suki asked.

"It's Sunday," Rachel replied.

"You look good enough to eat," Josh said, showing his approval with a wicked grin, and her face grew rosy hot with pleasure from his praise.

Putting down the spatula, he picked up a tall glass filled with a maroon-colored juice, stepped closer, and offered it to her. She wrinkled her nose and leaned away from it. "What's that? My stomach isn't ready for any surprises."

"Good morning to you, too, sunshine." Without warning, he leaned down and kissed her on the lips.

Closing her eyes, she leaned into him. A moment later, he broke contact, and she swayed on her feet, lightheaded. Josh put a hand on her shoulder to steady her and said, "This," he held the glass higher, "will help ease your hangover and smooth out the tremors in your tummy."

Turning her face aside as if the concoction were poison, she was tempted to drink a bottle of beer instead. Her eyes went to the old Electrolux refrigerator.

He laughed. "The hair of that dog will not help, but this might."

Looking doubtful, she dipped a fingertip into the concoction and sampled a drop. "I recognize the tomato juice," she said. "What else is in there?"

"Well," he said, lingering on that word, "there's water, spinach, a pinch of cayenne pepper, some oatmeal, and a banana. That mix came in handy during my early Marine Corps drinking years. A Filipino bartender in Okinawa near Camp Hansen showed me how to make it. Trust me. It helps rehydrate your body, boost blood sugar levels, and provides beneficial electrolytes." She took the glass and watched him turn to the griddle and flip one of the three pancakes that had bubbled.

He hummed a tune as he continued cooking. Rachel felt a jolt of energy as she recognized the song. It was Camila Cabello's "Consequences," about being in love and the pain that came with it. It was one of her favorites. She thought about Josh's battle scars and remembered what she'd heard last night about what it was like living with PTSD. The hangover remedy looked scary. Taking a deep breath to fortify herself, she drank the supposed hangover cure. To her surprise, it went down smoothly. Once the glass was half empty, she joined Suki and LG at the timeworn kitchen table she'd picked up at another garage sale. It could use a good sanding and a couple of coats of white paint.

The glow in Suki's eyes distracted her. *Wait a minute,* Rachel thought. *If Josh was in my bed with me, where did they spend the night?*

Suki leaned closer to Rachel and whispered in her ear, "We talked all night. Best conversation I've had in years. It was great! We're besties now. I wish LG had been my father, or at least a grandfather."

Rachel kept her expression neutral and thought, *How do you become best friends from one conversation?*

"What are your plans for today?" LG asked, with his eyes on Rachel. She noticed that for talking all night and probably not getting any sleep, he looked years younger. That must have been one hell of a conversation. If she'd been a mosquito on the wall, what would she have heard?

"Josh and I plan to attend the 2:00 p.m. Sunday services," she replied.

LG glanced at Josh for confirmation.

"Last night was not free," Josh said. "It came with strings attached, and I'm a man of my word."

"Why not join us?" Rachel asked.

LG and Suki's eyes met briefly before Suki replied, "We're headed west for the mountains to find a spot to camp for a few days and get away from everyone and everything."

*Whose idea was that?* Rachel thought and turned to Josh. "Did you know about this?"

He nodded. "They told me before you joined us." He filled a plate with eggs, home-fried potatoes, and two pancakes, then placed it in front of Rachel. "Dig in, hot stuff." He brushed her cheek with his fingertips, sending a shock wave through her. She felt her face glowing with heat again.

Her churning stomach soon calmed, and she ate with enthusiasm. Halfway through the meal, the 1959 Western Electric wall phone made a lame tinkling noise. That phone had been there since the house had been built.

Rachel watched Josh pluck it off its cradle and heard a thin, metallic voice ask, "Is my brother Josh there?" She hated the way people sounded on that phone, but her budget didn't allow her to waste money because she didn't like something that still worked.

"Why are you calling, Sammy?" Josh asked.

"Because I figured that's where you'd be when you didn't come home last night," Sammy replied. "Is Suki there too?"

"Yes, and we're eating breakfast for lunch."

"I'm calling from the bunkhouse because the local sheriff is talking to Dad in the main house. This line is separate, so I don't think anyone is listening." There was a pause.

Then Sammy continued: "He arrived with three deputies, and they're looking for you and your friend. Darwin Tweet's dad is claiming you two had something to do with his son's disappearance. He says you attacked his son in a bar in Great Falls. What's going on?"

Josh knew all about Dandy Darwin's dad. Charles Tweet was a libertarian billionaire running for the US Senate in Montana. He owned a ten-thousand-acre ranch in the state and, with help from dark money, was outspending the Democratic incumbent ten to one.

Tweet Senior also owned a thirty-room mansion in Gulf Breeze, Florida, and a three-thousand-square-foot, high-rise condo overlooking Central Park in New York City. A dues-paying member of ALEC, he also belonged to the hard-right Christian extremist sect called The Gathering. He'd made his wealth as the founder of a sketchy hedge fund.

"Nothing to worry about, brother," Josh replied. "LG and I were long gone by the time his son went missing, and we have plenty of evidence to prove that in court." He hung up.

Suki shoved her chair back, shot to her feet, and said in a loud voice, "They're lying...again!" Food spewed from her mouth, and her face flushed. "Darwin started it. LG and Josh were only defending me from that bastard."

LG's voice was soft when he said, "Suki, take a breath, sit down, and please finish your breakfast. Trust me. There is no reason to worry about Josh and me. We're more than capable of taking care of ourselves against the Tweet clan, no matter how much political power and money they have." He was busy slicing off a piece of pancake with a fork, spearing it, and soaking it in maple syrup before putting it in his mouth.

"How can you two be so low-key?" Suki's face was flushed with anger. "They're doing it again, and not just to me, but to my brother and you."

"LG's right," Josh said. "We have it covered."

"How?" Rachel asked as she hurried from the table to the living room's front window, where she peeked through the dusty, closed Venetian blinds. "They could be here any moment to arrest the two of you."

Josh had followed her and was looking over her shoulder.

The street was empty.

"If the police were closing in," he whispered in her ear, "my team would have warned us." He took her hand and led her back to the kitchen area. "We'll calmly finish eating and clean up before we go to church and they go camping. No problem."

Suki wasn't eating. Her hands were clenched together in her

lap, and she was staring at the floor between her feet, her face pale with shock.

"What about after church?" Rachel asked. "You can't go back to the ranch. That sheriff and his deputies will arrest the two of you."

With a miserable expression, Suki's lower lip trembled. "Charles Tweet owns the sheriff," she said. "He was one of their expert witnesses when I was crucified in court during the rape trial. He came up with a list of all the boys I had dated since middle school, making me look cheap. I'm not a whore! Why is it men can sleep around, and that makes them someone to admire, but if a woman does the same thing, she's a slut?" Her eyes were brimming with tears.

LG scooped up a forkful of potatoes and chewed. Rachel saw him swallow before he reached for Suki's hands, where they were trembling in her lap. "Suki," his voice was soothing, reminding Rachel of eucalyptus honey, "Josh and I have been through a lot worse than this. I'll call a friend of ours to come get us. The Viking has horses on his ranch. We'll borrow a pair and some gear, then vanish in the wilderness to camp out for a few days like we already planned. That will give our lawyers time to keep us out of jail."

"He's talking about Vick," Josh said. "LG calls him the Viking because the guy's ancestors originated in Norway. He served with us in one of LG's special-forces commands. When Vick retired after thirty years, we convinced him to buy one of the smaller bankrupt spreads a couple of hours from here."

Rachel sensed there was more to the story.

Suki said calmly, "Sounds like a good plan." But Rachel knew better. She could tell by the way her friend brushed her hair back with her fingertips and the look in Suki's eyes that she had locked a lid on the pressure cooker inside her head to keep it from exploding. She'd seen her do it before.

Everyone looked at LG as he clapped his hands together and beamed. "Good!" His plate was empty, and he slid it toward the center of the table. He picked up a mug of coffee and, holding it in both hands, sipped the dark, steaming brew.

---

Less than two hours later, Rachel parked her Shelby in the gravel parking lot of a small white chapel built in the middle of a few acres. She led Josh inside, where a congregation of about a hundred was already seated as the sermon was starting.

"Holy hell!" Josh said. He turned to leave, but Rachel, looking satisfied and sheepish, dragged him to the last pew where they sat.

Josh was staring at his mother, Judith Kavanagh, who was the pastor behind the pulpit. When he'd left home, she hadn't been a pastor. Back then, she'd been a dedicated Bible student and by now must have studied all 450 English translations of the holy book.

He watched as his mother scanned her flock until her eyes met his and stopped roving. She said, "Ephesians says, 'To put off your old self, which belongs to your former manner of life and is corrupt through deceitful desires, and to be renewed in the spirit of your minds, and to put on the new self, created after the likeness of God in true righteousness and holiness.'" She paused for a moment to let the words sink in before continuing, "As these new horizons are birthed, God offers all of his children a renewed life in His service."

The sermon didn't end there, but Josh stopped paying attention. Only his mother could make him feel shitty with her holier-than-thou attitude, and if it hadn't been for his promise to Rachel, he would've left.

When the chorus in the loft above them started singing, he

leaned toward Rachel and whispered, "How invested are you in my mother's moralizing?"

Without meeting his eyes, she replied, "I'm not born again, if you're asking. Your mother has always been there for me. It wasn't easy being a single mother. I couldn't have raised our children without her help, and the members of this church protected us from that asshole I married after I divorced him. I attend her services out of love and respect. I tricked you into coming here because it's time for you two to make peace. If you love me as much as you say you do, please do that for me."

Rachel didn't know that his mother had triggered the anger and rebellion that had driven him to join the Marines and leave home. The last straw had been his mother's endless preaching about what she called his sinful relationship with Rachel.

He wouldn't fall into that trap again. "I'll do it for you," he said.

She placed a hand on his knee and rested her head on his shoulder.

# CHAPTER 18

AFTER THE SERVICE, Josh watched the congregation leave the building through a narrow back door until he was alone with Rachel. He didn't want to disturb her. With her eyes closed, she looked pure, as he'd always remembered her. Her scent, her head on his shoulder, and the warmth of her hand on his leg had released a flood of memories from their youth. While he'd been with other women since leaving home, she was the only one who appeared in his dreams, and he lost her because of the dumb, immature decisions he'd made back then.

From where they sat in the last pew, he saw his mother standing outside talking to each member of her flock as they walked past her toward the shady picnic area behind the chapel. Her affection for them was apparent. She'd touched hands, elbows, and shoulders; kissed some cheeks; and hugged a few, probably her favorites.

She'd been strict with him and his brothers when they were children, always fast to quote from Proverbs. One, in particular, floated to the surface: "Whoever spares the rod hates his son, but he who loves him is diligent to discipline him."

She had loved him more than his brothers with the stout stick she used for her rod. He couldn't remember how many times he'd felt its sting when she'd punished him. For a brief instant, a flash of bitter resentment threatened to invade the calmness he'd worked hard to cultivate after leaving home. He swiftly dismissed those dark thoughts. Maybe his sister and Rachel were right, that his mother had changed and he should make peace with her.

It took a moment longer to figure out that something was off. For the last twenty-four years, he'd served in units where minorities made up a significant troop ratio. There weren't many minorities in his mother's congregation, but, for all of her faults, he knew she wasn't a racist.

Then, with a jolt, he remembered. Montana had a population of about a million, and almost 90 percent were white. After you subtracted the 66,000 Native Americans who lived in the state, there were fewer than 45,000 remaining to represent all the other minorities. Of course, not all whites were racists, but still.

Then he thought of Cheéte, one of his best friends. His right hand went to the Hog's Tooth, attached to a leather cord hidden under his shirt. It was a 7.62x51mm NATO round, the one fired by the M40A6 sniper rifle used by the Marines. He'd carried it with him since graduating from sniper school.

When Josh had been assigned to his first two-man Scout Sniper team, he met Cheéte and quickly learned that the Crow Indian's name translated into "Wolf" in English. During the years they worked together, they'd formed a strong bond. In time, Josh thought of this friend as a father figure, since his own father had been such a brooding, unhappy man during his childhood.

Cheéte had been twice his age when they first met. When his Crow friend retired from the Marines at the end of twenty-five years of service, he returned to the Indian reservation south of

Billings, Montana, where he'd been born. Because he thought of Cheéte as the father he'd always wanted, the phone calls, e-mails, and letters that should've been for Josh's family went to him. When Josh wanted to know how his family was doing, Cheéte had always checked without letting them know and reported back.

"Are we going to sit here for the rest of the day?" Rachel asked without moving or opening her eyes.

When he heard her voice, Josh's heart warmed. "I thought you were sleeping and didn't want to disturb you," he replied.

A smile flirted with her lips. Yawning, she opened her eyes and stretched. "Oh!" she said when she saw the empty chapel. "We better get moving. I'm hungry, and your mother will expect us."

"I'm glad you're feeling better, but there's something I want to talk about first," he said.

Rachel leaned back, and, with a stern expression, crossed her arms over her chest. "Are you thinking of breaking your promise?"

He shook his head and slipped off the hardwood bench to get down on his right knee. The one that had been replaced after a round had shattered the original joint. There was a twinge of pain, but he ignored it, as usual. He took her left hand and held it in one of his. "Rachel Cooper, I want to marry you." He turned over his free hand to reveal the engagement ring.

Josh had always wanted a family, and he'd loved this woman since grade school. He also loved another, but Mia had turned him down when he'd asked her to marry him a few months earlier. She'd clarified that she didn't want to be married to anyone or ever have children, but said it was okay to stay lovers.

He understood. He knew about her harsh childhood in Haiti and what had happened to her after she'd been abducted at fourteen. But since she had rejected him, he hadn't returned to France to be with her.

When Josh and Mia first met after he'd help free her from the traffickers, he'd just turned nineteen. After that night, they were friends for almost a decade before they became lovers. She was a few years younger and now lived near the parents who adopted her soon after he and Cheéte had rescued her and a few others.

Locking those memories away, he thought if Rachel said yes, he'd have his family, and she was still young enough to have more children if she wanted them like he did.

He saw her holding her breath as she stared at the ring. He hadn't forgotten what she'd said after kicking him in the balls in front of their heart tree: "We'll have to wait and see, won't we?"

Worried about her long silence, he said, "I have loved you since the first time I saw you. I didn't even know your name. The way I felt then has not changed. God knows I tried to forget you, but no matter who I was with over the years, I always thought of you first thing every morning."

Pressing her lips together, she studied the ring. "It looks expensive," she said. "It wouldn't be easy to buy a classy ring like this over the counter around here. When did you get it?"

"Eighteen years ago, after I signed up for my second enlistment. I bought the set in Dubai, where I was stationed."

Her eyes narrowed. "You got this for another woman, didn't you?" There was a warning tone of disappointment and suspicion in her voice.

He made sure not to break eye contact and risk tainting the truth. "No," he said. "I was due for a thirty-day leave and planned to fly home and ask you to marry me. When I bought the set, I didn't know you were already married to Luke. The only reason I found out was because I sent an e-mail to a friend I served with during his last tour and my first in the Marines. You've never met him, but he lives south of Billings. I asked him to be my best man. He was the one who told me what you did."

Josh didn't mention that his first reenlistment bonus had been $100,000. He'd been so depressed after hearing Rachel was married, he ended up spending his leave in Denmark with a prostitute who looked like a Victoria's Secret supermodel. He'd been tempted to throw the rings away but didn't.

Josh watched the tension drain from Rachel's face. "When you left without saying goodbye," she said, "I thought something was wrong with me."

He shook his head. "I'm sorry that happened. I want you to know that nothing was wrong with you. It was all on me. Is that why you married a loser like Luke?"

Her eyes teared up, and her voice cracked. "I didn't think I deserved anyone better."

"Let's start a new life together and put all of that behind us," he said. "Please, say yes."

She threw her arms around his neck and cried. As she sobbed, he whispered in her ear that he'd rather be dead than lose her again.

Clinging to him, she took several large gulps of air before she said in an almost inaudible voice, "Yes, any place and any time you want to get hitched, I'll be there."

He turned his hand palm up, so her left hand rested on top of his, and with his free hand, he slipped the engagement ring on her fourth finger. Then he leaned down and kissed her palm.

They both jumped when someone nearby cleared their throat. Turning, Josh discovered it was his mother. She was standing at the opening of the pew behind him. "I must confess. I heard everything," she said in a rush, "and I can't put words to how happy I am right now. I should cry joyful tears, but you guys have to get out of here. I just got a call on my mobile phone from a man who wouldn't identify himself. He said to warn you that the Sheriffs are converging on my chapel as we speak, and they have drones watching the place. He said don't take the Mustang, and there's no time to send in the bird. What kind of bird is that?"

"A helicopter, Mom," Josh replied, stifling a laugh.

"Why do you have one of those?" she asked.

"It's the business I'm in." His free hand went to his empty right ear. What the hell! He must've left his earpiece at Rachel's house. He remembered taking it out before showering, and it was apparent he hadn't put it back where it belonged. It had been so long since he'd been with Rachel that he'd forgotten how being around her always scrambled his brains.

"We don't have time to make a run for it," Josh said. "We better get out there and join the picnic, so there are plenty of witnesses. That way, Tweet's minions won't risk causing trouble, and I won't hurt any of them. During your sermon, I saw your old lawyer and his wife. Do you think he'll represent me?"

"I have a better idea," Judith said. "Follow me." She hurried toward another, smaller door to the left of the preacher's podium. That opened into a tiny office with one wall covered with floor-to-ceiling bookshelves. His mother knelt and reached under the bottom shelf. As soon as she stepped back, one section of books pivoted out of sight, revealing a narrow opening and a staircase leading down into darkness.

The sound of brakes squealing was followed by several tires crunching gravel in the parking lot in front of the chapel.

"Hurry," Judith said, breathless. "No one but Suki and Rachel know about this. I only took out a building permit for what's above ground. You never know when a 1200-square-foot survival shelter stocked with food, supplies, and medicine will come in handy."

"Sounds like you inherited some of Grandma Cat's paranoia,"

Josh said as he put a hand on the small of Rachel's back and guided her through the opening first.

"It's a good thing I did," she said and reached inside to flip a wall switch. "You'll need some light. It's a long way down, and I don't want my future daughter-in-law breaking a leg, or worse, her neck." Her eyes were glowing.

"What about me?" Josh asked.

Judith laughed. "From what I've heard about you from your sister, you're indestructible."

"Not quite," Rachel said. "I've seen his battle scars."

Judith looked startled as the bookshelf swung back into the opening and, with a click, sealed them in.

Rachel giggled, took his hand, and led him to the top of the stairs. "I've been down there. Once we reach the bottom, there's a long tunnel that leads to the shelter. The master bedroom has a queen-size bed, and I don't think anyone has ever used it."

# CHAPTER 19

TO AVOID Charles Tweet's goons, LG and Suki had disappeared into the Little Belt Mountains west of the Kavanagh ranch. This road-free mountainous wilderness covered about 200,000 acres of conifer forests.

Since LG had a lifetime senior pass honored nationwide at all parks, they didn't need to apply for one. Towing a horse trailer with a four-wheel-drive truck, the Viking had driven through the small village of Monarch, Montana. A few miles later, he left the paved road and headed into the wilderness, where he dropped them off with supplies, two horses, and a pack mule.

"Your friend looks like a Scandinavian pirate," Suki said as they watched Vick return the way they'd come. "He's tall, blond, burly, and has a bushy beard. The only things that don't fit the image are his glossy, spit-shined boots and perfectly pressed, spotless canvas coveralls. What does he do if they get dirty?"

"He has a dozen more hanging in a closet," LG replied. "Someone abandoned soon him after birth. He grew up in foster care and joined at eighteen. The military was his life for the next thirty years. He was a sergeant major when he retired, and those coveralls became his new field uniform. Never married. Has no kids. Enjoys living alone."

"What if we need help?" Suki asked. "How will you call him to come get us?"

LG unclipped a satellite phone from his belt and held it up. "We won't call Vick. If something unexpected happens, we're fifteen minutes' flight time from The Oath Group's MH-6 Little Bird in the pocket valley."

He didn't tell her about the microchip the size of a grain of rice powered by his body heat. They had injected it into the subdermal fascia between his thumb and forefinger on his left hand. On his other hand, he wore a ring that activated the chip. All he had to do was tap the ring on the spot where the chip was located. To turn it off, tap again. Everyone in The Oath Group had one.

Suki didn't know she had one of those microchips, too. Josh had injected it in the same location the first night she'd spent in the pocket valley. He'd waited until she was in her deep sleep cycle. Since she had blisters and was sore from working alongside his men, she didn't notice when she awoke the following day.

They rode single file up a slope with Suki leading, LG in the middle, and the pack mule last. LG wondered what hellish memories were festering inside her head. He suspected she felt responsible for being raped. When bad things happened to good people, they often thought it was their fault. Thinking like that could change her for the worse. LG didn't want that to happen—not to Josh's sister, not to anyone.

During their long early morning conversation back at Rachel's house, she'd kept the topic on Josh and what life was like in the military. Whenever he'd attempted to get her to talk about something closer to home, he'd failed. Not wanting to push it, he let it go.

He didn't know this young woman any better than she knew him. It took more than a few days to get to know someone. Still, he liked her for the same reason he liked Josh. He wanted to be her friend, and that meant he had to teach her how to manage her demons, as he'd always done for the troops he'd commanded. To do that, he figured he had to dig around inside her head, unnoticed. He wasn't Dr. Tate, but he wasn't a novice at dealing with trauma.

"You have said nothing about how you feel," LG said. He figured if he kept the conversation light, he might make some progress. That was how Dr. Tate started with him after Josh talked him into seeing her about his PTSD.

"What do you mean?" Suki replied as she glanced over her shoulder, grinning.

"You're on the run with a wanted man. Doesn't that bother you?"

Her expression revealed that was something she hadn't considered. "I kind of like it, but if you're asking, it must bother you."

Shit, he thought. She did it again, switched topics. I don't want this to be about me. "No...I'm just concerned it might bother you. I mean, roughing it like this isn't like a night out dancing. There are going to be bears, mountain lions, snakes, and ticks. We might not get to take a shower for days, but being in Special Forces for decades, I'm used to it."

"And I'm not because I'm a woman and a civilian?" The sharp tone of her reply warned him. In the age of the world's first mass movement against sexual abuse, her reaction didn't throw him. He'd just have to conduct his inquiry at a more cautious, slower pace.

She rolled her eyes and frowned. "Look," she said, "I've gone camping like this at least twice a year for most of my life. Our dad might not be the most pleasant person in the world to be around, but he was patient, teaching us how to survive in all kinds of hazardous conditions. I can make a fire with the right sticks and kindling, and I can survive in a blizzard because I know how to build a snow cave. Do you think Josh is the only one in this family who grew up with the skills of a sniper? He didn't learn how to shoot like that in the Marines. Just like Josh, I can run a trapline, easily shoot game at one hundred yards, and make a bow, including the string, just like the Native Americans did."

She made a dismissive gesture with one hand. "Roughing it makes me feel alive like nothing else does."

He raised his eyebrows in mock surprise, hoping to dispel the tension in her voice.

She burst out laughing and a moment later said, "I know what you're thinking."

It seemed his nonverbal ploy may have worked. "And what is that?"

"That I enjoy the wilderness more than civilization. That I'm a wild child."

He timed a proper moment of silence before replying, "And?"

"It's sort of true," she said. "I enjoy the wilderness more than civilization."

"Why's that?" he asked.

"There's no one out here to deal with."

That was his cue to lighten the mood, so he made an expression that signaled he might doubt her. "Most people aren't that bad," he said.

She chuckled. "Really, after you and Josh said you don't like crowds. Tell me what's to like."

It was his turn to laugh. "Touché."

They rode next to each other for a while. Since her expression looked lighter, signaling a good mood, he took a chance. "We have something else in common besides enjoying banter."

"Oh?" Suki tilted her head to one side and waited. Her cheesy expression urged him on.

"We're both rebels." He chewed on his lower lip to let her think he was afraid to speak, then urged his horse to move slightly faster, pulling away from her.

"What do you mean?" she asked. Soon they were riding next to each other again, and she was studying his face. "Go on, spit it out. Don't be shy."

"I'm afraid to ask. I don't want you to bite my head off again."

"Wait, a darn minute. I didn't do that."

"What did you call that lecture about your wilderness skills?"

"I was setting the record straight. I'm not a helpless damsel in distress, needing to be rescued. Try asking another question."

"I want to know what your life was like before Darwin Tweet came along."

"That wasn't a question, and it has nothing to do with being a rebel." Her expression sobered, and she broke eye contact. They rode in silence for a while before she said, "I was in my last year at Carroll College in Helena when it happened."

He knew that, but wanted to hear it from her. The Oath Group had a file on everyone linked to Suki's rape, including her. "What was your major?" he asked. He knew she had dropped out of college but didn't want her to know he knew.

"I was focusing on the biochemistry of neurodegenerative diseases," she said. "I was planning to get a job in biomedical research near San Francisco and live with my grandmas."

"Nothing is stopping you," he said.

Her body stiffened. "I don't want to talk about that. If I return to college, there'll be more guys like Darwin to deal with." She dug her heels into her horse's flanks, and it trotted away from him. They'd been riding up a gentle slope, and the trail had been narrowing, anyway.

Thinking her mood had turned chilly, he said, "I'm sorry. I didn't mean to upset you."

That was when he heard the warning buzz of a prairie rattler. Her horse panicked, leaped in the air, twisted like a pretzel, and threw her from the saddle. When she hit the ground, her head struck a rock near the thick-bodied snake that had spooked the horse. Before LG had time to react, he saw the olive-green rattler strike.

Before he reached the ground, the snake had released its fangs from Suki's leg. Using his retooled Special Forces M1911 pistol, LG blew the rattler's head off with a single shot from a dozen yards.

Glancing up, he saw her panicked horse tearing away at a gallop along the hillside until it was out of sight. Knowing the sat phone might take too long, he tapped his microchip with the ring on his right hand, and as soon as he reached Suki, he did the same with hers.

The microchips had biosensors and GPS tracking devices. By activating both of them, an Oath Group team would be in the air from the pocket valley within minutes. They'd see her vital signs and know she was in trouble. That meant a medic would be on the chopper with a kit that came with antivenin. LG estimated they'd arrive within a half-hour at most.

He searched the nearby area to make sure there were no more snakes. Then he hobbled his horse and the mule, found a blanket from their supplies, and wrapped Suki in it. Vick would have to return to find his runaway horse. It was probably chipped, too.

The blow to Suki's head had knocked her out cold, and she might have a concussion. After the chopper arrived and the medic treated her, she'd have to be taken to a hospital. He knew most deaths caused by rattlesnakes occurred between six and forty-eight hours after the bite. If they started the antivenin treatment within two hours, she had a 99 percent chance of surviving.

The best hospital in Montana was the Billings Clinic, so that was where she was going. There was nothing else to do. He settled beside her and worried. He felt responsible because he'd distracted her. It was obvious his probing questions had broken her concentration, and if not for them, she would've probably spotted the rattler and guided her horse around it. She'd also been riding an unfamiliar horse. If she died or survived with permanent damage, he'd carry that guilt with him to his grave.

He suspected her tough act had been a charade. Beneath the skin, she was hiding feelings of shame and self-blame.

From the report his NSA contact had put together about her rape, she'd been semi-conscious after being drugged. When Darwin finished, he told his bodyguards to have fun, too. It was brutal, and she'd been aware of everything that was happening with no ability to resist. Some of Tweet's victims hadn't been as fortunate. A couple of underage girls seen hanging around him had vanished. Without bodies, there was no evidence, and most parents didn't have the money to buy justice.

Suki had been cleaned inside and out. Then she'd been dropped off naked and battered in front of her mother's chapel during one of the Sunday potlucks. When she stumbled around the side of the building to the picnic area, she was half out of her mind.

LG used the sat phone to dial a number located east of Oakland in the San Francisco Bay Area. He had to do something, so he was calling his PTSD therapist's mobile phone. Suki was going to need an expert to help her rebuild her life if she survived this.

After Dr. Tate answered, he said, "This is LG. We're on a secure line. How much vacation time do you have? Josh's sister needs you ASAP."

"Where?"

"Montana."

"I'll be there as soon as you arrange for the Cessna Citation Bravo." Doctor Tate worked with many of the former Special Forces troops that were members of The Oath Group.

"I'm calling our pilot next," he replied.

# CHAPTER 20

AFTER TALKING to Dr. Tate in California, LG's second call went to the Viking, telling him to return and recover his gear, horses, and mule.

When the Little Bird arrived, two armed men sat on the fold-down benches outside the fuselage with room for four more on those seats. The US Army's elite 160th Special Operations Aviation Regiment had nicknamed the aircraft the Killer Egg. Its primary mission was to insert Special Operations Forces onto rooftops or on narrow roadways.

After Gary, the medic, treated Suki, he turned to LG and asked, "Do you want me to remove the chip before we take her to the trauma center in Billings?"

"Good idea. Do it," LG said.

After the DARPA chip in her left hand had been removed, LG ordered the other man to stay with the horse and mule until Vick arrived. "The Viking will give you a ride back," he said.

A medical team was waiting on the roof when the Little Bird arrived at the Emergency and Trauma Center in Billings, Montana, an hour and a half later. Suki, still unconscious, was moved from the co-pilot's seat to a gurney. LG and the medic stayed with her.

The hospital's trauma team must have seen the 10mm MP5 submachine guns inside the chopper. As they hurried across the rooftop toward the building entrance, LG thought most of the clinic's people looked nervous. It didn't help that his young medic wore washed-out camouflage combat fatigues.

The submachine guns stayed on the chopper, but LG and the medic carried concealed weapons. The Little Bird's crew of two flew to the nearest private airport to refuel before returning to the base camp in the pocket valley on the Kavanagh ranch.

The male nurse in charge of the trauma team said something to the others that LG couldn't hear. Whatever he told them eased the tension, and Suki was soon inside being treated.

LG moved closer to the lead trauma nurse and said, "For Suki's safety, my man or I will be with her at all times."

"I know who you are, General. My name is Jesus Lopez. I served several tours as a medic with the 75th Ranger Regiment in Iraq and Afghanistan. I'll make sure the doctor and the clinic's administrators understand."

Lopez, an active member of The Montana Racial Equity Project, knew about the Tweet family and also Suki's tragic story.

Lopez lowered his voice and continued, "Sir, it's all over extreme-right social media sites. Charles Tweet thinks you and Josh Kavanagh had something to do with his youngest son's disappearance after that bar fight in Great Falls. I don't care who started it. That family can rot in hell. If the police learn you're here, it won't be me who called them."

LG put a hand on the man's shoulder. "Thank you, Mr. Lopez. I appreciate your support."

Turning away from Lopez and toward his man, he said, "No matter what happens to me, I want you to keep the colonel's sister in sight at all times. Don't let anyone but doctors and nurses near her. Has Josh been notified?"

"No, sir. We lost contact after the raid on his mother's chapel. The local authorities didn't catch him. It seems he gave them the slip. We don't know where he went."

LG grinned. "Knowing Josh, I'm not surprised he avoided them." Then his expression sobered. "Keep trying. He's out there somewhere."

LG left the trauma unit to find the admissions office. Since they couldn't reach Josh, the responsibility to notify Suki's parents fell on him. He knew his career had been a success, but he refused to let that go to his head. To him, his Medal of Honor was stained with blood, and after he'd retired, he locked it away with all the other medals.

Suppose Suki dies or ends up with a permanent physical disability, he thought. In that case, I'll add her memory to all the others I lost and refuse to forget.

Before he reached the admissions clerk, he stopped in a hallway, leaned against a wall, and closed his eyes. He thought of the Bible, a book he'd studied with the same focus and discipline he'd applied to Sun Tzu's The Art of War when he'd been a West Point cadet. He wasn't a religious man, but he still agreed with George Washington that God was wise, inscrutable, and hidden from humanity, yet like an invisible shepherd, LG believed He guided the affairs of the universe.

Heal Suki, O LORD, he thought, and she will be healed; save her, and I will be saved.

Then he prayed for strength: Lord, I'm weary. My energy is sagging, and my motivation is lagging, and I need your strength and fresh touch to get back on course again.

"Are you all right, son?" a woman's voice asked.

LG opened his eyes and saw the concerned face of an elderly

black woman. "Thank you for asking," he said and smiled. "I'm fine, ma'am. Just tired." He moved on to admissions.

When asked for identification, he pulled out his Army USID card, revealing he was a retired lieutenant general and a Medal of Honor recipient.

The admissions clerk took the card and stared at it. "When Lopez called and told me you were coming, I didn't believe him," she said. "Thank you for your service, General. I lost my brother in Afghanistan. He was a Marine."

"I am so sorry you had to go through that," LG replied.

She blinked away the tears clouding her eyes and leaned closer to reread his card. Clearing her throat, she met his eyes and asked, "Are you related to the patient?"

"I'm a friend of the family," LG replied.

"Have you contacted them?"

"Not yet."

"What's her name, please?"

"Suki Kavanagh."

The clerk's fingers froze over the keyboard for a moment. Few in Montana didn't know about the Kavanagh ranch and what had happened to Suki. "My brother served under her brother Josh," she said. "He would've followed that man to hell and back." She dabbed her eyes with a tissue.

With her fingers still hovering over the keyboard, she made eye contact again. There was a depth of sadness there that could not be measured. After a moment of shared sorrow, she started typing.

"I haven't called her family yet. I'd like to, but I don't want to step on your procedures," LG said.

The clerk indicated he should call, and LG took out his satellite phone and jabbed the buttons. Josh's brother Sam answered on the second ring, and LG told him what'd happened.

"We'll be there as soon as I get the family in the air," Sam said and hung up.

The ranch had its own airstrip about a mile from the house. They owned a Beechcraft King Air 250, capable of reaching Billings in less than an hour. Both the father and Sam were licensed pilots. When not in use, the aircraft sat in a secure hangar.

Finished with the admissions clerk, LG returned to the trauma center, where he discovered Jesus Lopez standing beside his medic. Lopez said, "The doctor will wait for a family member to arrive before he tells them what he knows. We're not supposed to share this with friends of the family or strangers. In my book, that does not apply to you, sir."

"I appreciate that," LG replied.

"Just don't tell anyone I told you."

LG nodded.

Lopez continued: "She's awake but has a moderate concussion. No skull fracture and most of her trauma is from the snakebite. She's fortunate to have had an anti-venom shot as soon as she did. We're already seeing dramatic improvement in her neurotoxic signs. We'll give her a second shot in about four hours. As soon as her clotting profile returns to normal, we'll stop giving them to her."

"Any loss of memory?" LG asked.

"We'll have to wait and see, but she hasn't forgotten you. Although she appears confused, she's called for you several times. Am I correct in assuming she had the Armed Forces anti-venom?"

"No, I gave her CroFab," LG's medic said.

The Armed Forces' anti-venom was effective against India's four most venomous snakes: the cobra, common krait, Russell's viper, and the saw-scaled viper. CroFab was for rattlesnake bites.

Lopez nodded. "Good. One more thing, sir. The doctor wants you both to stay in the waiting room instead of in the trauma unit."

"Tell him we will not do that, but we'll keep out of the way."

"I understand, sir." Lopez returned to Suki to help treat her.

LG turned to his man. "Gary, the Tweets are going to learn I'm here and send whoever their pet law enforcement is to arrest me. Have our people monitor all their calls, so I'll know how long I have before they arrive."

"Yes, sir. Do you want your microchip deactivated?"

"No, I suspect I'll need it in case I vanish after I'm arrested. That way, our people will know my location."

Every member of The Oath Group on this operation knew that Charles Tweet acted like a feudal lord and treated Montana as his fiefdom. He wasn't the only one. A couple of dozen multi-billionaires seemed to be buying the two major political parties by getting as many of their minions elected as possible. LG and Josh belonged to a small, secretive group of patriots called The Paul Revere Network, scattered throughout the FBI, DOJ, CIA, DARPA, and the DOD. They were monitoring those billionaires and their elected flunkies.

Lopez had returned. "What happens if Riley Pearl gets hold of you, sir?"

"Why did you mention him?" LG had been one of the five officers sitting on the jury panel for Pearl's court-martial. The verdict had been unanimous.

"Because the pretender gets financial support from Charles Tweet."

LG didn't know that. "Thank you, son."

"My pleasure, sir."

Pearl had been a lieutenant colonel in the Air Force, not a pilot. After the general court-martial found him guilty of racist comments online and racist behavior toward minorities in his unit, they gave him an officer discharge. Commissioned officers cannot receive a bad conduct discharge or a dishonorable discharge like an enlisted man. As officers, a court-martial can't reduce them in rank. Still, a dismissal notice was the same as a dishonorable discharge.

Once Pearl left the Air Force, LG had kept track of him until he dropped out of sight. He knew Pearl had ended up in Montana and joined a neo-Nazi white supremacist militia group on a remote ranch near the Canadian border. Their website listed several combat medals that Pearl hadn't earned. He never saw combat, but on the militia's site, his photos made him look like a total badass. Since he'd lied about his military honors, he violated the Stolen Valor Act.

LG wondered what Charles Tweet and Riley Pearl were up to. He had to make more phone calls and see what else he could learn. He didn't like the idea of those two working together—no telling how much trouble they'd cause.

# CHAPTER 21

TEN HOURS after the rattler bit Suki, The Oath Group's Cessna Citation Bravo left Buchanan Airport in Concord, California. Doctor Janet Tate, the only passenger, couldn't help thinking of the money this flight was costing. That cash could've helped a homeless vet she was counseling. The man, his girlfriend, and her two children lived in a 1978 Dodge van.

Dr. Tate had served in the Air Force for twenty years before retiring. She also answered her phone at any hour. A crisis triggered by PTSD was unpredictable, and the suicide rate among veterans was more than twice that of civilians.

This was the first time she'd flown on a small private jet designed to carry only eight passengers. The noise and intense turbulence interfered with her ability to focus and relax.

With the aircraft on autopilot, the pilot left the cockpit and made his way aft. "Ma'am, would you like something to eat and drink?"

"Thank you, but no," Tate replied. "It was a tough day, and I'd like to take a nap." Her workdays at the Vet Center often ran ten hours or longer. She'd also skipped her lunch break today because one of her female vets walked in without an appointment. The young woman had served one tour in Afghanistan. Her duty station had been at Bagram Air Base, where she'd been gang-raped. When her attackers dragged her from her bunk, they covered her mouth with duct tape and slipped a pillowcase over her head. She didn't know who they were or where she'd been taken. The base covered six square miles with a population of 40,000.

After being released by her abductors, she reported what had happened to her commanding officer. The lieutenant colonel refused to let her be checked by a nurse or doctor and filed charges against her for being absent without leave. He then had her locked in a cargo container for several days, as if she were the criminal.

If it hadn't been for a friend telling her boyfriend and his Delta Force team raising hell, she was convinced she would've been killed and her body dumped somewhere. No charges had been filed against the officer she'd reported the incident to, and she'd received death threats. One of those anonymous calls had triggered her latest trauma.

She hadn't told her boyfriend about the threatening phone calls because she was afraid of what he might do. When Tate asked her why not, the girl replied, "With help from Colonel Kavanagh, he might trace who made the call and deal with it his way. I admit the idea is tempting, but I don't want that kind of justice. I've already talked to a lawyer referred to me from the National Women's Law Center, and I like her. She's tough as nails. If anyone can fix this, she will."

"How long will we be in the air before we reach Billings?" Tate asked the pilot.

"About two hours, ma'am," he replied.

"That fast? I expected it to take longer."

"Well, ma'am, we don't have to deal with the same crap most

commercial aircraft do. You sure about that drink and some food? What about music? Do you have any preferences?"

She shook her head. "No, that's okay. I had supper already. How about dimming the lights, though? And I'd like a blanket if you have one. Do you have a noise-canceling headset or earplugs?"

The pilot got the things she wanted and turned down the lights. Before he returned to the cockpit, she asked, "Where's the co-pilot?" She'd seen The Mountain Between Us and didn't want to end up alone in the wilderness struggling to survive.

"No need for one. They designed this aircraft for single-pilot operation. Have a nice nap."

He better not have a stroke, she thought. I'm going to be really pissed if he does. Tate glanced out the porthole window next to her and marveled at civilization's light show spread out below the aircraft. It would vanish soon enough once they left the airspace over suburbia. There was a lot of uninhabited wilderness between the Bay Area and Montana. With the blanket wrapped around her, she reclined her seat and stretched out.

She wanted to sleep, but her thoughts wandered. Tate suspected The Oath Group was involved in the CIA's global shadow war. It was a safe bet the group worked for the DOD, too. She'd read a report that said the ratio of contractors to troops in combat zones was three to one. Having a retired three-star general with The Oath Group probably meant they had deep connections. She didn't know the details and didn't want to know. She knew that Josh's Oath Group was big enough to have its own little air force. That didn't surprise her. A recent Congressional Research Service study had revealed that about half of the Department of Defense's budget went to contractors, more than $300 billion.

Her smartphone vibrated. It was a text from one of the Vietnam vets she worked with. Jim had served two tours in 1967 and

'68. He'd recently read his DD-214 for the first time, and it didn't list most of the operations he'd witnessed when he'd been an Army combat photographer and artist.

She texted back that if he wanted to correct the DD-214, they'd request a DD-215 form. She asked if anyone had let him review his paperwork before he left the service.

He texted back, "No."

She shook her head. That was not uncommon for Vietnam vets.

Jim texted again: "Dr. T, I'm screwed. Someone fucked up my file, and I'm having trouble with my VA benefits because of it. This is giving me headaches and I can't sleep."

Tate smiled. Most of her combat vets worked hard, were modest, and avoided stressful situations when possible. Getting them to open the snake pit inside their heads wasn't easy since a lot of what had happened to them in combat was buried deep.

She texted, "I'll be back in my office in a few days. Call and make an appointment. We'll talk, and I'll guide you through the paperwork."

"Too complicated," he replied. "I don't want to bother you."

"We'll talk when I return. Make an appointment, Jim! Don't let this slide."

A moment slipped by before Jim texted back: "Okay, Doc. See you."

She closed her eyes, and the next thing she heard was the pilot telling her to put her seat in the upright position and buckle up. They were minutes away from Billings Logan Airport.

After landing, she found herself on the tarmac in an isolated, gloomy area. One of Josh's men had been waiting in a Chevy Tahoe SUV that looked sinister with black wheels, black Chevy-logo bow ties, a black mesh grille, and a black roof rack with cross rails. It was apparent the SUV wasn't standard. She wondered if it was armored, maybe with Kevlar or something else, since Josh had a connection with DARPA. She did not know what he did for the Defense Advanced Research Projects Agency and didn't want to know. With need-to-know secrets, it was safer not to be curious.

The friendly face that greeted her was one of her patients, and Tate immediately asked, "What's the reason for the heavy weapons?" It was impossible not to notice the MP5 submachine gun clipped to a spot the driver could easily reach. Under his left arm, there was a shoulder holster, and she recognized the Glock's black polymer frame. That wasn't all. When she'd slipped into the front passenger seat, she'd seen the M32 on the floor behind her. The dark, skimpy towel that was supposed to conceal the weapon had slipped off.

Why do they need a multiple grenade launcher in Montana? The M32 could fire two 44-mm grenades a second, with devastating results.

"What heavy weapons?" the driver replied.

"Oh, crap!" she said. "Don't bluff a bullshitter. You need a bigger towel to cover the M32." She jabbed a thumb over her left shoulder toward the back seat.

"Dr. T, this is Montana, and your safety is my responsibility. That means we need to keep a low profile and avoid trouble. There are too many white extremists in this state, and with Trump in the White House, they're bolder than ever. It's safe to say that this state is not friendly to Jews and Black Americans like us."

Tate thought Montana couldn't be that bad, but her clients were hypervigilant and on guard no matter where they were. The driver was six foot three, about eight inches taller than her. When she received his file from the VA, a lot of the information had been redacted. Come to think of it, the same was true of all the men she knew who worked with Josh. Something was going on in Montana besides Josh returning home to offer moral support for his sister.

"Will LG and Josh be at the hospital?" She was an expert at body language, and the driver's expression took on stress around his eyes.

When he replied, his strained monotone signaled reluctance. "They're not there, Dr. T."

"Why didn't Josh call me instead of LG?"

He stammered, "I...don't...have an answer."

She softened her voice. "I worked in Air Force Operations Intelligence for most of my military career, and I haven't lost my top-secret clearance. I might look stupid, but I'm not. Something is going on here that no one is telling me. Also, I'm your counselor, and unless you're in an obvious danger to yourself or someone else, what you tell me will be kept confidential. Did you notice I'm not taking any notes?"

"You don't look stupid, Dr. T," he replied, "and I'm not allowed to talk to you about this operation." A moment later, he added, "Shit!"

His slip with the word "operation" gave it away, and Tate took out her mobile phone and called two numbers. When no one answered, she asked, "Why aren't Josh and LG answering my calls? They always pick up."

The driver glanced warily at her. "We don't know where Josh is, and LG was taken into custody by DHS agents a few hours ago."

That got her blood pumping. "Are we driving into a goat fuck?" When he didn't look at her or reply, she said, "Then who is your ranking officer? Is he one of my vets too?"

"Captain Forest," he replied.

"Thank you," she said. Forest was another one of her vets. She wondered how many of her clients belonged to The Oath Group and was willing to bet Josh had recommended they see her without letting Tate know he'd done it. In fact, Josh referred the young woman who'd been raped in Afghanistan. That meant for sure he knew her boyfriend in Delta. The rapists must be running scared now that they knew who he was. Delta Force was elite, even among Special Forces units. It also convinced Tate that her commanding officer already knew his career was over. LG would've seen to that. With no chance to move up in rank, that lieutenant colonel would have to retire early.

Josh and LG only recruited from the Marines, SEALs, and Special Forces. Forest was a former Marine and Scout Sniper. He and Josh had been on over one deployment together. She even knew that Josh called the captain Popsicle Dick. She didn't want to know the story behind that nickname. Still, she knew enough about Forest that no one on Earth would get away with calling him that unless they were closer than brothers, thicker than blood.

Tate speed-dialed Forest, and he picked up immediately. "What's up, Doc?" he chuckled.

That tempted her to say she wasn't Elmer Fudd, and he wasn't Bugs Bunny, but she resisted the urge. "I called to ask you the same thing."

There was a moment of silence. "Are you at the hospital?"

"Still in route."

"I'll see you there in a few," he said, "and I'll have some answers for you, depending on what you ask." He hung up.

What the hell have I gotten myself into? This time, when she looked through the SUV's windshield, she noticed all the threatening red taillights in front of them and sensed the danger they might be in.

"Is this SUV armored?" she asked.

"Yep," her driver replied. "It even has ballistic glass."

# CHAPTER 22

CHEÉTE, his wife, and three of their youngest seven children witnessed Josh marry Rachel in the secret underground survival shelter. Two days earlier, the sheriffs had searched the chapel.

Before the ceremony, Cheéte pulled Josh aside and asked, "Did you know you're part Crow?"

Josh studied his friend with one eye closed, wondering if this was another example of Cheéte's odd sense of humor.

"No joke." Cheéte grinned. "I'm as serious as syphilis."

"How can you know I'm part Native American?"

"Well, back when we were a team, I was curious because of two things: you fight like one of us, and you have subtle features that made me suspect you might have some of our blood. When we were in Afghanistan, I waited until you were wounded and borrowed a sample of your blood for a DNA test to determine your ancestry."

"Wait..." Josh said, interrupting. "How did you know I was going to get wounded?"

"You always got wounded at least once during every deployment when we served together, Baby Bro. It was inevitable. It's like you were having a love affair with bullets and bombs. Besides, most of them were flesh wounds."

Josh hadn't heard the Baby Bro tag for about two decades. When he'd served with Cheéte, the older, taller sniper called him that because of the difference between their age and height. His friend was a couple of inches taller than him.

Cheéte continued, "I also did some research into your family history and learned that several of your ancestors married our women."

Josh raised his eyebrows. "Who helped you get a sample of my blood?"

"Our corpsman. He owed me a favor."

"You'd make a superb poker player," Josh said. "Except for the scarce grin that never matches what you're saying, the look on your face almost never changes. What did the test reveal?"

"That you're 27 percent Apsáalooke. It seems you Kavanagh men really like our women. I want you to apply to get a certificate issued by the Bureau of Indian Affairs. Then we'll really be brothers. That blood connection helped me recruit the team for this mission...Ah, do you know how I figured out that Kavanagh men are attracted to our women?"

This better be good, Josh thought. "How?"

"Because of Rachel. Where do you think she got her gorgeous, glossy black hair and those high cheekbones? Her male ancestors also liked our women."

Josh couldn't help but glance at Rachel across the room, where she was talking to Cheéte's wife. It was true. "Maybe there was a shortage of white women back then." Josh was half-joking.

"Nah, our women are just better looking and better in bed," Cheéte replied. Leaning closer, he lowered his voice to a hush. "Why are you really here, Bro? I don't see you returning home to mellow out in a rocking chair. Not at any age. Sitting on porches waiting for time to pass is not for guys like us."

Josh glanced around to make sure no one was close enough to hear his answer: "For two decades, domestic counterterrorism strategy in the US ignored the rising danger of far-right extremism. They have unofficially tasked The Oath Group to gather info on these organized militias. Depending on what our undercover operatives learn, we're allowed to probe a few targets. We started in Montana."

Cheéte was silent for a moment. It was clear from his half-closed eyes he was thinking. "Well, if you're going to go after some of these assholes, me and my warriors want in on the action."

Josh felt his heart swell with gratitude. "We'd be honored. Although I think you, being the tribe's only living war chief, was probably a major factor in getting your men to agree."

Cheéte's nod of agreement was almost imperceptible. "If Joseph were still with us, he would've given his blessing."

Josh had learned about Joseph over the years through e-mails from Cheéte, who was close to the old warrior. Josh regretted never meeting the legendary hero, who became one of the last war chiefs of his tribe when he stole fifty horses from the Nazis during World War II.

In traditional Crow tribal culture, if a warrior accomplished four significant deeds on the battlefield, he became a war chief. Cheéte had earned that honor, too. The last member of the tribe to receive it before him was Joseph Medicine Crow, who died in 2016 at 102. Whenever he went into battle, Joseph wore his war paint, two red stripes on his arms, and a sacred painted yellow eagle feather under his helmet.

One of the four deeds was to steal an enemy's horse. With the end of mounted soldiers in World War II, that became almost impossible—until Cheéte started stealing horses from the Taliban in Afghanistan. Before taking the first horse, the first deed was to touch the still living Taliban, counting coup, and knocked him off his mount. Then, without killing the man, he took his weapons, accomplishing three of the four. Leading a successful war party was the fourth requirement.

"Because you're eligible to join the tribe," Cheéte continued, "your siblings and father probably are, too."

"My sister and brothers might be interested, but not my dad. Mom wanted him to get one of those tests decades ago, but he refused." Josh thought that was probably why no one in the family ever talked about the possibility of being part Native American.

After the marriage ceremony, they waited for the all-clear from Cheéte's team before embarking. Cheéte had arrived driving a Toyota Highlander with over 150,000 miles. It was dinged and scratched, but reliable.

Cheéte and his family had not come alone. Four other vehicles were carrying a dozen armed Apsáalooke, the original name of the Crow tribe. All the former US Marines and combat vets had arrived hours earlier, taking up concealed positions around the chapel. There was no shortage of combat vets on the reservation, since more Native Americans served in the US military than any other ethnic group.

Josh and Rachel shared the second row of seats with one of Cheéte's daughters, a stunning twelve-year-old, who revealed what her mother must've looked like when she was younger.

Cheéte's wife, Raven, was forty-three, twenty years younger than him. She literally rode shotgun in front. It was legal to carry firearms inside a vehicle without a permit in Montana, as long as they weren't concealed. Her DP-12 double-barreled pump shotgun looked more like a machine gun. It came with one trigger and a two-tube magazine that held fourteen rounds, not counting the two in the chambers. Each tube fed its own barrel.

Cheéte brought two weapons—a .50 caliber Israeli Military

Desert Eagle and an M-40A1 Marine Corps sniper rifle—and clipped them to the dash next to his wife's shotgun.

The two lead vehicles were out of sight, and the others spaced out behind them, so it wasn't obvious they were a convoy. They were linked through walkie-talkies and only spoke the Siouan language.

---

When Cheéte had dropped Josh and Rachel off at a remote cabin on the 2.3-million-acre Crow Indian Reservation south of Billings, Montana, he'd pointed west. "Eventually, you're going to get cabin fever. You'll find a trail over there about a quarter-mile. It looks like an animal track, but with your skills, you can't miss it. If you walk southwest on that path for an hour or two before returning to the cabin, it should be safe."

Almost 8,000 members of the tribe lived on the reservation, with a few thousand more outside its boundaries.

Now, a few days later, they set out on foot with sunset less than a half-hour away to lower the risk of drone exposure. They paced themselves to enjoy their first walk as a married couple. They talked little at first, as daylight fled and the low 80s gave way to cooler temperatures.

They were both armed. Cheéte had loaned Josh one of his .50 calibers. "What do you expect me to do with this cannon... stop a tank?" he'd asked when his friend offered him the large revolver.

"You never know what you'll run into, Baby Bro. Yellowstone isn't that far, and the grizzlies don't stop at the park boundary. There are also wolves, coyotes, and cougars. You might even bump into a white neo-Nazi looking for one of our women to rape and murder."

"You're kidding, right?"

"Do I sound like I'm kidding? What would you do if one of them raped Rachel?"

"I'd want them to suffer for as long as possible." Josh hefted the five-shot S&W500 with its 8.38-inch barrel and aimed at an imaginary target. "But I'd rather use bear spray than this and take my time dismembering them. I'd start with their fingers, one digit at a time, until all ten were gone, and then I'd move on to their toes. I'd let Rachel castrate the bastard, and knowing her, she'd make him watch as she gelded him."

His friend grinned. "I like your thinking. I'll be right back."

A moment later, he'd returned from the Toyota with two ten-ounce canisters of Counter Assault pepper spray with hip holsters. Each canister had a spray distance of forty feet. "One for each of you," he'd said.

During the hike, the Smith & Wesson hung from a sling around Josh's neck. Rachel carried his Glock in an underarm shoulder holster.

Wearing floppy hats to hide their faces from the sky, they held hands as they walked. Josh ran his thumb over the diamond of her engagement ring and the marriage band below it on the same finger. Just touching her aroused him, triggering guilty memories of walks with Mia. It was taking too long to get over his last lover, and he had no intention of telling Rachel about her.

They'd been married almost a week, and Josh was having trouble believing he was finally hitched to the girl he'd been in love with since grade school. It was true they weren't legally married yet, but his mother had said they'd get the license later.

"What counts, son," she'd said, "is that you two are married under God. We'll take care of Montana's paperwork after our lawyers get that billionaire off of your back."

"Rachel," Josh said, "before we said 'I do,' Cheéte told me we could become members of his tribe."

She shrugged, and a ghost of a smile flirted with her lips. "I already knew about me," she said. "I'm glad you share that blood, too."

The trail crossed a meadow filled with the strong, sweet scent of lupine. There was also a slight aroma of vanilla from nearby Ponderosa pines. He stopped, faced her, and took both of her hands in his. "How did you know?"

"I had one of those tests years ago because I wanted to find out. I hoped I'd end up being part Apsáalooke instead of one of the other tribes."

"What did you have against the others?"

"Nothing," she replied, "but I fell in love with Cheéte's tribe when I was seven, the first year my family went to the Crow Fair Powwow and Rodeo." She squeezed his hands. "You know, the hundredth annual fair takes place this August. If we dress in traditional Apsáalooke costumes, no one will recognize us. Cheéte's wife offered to get them for us if we want to join them."

A wolf howled. Another wolf answered. Then they heard the distant sound of coyotes yipping and barking. They'd been out for over two hours, and the only light was from the stars spread across the night sky. "I think it's time we started back," she said.

Josh leaned down and kissed her before they turned around. Every time they kissed, the touch of her lips sent an electric thrill through him, and he couldn't get enough.

# CHAPTER 23

MINUTES TO MIDNIGHT, The Oath Group's black Chevy Tahoe parked in front of the main entrance to the Billings Clinic. The first thing Dr. Tate noticed were several Ford sedans with exhaust billowing from their tailpipes. They were parked along the curb at the far end of the covered portico's in-and-out entrance.

She rummaged in her purse for her reading glasses and slipped them on. The license plate on the closest car said US Government, and below that was DHS, followed by a number. The prefix told her the cars belonged to the Department of Homeland Security. Some of her vets thought DHS meant Dick Head Syndrome. They weren't alone in their opinion. Tate didn't trust this federal agency, either. Less than two months after the September 11 attacks, it had been created by the Patriot Act and was allowed to get search warrants from judges without showing probable cause, ignoring the US Constitution's Fourth Amendment.

There'd already been court cases where federal judges struck down several key provisions as unconstitutional. The department's inspector general was also investigating hundreds of corruption cases.

Two more Oath Group men materialized out of the shadows and opened the passenger door. Instead of exiting, she stared at her driver. The burly man sighed. "What do you want to know, Dr. T?"

"How long has it been since LG was taken into custody by them?" She jabbed a finger at the parked DHS cars.

"Several hours, ma'am."

She noted the change from "Dr. T" to "ma'am." Her simple question must've strayed into operational territory, but why was Homeland Security still here?

Several plain-clothed DHS agents with IDs hanging from neck lanyards spilled from the unmarked cars. They hurried toward the Chevy Tahoe under the covered portico.

"Those fools have been waiting for Josh to show up so they can arrest him!" Her driver said, ready for a fight, yet Tate knew he was in total control. Special Forces training lasted sixty-three weeks compared to the Marine Corps' twelve-week boot camp and the Army's ten.

The anger she heard in his voice wouldn't dictate his actions. His martial arts skills included boxing, Muay Thai, Brazilian Jiu-Jitsu, and more, including avoiding starting a fight in a situation like this one.

Three more camouflage-clad Oath Group troops appeared from the hospital's entrance and joined the others to form a defensive line. Facing each other, the two groups squared off. One of the DHS agents asked in a gruff voice, "Who's in there?"

"None of your business," one of Tate's men replied in an unruffled tone.

Leaving the SUV, Tate slipped between two of her men to confront the feds. They needed to shave, shower, and get haircuts. With their rumpled clothing, they looked like undercover narcotics officers from central casting on the set of a sleazy Hollywood TV crime show. She noticed the stress in their body language, or was it fear?

"Do I look like Josh Kavanagh?" she said, making eye contact with the agent in charge, since he was the only one talking.

His upper lip curled in a sneer, and his mouth formed unspoken words that looked like "damn uppity niggers." He turned his head to the side and spat in the demilitarized zone between the two groups. Then his charcoal-colored eyes bored a hole through her, and she felt a chill. He said, "Step aside! We're inspecting this vehicle."

"Like hell you are!" one of Tate's men replied. They moved around her until they were closer to the feds, and she was behind their defensive line again. The DHS agents took a step back. The feds were armed, but so were her men. No one had pulled a weapon, but the tension between the two groups was like hot, sputtering bacon grease ready to explode.

"Don't provoke them," she said. Tate knew her men and what they were capable of. These feds didn't stand a chance.

"Ma'am," her driver appeared beside her, "Suki's family is waiting. Come with me."

She hadn't noticed how tense and stiff she was until they entered the hospital's warmth. Before going inside, she heard one of her men say to the DHS agents, "If you don't have a proper warrant that shows probable cause, you don't search our vehicle."

"Like hell," the fed replied. "We don't need no search warrant." Then the hospital's door closed behind her, and it cut the voices off.

She didn't doubt that if it got violent, the feds were going to lose. While climbing out of the Tahoe, she'd spotted the tip of a sniper's rifle poking from the Cherry Tree Inn's flat roof across the street from the hospital. The weapon was pointed at the feds. She hoped they loaded it with non-lethal rounds.

"Why so much anger?" she asked her escort as they crossed the hospital's vestibule.

"Dr. T, we respect and love the general and didn't want to let those assholes take him."

"You're itching for a fight?"

"Yes, ma'am."

Back to ma'am again, she thought. "Don't start a war with Homeland Security. Whoever is paying The Oath Group to be in Montana would disapprove of that. They'd want you to keep a low profile."

"We understand, and you can take it to the bank, that we won't start anything—but if they do, we'll finish it."

Two men in expensive-looking suits appeared from the elevators and passed them at a brisk walk toward the exit.

"Are they part of this drama?" she asked.

"The younger guy is our lawyer," he replied. "We have a fancy west-coast law firm on retainer. The older gentleman represents the Kavanagh family. If it weren't for them, those feds would still be planted in the hallway outside of Suki's hospital room. Have you ever met Josh's parents?"

"No."

"They're camped in the waiting room near their daughter. She was improving when LG was with her, but after the feds took him, she fell apart. And when she heard them say they were taking her, too, she became hysterical."

Tate blurted out, "Why would they want to do that?" She hated to admit it, but this was better than her favorite TV series.

"The doctor wouldn't release her," he replied, "and if it hadn't been for Audie, the nurse was going to sedate her. While the nurse was getting the syringe ready, the dog jumped on the hospital bed and situated himself between them. That helped calm Suki. It was really tense. Those feds are assholes."

"You think?" she replied. "This is a clusterfuck ready to go bat shit ballistic. And I seriously doubt any of those feds are to be trusted. I felt as if I'd been dropped in the middle of the Deep South during Jim Crow."

"I know what you mean," he replied. "I was on duty outside Suki's room with two others when the feds arrived. There were twelve of them and three of us. It was getting ugly until the rest of our team arrived."

That explained the sniper she'd spotted on the motel's roof. A Special Forces team comprised twelve men—two officers and ten sergeants. Even though The Oath Group was a private company, they organized it the same way.

"We better get upstairs," her escort said.

A burst of flashing red, white, and blue lights filled the lobby, and they both turned to look through the floor-to-ceiling windows facing the street.

Several black squad cars with Billings Police printed in large white letters on their sides had flooded the street in front of the hospital. There was also a white police SUV. Uniformed officers left the squad cars and gathered around the SUV until a tall man with glasses and gray hair stepped out. He was followed by a policeman in a uniform who looked like he might be the city's police chief. The uniformed officers escorted the suit and the chief to the standoff.

While the suit talked to the DHS agents, she watched Josh's men fall back until they were behind the local police. Looking deflated but still angry, the federal agents returned to their idling sedans and drove off. The suit then shook hands with the lawyer, who represented Josh's family. It was apparent they knew each other.

"A few hours ago, the Kavanagh's lawyer made a phone

call," her escort said. "We don't know the details, but we think the suit with Billings' police chief is Montana's attorney general."

"Did your lawyer call anyone?" she asked.

"Yea, but I can't talk about that, ma'am."

"Did you notice that tall, thin guy over there hidden in the shadows watching us? Is he one of ours?"

"We don't know who he is. He showed up soon after the feds took the general, and hasn't moved from that spot."

"His body language is giving me the creeps," she said.

Her escort's eyes widened. "Then we're going to keep a closer watch on him." He touched his earbud and started talking. Tate couldn't hear what he said. Once he finished, he led her to the room where the Kavanagh family was camped out.

The first person Tate saw was Josh's mother, just inside the entrance. This family had a Facebook page with photographs, so she knew what they looked like.

Judith's auburn hair was tied in a bun, and she was staring at the floor. Her husband was sitting across the room reading a Field and Stream magazine. Samuel was slouched in a chair across from his father with his eyes closed. The youngest brother, Mel, wasn't there. Audie wasn't either. What she knew of them was the image Josh had painted during their sessions together. This family was struggling.

"Mrs. Kavanagh," Tate said.

Josh's mother looked up, and their eyes met. A smile blossomed on Judith's face. Her eyes were a crisp brown with dramatic hints of jade green that Tate had never seen before. Judith stepped forward and folded the short, stocky therapist in her arms. "LG told us you were coming, and that Josh wanted you to help Suki." Her voice cracked with emotion. "I'm so thankful you're here, Dr. Tate. From what I've heard about you, I think you are God's answer to my prayers."

Judith stepped back but held on to one of Tate's hands. There was nothing but warmth in the older woman's face.

"We don't need her!" a resentful voice said.

Judith turned to her husband. "We've already had this conversation, Ash, and we will not have it again."

"We don't need someone from the VA meddling in our family's affairs!"

"You aren't paying for this!" Judith's warm voice had been replaced with rebar and concrete.

"Fine," he said and gave Tate a sharp look as he left the room.

I need a smoke, Tate thought. She hadn't had a cigarette since leaving California and was feeling edgy.

"Ignore him," Judith said. "He gets that way when he hasn't had enough sleep." There was no sign of the iron that had been in her voice a moment before. "I'll take you to Suki."

Tate glanced at Samuel. With his eyes closed, his features relaxed, his mouth hanging open, and the heavy, slow breathing, it looked like he was in a deep sleep. But she was wrong. She followed Judith toward a hallway on the lounge's far side and heard Samuel say, "Dad never gets enough sleep."

Startled, Tate looked back. Josh's brother hadn't moved or changed position. His eyes were still closed.

"Don't mind him," Judith said. "He's not like the rest of us. He can sleep anywhere and wake up in a flash. We all envy Sam for that."

"Where's your youngest son?" Tate asked. She knew that after they raped Suki, Mel had confronted Darwin Tweet. His mistake was going alone. With no witnesses and cameras, Tweet's bodyguards had beaten him savagely. He might never walk again.

"He's with Suki," Judith replied.

Tate had an epiphany. Judith and Ash were still together because of the children. Her religious beliefs played a part in that, too.

A moment later, they were in Suki's room. Mel was in his wheelchair next to the bed, and the service dog was between Suki and her brother. His muzzle rested on Suki's stomach, and the young woman held the dog with both arms. Mel was close to the bed and had an arm draped across the dog's back. It looked like Audie was their guardian angel.

The dog noticed the new arrival and Audie slipped out from under their arms in a smooth, flowing motion, then left the hospital bed and crossed the room to greet Tate. She knelt and rubbed the back of the dog's neck. "How are you doing, guy?"

The service dog stared into her eyes. After a moment of this, Tate heard the wall clock ticking. It was that quiet in the room. Then Audie shifted his gaze to Mel and Suki. After that telling moment, the dog returned to his spot on the bed between the two he was supporting.

Audie's pale-blue eyes expressed sadness and concern, which triggered a warning in Tate's mind. She'd never seen this service dog unhappy. He was always upbeat, supportive, and loving. Something was bothering him, and the dog didn't have words to express himself.

"Dr. Tate, I presume," Suki said, and the young woman held out a hand. The way her head dented the pillows made her look fragile. Then her face crumpled, and the look of deep sorrow and guilt triggered a lump in the therapist's throat. Tate took the girl's hand in both of hers and held it. She feared she didn't have the magic this girl needed. It was apparent that Suki was severely traumatized.

Judith had positioned herself at the foot of the bed.

Suki cried and talk at the same time. "Do something, Dr. Tate...Save him...No one will listen to me, Dr. Tate. They think I'm crazy, but I know. Right before they took him, I could see it in his eyes, Dr. Tate. He felt death was near, and he was ready to stop fighting. Audie knows. He'll tell you, Dr. Tate."

Josh's sister kept using Tate's name as if it were a benediction that turned wishes into miracles. Oh shit! She knew what Suki meant. That's what the dog had tried to tell her. Tate wanted to shout "Fuck!" but didn't.

She looked at the door and saw her escort in the hall. "Tell Captain Forest to get here ASAP," she told him.

"He's on his way, Dr. T. The chopper can't fly any faster."

"I have to talk to Josh." She knew Forest wasn't the one to handle this shitstorm. The captain was a good team leader, but Josh was ten times better. That's why LG had mentored him. If he'd stayed in the military for another decade, he would've retired as a general with at least two stars. Josh had already earned his silver oak leaf months before he retired. The Marines had offered him eagle's wings to stay, but he turned the promotion down.

"Captain Forest doesn't know where my son went, but I do," Judith said in a soothing voice. Every eye in the room turned to her, even Audie.

# CHAPTER 24

JOSH SAT at the small table, studying the chess pieces squatting on their black and white squares. He glanced at Rachel, napping on the narrow bed. With her eyes closed and features relaxed, she looked innocent and sexy, his favorite combination. He was tempted to join her, but after last night's marathon on that lumpy mattress, she needed the sleep.

He took a sip of bitter, lukewarm coffee before focusing on the solo game. The brew tasted foul, but he never wasted food or drink unless it was worse than rotten. While on deployments in third-world countries, he'd witnessed too much extreme poverty.

Just as he reached for a black castle to make another move against his white army, there was an unexpected knock on the cabin door.

Startled, Rachel jerked awake and said, "What?" Her dark hair was a tangled mess, her words slurred.

Josh placed a finger across his lips, signaling silence. She stared at him, blinking several times before nodding. Her eyes were bloodshot.

With pistols ready, they took up positions on both sides of the door. Once the Morse code tapping for BFF repeated the second time, Josh slipped his weapon into its shoulder holster and opened the door to reveal Cheéte's grim expression. "Your mother called," his friend said.

Josh stepped aside, and Cheéte brushed past him. Rachel moved behind Josh and slipped her arms around his waist, kissing the back of his neck. Cheéte gave her a greeting gesture before continuing: "LG was arrested by Homeland Security agents at the hospital in Billings. Forest said the GPS chip shows they took our friend to a remote area near Lake Koocanusa."

Josh cursed, then asked, "Why did they take him there?"

Rachel let go of Josh and turned to the only mirror in the cabin. She leaned close and squinted. It was ancient and only reflected fuzzy images. When she saw the mess her hair was in, she grabbed a brush and untangled the knots.

"It's a neo-Nazi militia training camp," Cheéte replied. "That's all I know, but your Captain Forest probably has more details."

"Why was LG at a hospital in Billings? He was supposed to be camping with my sister."

Cheéte told him what happened to Suki and the details about Tate's run-in with Homeland Security. He included the fact that she'd suspected a strange guy she'd spotted in the hospital's lobby. "This dude gave Tate a creepy vibe," Cheéte continued. "A couple of your troops were assigned to watch him, but he gave them the slip."

"It isn't easy giving our tier-one units the slip," Josh said. "That takes skill. Dr. T is an expert at reading body language. We suspected Charles Tweet might have sources in Homeland Security. Now that we know, we can't ignore this stranger. Is there anything else you can tell me about him?"

"Only that Tate said he was tall, maybe six foot six, and thin like a straw."

"Anything else?" Josh asked. "Any details help."

"Yea, she said his face was ash-colored, like it had been blanched in boiling water."

Josh stared at the ceiling for a moment. "That sounds like someone I've dealt with before. That means we may be dealing with the CIA's Special Activities Division. Even if it's a long shot, we can't afford to ignore it. Too risky. I have to do some serious thinking." Josh tuned them out and started pacing from one end of the cabin to the other while staring at the floor.

Rachel said to Cheéte, "I don't understand what's going on. I thought the CIA only worked in other countries."

"The president can directly task SAD to conduct covert military missions: raids, ambushes, sabotage, targeted killings, and unconventional warfare. It's also one of the most mysterious branches of operatives in the world. Most of them came from Delta Force and Navy SEAL Team Six. In fact, SAD invited Josh to join, but he turned them down."

She looked stunned. "That's scary considering who's in the White House."

"True, but nothing we can't handle," Cheéte replied.

Rachel brewed fresh black coffee, and soon after, she and Cheéte sat at the small table sipping from their steaming mugs and watched Josh chewing his lower lip as he continued to pace back and forth.

She leaned toward Cheéte and whispered, "How long can he keep this up?"

Cheéte shrugged. "That depends on how long he takes to make sense of what little intel he has and come up with a plan."

A moment later, Rachel spilled some of her coffee when, with a snap of his fingers, Josh shouted, "Got it!" He lowered his voice and continued, "Don't talk while I make this call."

The cabin was not connected to the grid, so Josh used his satellite phone. They couldn't hear what he was saying. A few minutes later, Operation Recover Paladin was born, and orders were flowing from US Special Operations Command.

When Josh hung up, his eyes glowed with an intensity Rachel hadn't seen before. "We're fortunate that SAD and SOCOM are still having disagreements. Before I explain what we're going to do, I have a few more calls to make." He started pushing buttons on the phone and turned his back on them.

"What's SOCOM?" Rachel asked, taking a sip of coffee.

Cheéte whispered an explanation: "It's the acronym for United States Special Operations Command. They're responsible for planning global operations against terrorist networks. For that reason, they sometimes run into the CIA doing secret shit, and they squabble over who has control. If friendly fire is involved, the temperature goes way up."

While they talked, Josh made phone calls to his Oath Group teams in Montana and Idaho. He gave orders for the base camp in the pocket valley on the Kavanagh ranch to be evacuated. "Leave no evidence that we were there," he said, "and hide the entrance to our cash cow."

Finished, Josh turned to Rachel and said, "I want you and our family to stay with my grandmothers, Clay and Cat. They have a three-story Victorian close to Golden Gate Park with a full-size basement garage where they keep their cars. There's a fortified safe room down there, too. Think of it as a vacation. Summers in San Francisco are mostly refreshing and cool."

"It won't be any fun if you aren't there," Rachel said. "I'm staying with you."

By then, they were facing each other. Josh put his hands on her shoulders studying her for a moment before saying, "It's going to be dangerous."

With a stubborn expression, she stiffened her back. "You think that scares me? I'm a better shot than you, and you know it. You need me."

"Really?" he replied. "Do you think you're immune to bullets and shrapnel? You saw my scars, and I like the way you are. Also, I won't be alone." He gestured at Cheéte. "With his men, I'll have seven teams—one of the best fighting forces in the world."

He could see he wasn't changing her mind. "I'll tell you what," he said, "we're going to have ourselves a shooting competition, and if you beat me, you can go with us. In fact, in this match, we'll use the same rifle we did when we were kids. We'll have to risk going back to the ranch, but we won't stay long, an hour or two at most. Once there, I'll shoot first, so you have the advantage and know the score you have to beat."

A lot had happened since Josh had left Montana when he was eighteen. They had trained him as a Marine Corps Scout Sniper. Four years later, he switched to the Navy and survived the training it took to become a Navy SEAL. Several years later, he returned to the Marines as an E-8 Master Sergeant before transferring to the Army as a second lieutenant in the Green Beret. Before that tour of duty ended, Delta Force recruited him. He joined them as an Army captain. After Delta, he returned to the Marines as a major. He finished his last few months as a lieutenant colonel and the XO to a Marine Raider Regiment. Now, after all of that, he was having another shooting competition with Rachel.

They returned to his family's ranch, and Rachel lost the shooting competition, but not by much. Pouting, she reluctantly agreed to go to San Francisco.

"Babe," Josh said as he kissed her, "I want you to keep my Glock with you at all times. Even in the house."

She stared at him as if he were crazy. "Why do you want me to carry a gun?"

Josh kissed her again. When their lips parted, he said, "I'm going to miss that." That brought a smile to her lips, but her eyes still expressed doubts.

"Don't worry," Josh said. "Grandma Cat will understand. She was victimized more than once when she was in her teens and twenties. She always carries a weapon of some sort, even if it's an illegal spring-loaded baton. If the Glock is in your bedroom on the second or third floor, and something happens when you're on the ground floor or in the basement, there won't be time to get it. If you go out, take it with you, but use the shoulder holster under a shirt or jacket. California has some of the most restrictive firearm laws in the country. I don't want you ending up in jail, but I also do not want you kidnapped, dead, or wounded."

"Dear God," she said, "you're scaring me. Are these SAD people that dangerous?"

He nodded. "If Strawman is in charge, it could be worse than dangerous. He's a deranged, sneaky bastard."

"Who's this Strawman?" she asked.

# CHAPTER 25

JOSH AND RACHEL went with Cheéte's twelve-man team of Crow warriors in three vehicles to Laurel Municipal Airport, outside of Billings. The Oath Group's Cessna Citation Bravo that had flown Tate from California to Montana was waiting.

Minutes after arriving, a Chinook landed with Forest and most of Josh's family.

"Where's my dad and Sam?" Josh asked Forest after his mother, Tate, Suki, and his youngest brother left the big bird. The last to disembark was LG's service dog, Audie.

"Your father refused to leave." Forest replied. "Then he blew a cork when we discovered someone had sabotaged his plane and couldn't fly back to the ranch without repairs. Sam returned to the ranch with him, and I assigned three of our people to tag along."

"SAD and the Strawman might be behind the sabotage to the plane," Josh said.

Forest's face turned grim. "Those assholes...again!"

"You have your orders, Captain," Josh said. "Return to the pocket valley and move our gear out of there."

Shaking his head, Forest returned to the bird.

Glancing around like he expected bullets to fly, Josh stood by the small passenger jet as his family boarded. He shook hands with Mel and leaned down so Suki could kiss him on the cheek. "Bring LG home," she said, her eyes glistening with tears.

"We'll do our best," he replied.

His mother gave him a hug and spoke in a whisper so only he could hear. "You're my oldest, and I made most of my biggest parenting mistakes with you. Please forgive me."

She didn't offer time for a reply, and he stared as she climbed into the jet. Wow, he thought. Not one passage from the Bible. That was a first. Was Grandma Clay right that his mother's born-again fever was cooling off?

Sniffling, Rachel slipped into his arms and clung to him for a long time before she reluctantly let go and, avoiding eye contact, disappeared into the jet. He was already missing her. Their honeymoon should've been longer, like a few years. The time they had spent in that cabin had been glorious. Even his adolescent fantasies didn't compare.

Tate was the last to embark. She planted her feet in front of him and said, "We have to talk."

"There isn't time for this, Doc," he replied. He knew what it was about.

"I'll keep it brief."

Shit! Josh glanced at the aircraft's open hatch. "Not here." He led her away from the two noisy aircraft to a spot where he could see Cheéte watching them from inside the Chinook. There was no way anyone could hear what they said to each other.

"Let me have it," he said, resigned.

"When are you planning to let Mia know you dumped her and married your childhood crush?"

A little more than half his age, born into poverty and raised in

Haiti, Mia was a singer-songwriter popular in the EU and Brazil with a small, loyal following in the United States. She spoke fluent English, French, Portuguese, Spanish, and Haitian Creole. There was also the dangerous work she did to combat sex trafficking. Her fans didn't know about that, but he did.

Tate had been instrumental in helping them survive as a couple. It hadn't been easy. The tone of his voice climbed when he responded to her. "Seriously, Doc, what I had with Rachel was more than a crush. I loved her for more than ten years before I left for MCRD. And, to set the record straight, I didn't dump Mia. She dumped me."

"Don't get testy with me," Tate said. "You've been with Mia for more than a decade, and what you have with her is not a traditional relationship. She called last week, and based on what she said, it didn't sound like it was over for her. She was worried because she hadn't heard from you in weeks."

"I still love her. Next time you two talk, find out why she turned me down when I asked her to get married."

"When did that happen?" Tate asked. "I thought we hashed this all out, and you knew better than to do that."

"We don't have time for this. Go home, Doc. It's risky for anyone close to me to stay in Montana. We did not know Charles Tweet had his tentacles into Homeland Security, and we still don't know how far his influence reaches. It also doesn't help that SAD might be involved."

"You will not distract me," Tate said. "You haven't told Rachel about Mia, have you?"

His expression answered for him.

"I thought so," she said. "When this operation ends and your adrenaline rush fades, I want you to think about what you've done. I respect Mia, and even if she said no to a wedding, that doesn't mean she stopped loving you. We both know what she thinks about marriage."

Josh broke eye contact and stared at his feet. "I thought I'd give it a chance anyway," he muttered. "I wanted more."

"I know what you're thinking. You can't keep them both. We'll talk about this again." Her voice softened. "Those Homeland Security agents worried me."

"We have an edge, Doc. With support from SOCOM, I'm getting some special toys from DARPA, and that's all I'm going to say. Go!"

With a nod, she sprinted for the passenger jet. Once Tate was aboard, the hatch closed, and the aircraft took off. Josh watched until it climbed out of sight and was safe from shoulder-fired, ground-to-air missiles. With the Strawman, Josh followed one rule: Never underestimate what that freak of nature was capable of. For that bastard, there were no rules. Although the CIA's focus was to gather intelligence in foreign countries, the agency also conducted covert operations in the United States to achieve its goals.

As soon as Josh was on the Chinook sitting next to Cheéte, his old friend leaned close and said in an undertone, "I read lips. What's going on with Mia? Tell me all the sordid details. Dr. Tate was wrong. There is no reason you can't have both."

Josh burst out laughing. When he calmed down, he said, "That never crossed my mind before Tate mentioned it. I admit it's an appealing idea, but I don't think Rachel would agree to sharing me with another woman. My French lover might though."

"Look, you don't have to tell Rachel about Mia. Hey, if it hadn't been for me, you'd never have met her. Once you're one of us, you can have more than one wife. In our culture, all people are equal. Before the White man, plural marriage was fairly common throughout Native America. But, since the invaders still control us through their laws and religions, you'll have to keep it a secret."

Josh had an idea, and his expression sobered. "Do you have more than one wife?"

Cheéte looked coy. "Maybe, but don't mention that to my Crow wife. She's a born-again Christian." He paused for a moment, then added, "But not the Trump type." With a sorrowful expression, he continued, "See what the White man has done to our culture?"

Josh held up an index finger, indicating a pause in the conversation. "We can continue this when we're airborne." He took out the satellite phone to call another friend who owned an elite private security agency in the San Francisco Bay Area. She was a former Secret Service agent who retired at fifty after serving twenty-eight years. He wanted her to provide armed security for his family in San Francisco.

His friend refused to charge him and said she'd assign her best people to the job. Josh knew what that meant. One day, she'd call him asking for help from The Oath Group and expect the same courtesy, and, of course, he'd agree without hesitation.

"Nancy, I have one more question," Josh said. "Correct me if I'm wrong, but don't you still have a close friend in the CIA?"

"I do," she said, her tone becoming guarded.

"If she's willing to find out, I'd like to know if Damien Bran is still with SAD."

"Why not ask someone in the CIA who belongs to the Paul Revere Network?" she asked. She knew their call was encrypted, or she wouldn't have mentioned the PRN. Nancy and Josh were members of a secret group supporting the Constitution with a website on the encrypted dark web that traditional search engines couldn't find.

"I'd rather go outside of our network first."

"I'll ask, but I can't guarantee an answer."

"I understand," Josh replied, and the call ended.

---

It surprised the Air Force colonel commanding Malmstrom Air Force Base in Montana when she received orders Sunday night from SOCOM.

The colonel immediately called the chief of staff of the US Air Force to verify what she'd been told. Her general said she didn't need to know what was going on. That once they concluded the operation, the material and equipment already on its way would be removed, leaving no evidence that anyone had ever been there.

She was informed that unauthorized disclosure of this operation would cause exceptionally grave damage to the national security of the United States.

Before dawn on Monday, a Navy Seabee company arrived at Malmstrom Air Force Base on a flight of Marine Corps King Stallion helicopters. The Seabees built military bases, airstrips, roads, bridges, and field hospitals.

Malmstrom had been in use since 1941 and covered an area of 5.2 square miles. It was one of three US Air Force bases that maintained and operated the Minuteman III intercontinental ballistic missile. Next to Great Falls, it was one hundred miles south of the Canadian border and close to the neo-Nazi training camp that was The Oath Group's target.

A flight of unmarked, flat-black Chinooks soon followed the Seabees that unloaded MIL Recoverable barrier units in a field near the southeast corner of the base inside its perimeter. Seven feet high, there were enough of them to form a perimeter surrounding twenty-three acres.

The flights continued throughout the day and into the night, delivering containerized housing units slightly larger than commercial shipping containers.

Within twenty-four hours, the work was completed, and a company of US Marines had set up a razor-wire no-man's-land around the MIL barriers. The only way into the compound was to get past the Marines, climb over the dirt-filled wall, or fly in by helicopter.

# CHAPTER 26

DRESSED in black and wearing a ski mask, Arnold was waiting until dark before moving out of the dry streambed north of Malmstrom Air Force Base. Concealed under natural and artificial camouflaged netting, he'd been watching for hours. He was near the base's northeast corner and debated infiltrating there instead of closer to the objective. The Strawman, Damien Bran, said not to do that because most of the base's personnel lived and worked near the north end. The risk of getting caught was higher if Arnold infiltrated there.

Glancing at the horizon, Arnold noticed the sun was almost down. That meant he had about an hour before it was dark enough to move out. He didn't know the reason for this insertion, but that wasn't a surprise. The Strawman worked that way. Bran compartmentalized everything and assigned bit parts to each member of his team. No one knew the whole script but him.

Arnold's task was to find out what was going on inside the acreage recently enclosed by a perimeter of MIL Recoverable barriers. He and Lena had already taken photos from the van as they drove slowly along Highway Road, less than a mile from the base's southeast corner. That'd been a waste of time.

Soon after dark, an irritating buzzing made the inside of his ears itch. It was unnerving. Seconds later, the sensation faded. That hadn't happened before. Maybe he was here to find out what caused that.

If he disobeyed the Strawman, he'd infiltrate the base near here and sneak from building to building instead of crawling through the dirt outside the wire. He hated bugs. He wasn't afraid of them, but some pests stung.

If he got caught, Bran wouldn't hesitate to have him silenced. The Strawman probably had someone inside with orders to eliminate him if that happened. Arnold had done it twice to compromised team members on missions. He didn't want to die, but understood the reasoning. The little he knew was still too much.

Just thinking about dying caused the back of his neck to tingle. The assassin's touch would be there, so he wouldn't see it coming. That was the way he'd done it. Wearing a thin, tight glove, he'd lightly caressed the back of the target's neck, administering a toxic lotion that the skin absorbed. In mere seconds, the convulsions started, and an instant later, death.

Arnold decided not to enter the base here.

If it came to that, he hoped the assassin wouldn't be his partner. Arnold didn't love Lena, but heck, they'd worked together for a couple of years, and her stocky body excited him. He liked his women wide across the hips and shoulders with big, soft hooters, more to hold. Skinny women with tiny titties did nothing for him.

Since it was too dangerous to have relationships with anyone on the outside, Bran encouraged his people to be sexually active with each other. That's why the Strawman paired his men with willing sausage wallets.

It occurred to Arnold that the only place he'd probably be safe as a prisoner was inside the compound he'd been sent to spy on.

It was going to take hours to reach that spot undetected, and even then, he might learn nothing. The Strawman hated failure and excuses. If Arnold couldn't learn what was going on from outside the fence, he'd infiltrate the target. To do that, he had to penetrate the base's perimeter, slip through the second barrier of coiled razor wire, and avoid the Marine sentries. Then he'd climb over one of the dirt-filled MIL containers, all while avoiding discovery.

If Arnold hadn't lost the coin toss, Lena would be here instead of him. He knew what she was doing. It was the same old routine. After dinner at some fast-food joint, she could have one beer in a sleazy bar. Then she'd be alone in their motel room by ten. It was what Bran expected everyone to do without exception. Another one of the Strawman's rules said don't talk to strangers because you might be under observation by another team. No matter what you said, your loose lips could get you ended.

It was time to leave the dry streambed that fed water into the Missouri River when it rained. After he folded his lightweight camouflage netting and stuffed it in a pouch, he started crawling on his side in the furrows between rows of waist-high plants. He stayed low and moved slow avoiding being spotted with night-vision gear or by motion detectors.

Every time Arnold stopped to listen, he checked the time. After an hour, he heard what sounded like a flock of mosquitos inside his ear canals. The sensation was more intense this time, but it didn't last long. When it ended, he was lightheaded, and out of nowhere, laughter bubbled up inside his chest, threatening to escape. What the fuck? he thought. Where did that come from?

Side crawling was tedious work, but he didn't want to leave a slug trail for one of the base's patrols to spot. During one of his stops, his mind drifted. He was a UFO buff and thought about the 1950 saucer incident caught on film near this base. The Air Force examined the film and claimed it was caused by the reflection of two F-94 jet fighters. Still, when the film was returned to the civilian who took it, several feet were missing.

That was one reason Arnold joined the Air Force after college and became an intelligence officer. In time, he learned the two F-94s weren't near the spot where the UFOs had been caught on film. A decade later, he switched to the CIA, hoping to learn more about aliens visiting Earth. That didn't pan out, and eventually, Bran recruited him as an operative in the private sector. Their only client was a billionaire, and the pay was incredible. He didn't know the money man's name and didn't care, as long as the tax-free cash kept coming.

He checked his wristwatch. Damn! It was almost midnight. He was doing too much daydreaming. That wasn't like him. Arnold checked his GPS navigation device to see where he was located. Shit! He still had too far to crawl. There'd be no more stops until he was in position.

If he got caught...well, fuck, he didn't want to think about that again. He'd never been caught before, and it was going to happen this time.

As he moved closer to the target, he knew from Google Maps that a narrow, rectangular peninsula of cropland crept closer to the base perimeter near the objective. Once there, he hoped he'd discover something useful without having to sneak on base.

At two in the morning, the buzzing returned, more intense. He stopped until the dizziness left, but he also felt sick to his stomach. Once he recovered, he moved out again.

Almost to his destination outside the wire, Arnold heard a soft whooshing sound, followed by an unexpected current of warm air that washed over him. He rolled to his back and studied the dark, starry sky. When a black oval shape blotted out the stars, his breath froze in his lungs. The thing was about thirty feet above him, and it looked like it was longer than sixty. There were no running lights, and it was moving toward the base. A similar form followed the first one, and there were others. They were moving too fast to spot any details. He'd witnessed nothing like it before.

His heart started thudding. What if they were real UFOs? What if that compound had been built to hide visitors from another planet? Maybe that explained the buzzing inside his head.

The film Iron Sky popped into his mind. He imagined the aliens in these UFOs were humans from a secret base on the moon's far side that Nazis builtin 1945. But this time, when they invaded with their armada of flying saucers, they'd win. The planet would be ruled by Caucasians again like it had for centuries, when European empires were colonizing the world and enslaving the inferior races. It was a farfetched idea, but if true, that explained why Bran and his boss, that unnamed billionaire, wanted to know what was going on in that compound. The Strawman didn't want to stop the aliens. He wanted to help them take over the planet.

Arnold jerked when something stung his neck through the knit mask. He slapped a hand on the spot and yanked a small dart out. The strength drained from his body in a handful of heartbeats, and the dart fell from numb fingers. Then his bladder and bowels released, flooding his crotch with warm, foul-smelling soup.

He sensed someone approaching but saw nothing until two fuzzy phantoms were hovering over him. Blinking, they vanished. He blinked again and saw asphalt-colored spacesuits with no visors.

*God, help me,* he thought. What if these suits held real extraterrestrials, and they weren't Nazis?

One shape leaned closer and touched the side of his head above his left ear. Were they telepaths like Spock in Star Trek? What if they ate human sushi just like those aliens from The Twilight Zone episode "To Serve Man"?

Arnold tried to scream but was struggling to breathe and couldn't.

# CHAPTER 27

CHARLES TWEET AGREED to pay Damien two million dollars to kidnap Susan (Suki) Kavanagh. Of course, Bran knew the billionaire wouldn't honor his end of the deal. After all, Tweet cheated everyone he did business with.

That's why Bran asked for twice what he thought the job was worth. Half the amount had to be deposited in one of his offshore accounts before he launched the mission. After the job, he'd ask for the last payment and look annoyed when the mogul refused to pay another cent.

Bran's attempt to abduct the Kavanagh girl in Billings had failed when he was spotted in the hospital. Now, he was in San Francisco in a parked van half a block from the Victorian house where the target was located. Being in this city irritated him. The only thing he liked about the place was the cool summer weather and the fog that made it easier to go unnoticed.

This was his first visit to San Francisco, a city with the highest percentage of people in the country who claimed to be rug munchers and ass bandits. They made up less than 7 percent of the population, but that was still too many for Bran. If he got his hands on a nuclear weapon, he'd destroy the place to get rid of them. Maybe Tweet would make a deal for that job, too. Bran already had a name for it: Babylon by the Bay.

When he was on a stakeout, Bran spent a lot of time reliving his glory days. At the moment, he was thinking about his first assignment in 1959. That was the year he'd met his mentor, teacher, and future father-in-law, Reinhard Gehlen, the CIA's European spy chief.

During World War II, Gehlen had been a lieutenant general in Hitler's army. Thanks to Operation Paperclip, he was one of over 1,600 Nazi war criminals recruited by the CIA, the FBI, and other US intelligence agencies after the war. Even though President Truman ordered the agencies not to hire former Nazis, they actively recruited them anyway.

It helped that Reinhard had been involved in a plot to assassinate Hitler. When it failed, he avoided Hitler's revenge on the officers and their families who had been behind the attempt.

Bran worked with his father-in-law until forced to retire in '68. Then Damien returned to the US with his German wife. She was a good girl and knew what he expected of her. Her father had raised her properly.

After a stint at Langley, Bran's next assignment had been Operation Condor in South America. He was proud of his targeted abductions, interrogations, and torturing leftist sympathizers from 1975 to 1989. Those were his glory days. Almost half a million people went to prison without trials, and sixty-to-eighty thousand had been killed. By the time Condor ended along with Argentina's military dictatorship, Bran was an expert at torture and making people vanish. His favorite method was throwing them out of an aircraft a few hundred feet above a lake or the ocean. When they hit the water, it was as if their bodies had slammed into concrete.

Bran had retired from the CIA at seventy-three in 2009, the

day before Barack Obama took the Constitutional Oath of Office. He refused to serve under an African-American president, but he didn't want to stop doing what he loved. So, he'd taken his skills to the private sector and found Charles Tweet.

Soon after the fog arrived between five and six every night, he parked the van down the street from the three-story house that belonged to Judith Kavanagh's female humanoid mothers. They were leftists, and he'd welcome the chance to make the two rug munchers collateral damage. To him, women who weren't grateful for a man's attention deserved to suffer. The vagina was an empty vessel with no identity until a man filled it with his essence.

While surveilling the house, his thoughts returned to Montana. Because of what had happened between Susan and Darwin, Charles Tweet's youngest son, the billionaire thought Josh Kavanagh was behind Darwin's disappearance from that bar in Great Falls. The billionaire wanted the Kavanagh girl as a bargaining chip to get his son back. Taking Susan was Tweet's way to teach the Kavanagh family a lesson. No one messed with Charles, and he always got revenge, even for imagined transgressions against him and his family.

Having corrupt Homeland agents grab the general had been another big win for the billionaire, but Graves hadn't talked yet. Bran was confident that Riley would break the man eventually because he'd been his teacher. Graves would say anything Tweet wanted to hear when Riley finished with him, even if it was all lies. Bran saw nothing wrong with deceiving a cheater.

Bran knew little about Josh's elite, secretive Oath Group, but he knew they worked for the CIA and DOD outside of the United States as military contractors. It made little sense that they'd be operating in the States, but Tweet was still suspicious.

When Bran's contacts in the agency had recently attempted to discover what the Oath Group was doing in Montana, they were quickly put on paid administrative leave. That was alarming, because both men had spotless records. But getting punished for just asking about something under need-to-know restrictions told Bran that Josh Kavanagh has some powerful allies.

This was the third night he'd been watching the house. During the day, Bran used local neo-Nazis to monitor the place. He had to establish the inhabitants' routines and find a weakness. There were five women, one young man in a wheelchair, a dog, and three cats in the house. They'd not be a threat to his team, but because of the Oath Group, Bran was taking precautions. That meant when his team grabbed the girl, he was going to stay in the van. He'd warned Tweet not to mess with Josh because of the Oath Group. Still, the billionaire never listened to advice from anyone. He preferred to rely on his gut instincts and said they never failed him. Tweet thought he was invincible. He'd been born into wealth, and with wealth came power and privilege, even for fools.

When Bran had strolled leisurely past the Victorian on his first night in San Francisco, he'd spotted surveillance cameras too high to reach. When his Russian hackers attempted to break into the security company's computers, they ran into a firewall they couldn't crack.

His team had scanned the house with through-the-wall sensors, so the only area they knew nothing about was the underground garage. The house had an elevator, a dumbwaiter, and two sets of stairs. The odd thing was a firefighter's pole close to the target's bedroom on the third floor. It led all the way to the basement. Then there was Graves's service dog.

Bran didn't mind eliminating people who got in the way. Cats were all cowards, so they'd hide once the operation was underway, but he loved dogs. He even told his wife she was fortunate that he thought she was equal to their German Shepherds. His wife and five dogs lived at their secluded house outside of Three

Lakes, Wisconsin. She loved working in the garden and going on hikes while waiting for him to come home so she could service him.

As time slipped by while he was watching the house, the idea of killing the dog continued to bother him until he decided his team would sedate the animal with an M99 dart. He'd also have them use the etorphine on anyone in the house who got in their way. It was a synthetic cousin to morphine and thousands of times more powerful. A smile split Bran's thin lips as he thought how the semi-synthetic opioid was crazy, lethal for humans. The dose was low for a dog, but one drop was more than enough to kill a human. Dart guns would also be quieter. He didn't want the neighbors to hear gunfire and call 911.

If everyone in the house died, it would end up as another home invasion gone wrong. But if they killed off most of Josh's family, there was no telling what the Tier One Operator would do to retaliate. Josh had the resources to do a lot of damage to Charles Tweet and also come after him. Bran knew he'd be on the run, looking over his shoulder for the rest of his life. The billionaire should've listened to him and left the Kavanagh family alone. Tweet's lawyers had won in court by making the girl look like a whore. That should have been enough.

Even though Bran knew little about The Oath Group's activities, he knew the basics of Josh's career in the military. He'd served in the Marines as a Scout Sniper. After his first tour, he'd become a Navy SEAL, followed by a transfer to the Green Beret a few years later, and then there was his time in Delta Force. Even though an individual could serve in multiple special mission units, it was improbable. Before Josh, the only other man who had accomplished a similar feat had been Kevin Holland, who barely survived a crippling wound that should've killed him. Holland was retired now.

Bran grudgingly admitted that Josh might be more dangerous

than him. He'd already decided that if Charles Tweet offered him a billion dollars to go after him, he'd say no. Money was useless if you were dead.

For the last decade or so, Josh had also been involved with DARPA. Bran didn't know what Kavanagh was doing with them. However, he had his suspicions and was aware of the agency's Warrior Web project focused on creating superhuman enhancements. With his military history, Kavanagh might be one of the first human terminators.

The glare of headlights in Bran's rearview mirror snapped his attention back to the present. He watched as the car cruised slowly down the fog-shrouded street, past his van, and pulled into the target's driveway. The driver was Dr. Tate, the coon-assed bitch working for the VA treating combat veterans for PTSD. She was the one who messed up his plans for snatching the Kavanagh girl from her hospital room in Montana.

A moment later, a black Ford van with large white letters on its side revealing it belonged to a plumber moved down the street and out of sight. It was one of the neo-Nazis Bran had hired to monitor the nigger.

The garage door rolled up, and Tate's car moved inside and down the ramp, out of sight. She'd also arrived last night at the same time. If her visits were routine, that might offer Bran easy access to the house without setting off the alarm. He'd have the neo-Nazis grab Tate and her car at a nearby stop sign while his people were waiting to rush in behind them and take the house. The garage door operated with a retina scan. That meant one of Tate's eyeballs would have to be plucked out before stuffing her body in the trunk.

# CHAPTER 28

THE FLIGHT of DARPA super-stealth helicopters, silent as gliders, had flown over Arnold at 0300. Their graphene-fiber airframes were six times lighter and 200 times tougher than steel. The birds looked like they were from another planet. Instead of a loud turbine engine, they had electric motors powered by graphene-foam batteries.

After landing near the northeast end of the airbase, they hooked the batteries up to recharge.

---

Once he came to, Arnold's first thought was of being shot with a tranquilizer dart. He heard a stifled groan, and the poor bastard sounded so miserable he felt sorry for him. It took a moment before he realized he was the stupid motherfucker making the noise. He tried opening his eyes but couldn't. After a failed attempt to move an arm or leg, he concluded they strapped him to a hard, smooth surface. Something was covering his head, and it was freezing cold.

DARPA's advanced fMRI helmet on Arnold's head could read his thoughts as they occurred. To work, his head had to be chilled and immobilized. Every thought appeared in print on a screen he'd never see.

"What are you doing to me?" he asked, but only heard a series of guttural sounds. There was something rigid and rubbery filling his mouth. Terrified, his heart thudded like it was going to burst out of his chest.

"Calm down," a dry voice said. "We don't want you to have a stroke."

There were other voices, and they didn't sound human. Arnold thought of the two aliens in the shadowy spacesuits. He didn't know he was listening to Crow Indians speaking their native language.

A moment later, wet drops flooded his eyes, and whatever had glued them shut dissolved. Then, as his vision cleared, the first thing he saw was a nightmare.

Cheéte's Crow combat team had painted their faces with traditional war paint. The nose and cheekbones, all the way to the thick, dark, braided hairline, looked burnt black. Below the nose and ears, the skin was covered with a dirty white color. A haunting purple haze surrounded the eyes. What looked like rivulets of blood ran from the hairline to the chin.

Thinking he was going to be the main course for extraterrestrials, Arnold fainted. When he awakened, the dry voice whispered in his right ear, "We will not eat you."

Another figure moved into view. This one was wearing the fuzzy spacesuit he'd seen outside the base perimeter.

"He sees you," the dry voice said.

"Then the suit needs another adjustment," a metallic voice replied.

The rubbery thing in Arnold's mouth was removed, and he said in a rush, "Let me go. I'll tell no one what I saw. I promise."

"I don't want to disappoint you, Mr. Schleicher," the alien's metallic voice said, "but we're going to ask you questions, and you will answer truthfully."

"I want a lawyer."

"We know how Damien Bran operates. That means there will be no lawyers."

The shock of hearing his boss's name caused Arnold to hyperventilate. Then, someone placed an empty bag over his mouth, and a moment later, his breathing was normal again.

He saw the spacesuit vanish as if someone had flipped a switch. "Can you see me now?" the metallic voice asked.

"No!" He thought for a few heartbeats. "Are you human?"

"We are asking the questions," Josh replied with the metallic-sounding voice. "Tell us why you were sent here to spy on us." He was wearing a prototype of a combat stealth suit being developed by DARPA that included a nanotechnology camouflage material, making its wearers invisible by bending light waves around them.

"I don't know what you mean. I only wanted to see an ICBM." Arnold had been through SERE Level C training. The last phase had taken place in a mock prisoner-of-war camp. He was proud of his ability to resist. He was confident these aliens would not get him to give up information easily. No matter what they asked, he'd stick to his script.

"He's lying," the dry voice said.

"Give him more truth juice," the metallic voice replied.

An instant later, Arnold heard his voice say, "Director Bran sent me to find out what was going on." What the hell? That wasn't what he was going to say.

"What is Damien doing in Montana?"

"I don't know."

"Why not?"

"He only tells us what we need to know, and nothing more."

Arnold was desperate to stop talking. He tried to bite off his tongue, but his body refused to cooperate. He didn't know there was a cocktail of drugs dripping into his veins. The truth juice wasn't the only one. Medications were controlling his impulses, too.

"Tell us why Bran had you spying on our compound inside Malmstrom Air Force Base," the metallic voice asked.

"Director Bran has a wealthy client in Montana who wanted to know what the sudden activity on the base was about."

The dry voice asked, "Why does this Bran guy have his flunkies call him 'director'?"

Before Arnold could answer, the metallic voice did it for him. "When Damien retired from the CIA, he was the Deputy Director of Operations for the Clandestine Service."

"That was a secret!" Arnold heard himself shouting. "How did you know that?"

Ignoring the question, the metallic voice asked, "Was this rich client Charles Tweet?"

"Director Bran never told us his name."

"What else do you know about this client?" the metallic voice asked.

"He pays the director a lot of money to do illegal stuff." Arnold didn't believe he'd said that.

"Have you heard of Josh Kavanagh?"

"No."

"Have you heard of The Oath Group?"

"No." Arnold thought of the thing strapped to the top of his head. Had they drilled holes through his skull and plugged his brain into a computer, turning him into a zombie?

"His answers match what we're getting from his partner," the dry voice said.

They'd divided the portable housing unit into two soundproofed, shielded rooms. Lena was being questioned in the other half.

With a jolt, Arnold thought, They have my partner! "Whatever she told you is a lie!" he tried to shout, but failed. "We are just tourists. Lena is my dumb girlfriend!" He started coughing as if something had trapped the words in his throat, and he couldn't spit them out.

"Stop with the deception," the dry voice said, and Arnold's eyes bulged when he couldn't get another lie out.

"Make sure he doesn't blow a gasket," the metallic voice said. In seconds, Arnold's panic vanished as the drip for the anti-anxiety drug increased.

"You know that the more truth juice we feed him, the longer his recovery will take," the dry voice said. "Tomorrow, he'll be one sick mutt, and his brain might be permanently impaired."

"Considering who he works for, he earned it," the metallic voice replied.

---

Josh stepped away from the prisoner and turned off the power-hungry invisibility function of his suit. "Take over the interrogation," he said to Cheéte. "Finish the list of questions and ask anything else you can think of."

"Anything?" Cheéte asked in a surprised tone.

"Yea, have some fun. Find out about his sex life and any other dirty secrets stuffed in that head. When you're done, push that button to flush the drugs out of his system. Then he'll get the concoction that will erase his memories from the last twenty-four hours."

"This gadget is PFA," Cheéte said. "How accurate is it?"

"It can give us false positives when the detainee thinks his lies are the truth. Oliver Sacks proved we can revise and even fabricate memories and think they're real. Our friends at Area 51 will be interested in the results since this is the first time their mind-reading device has been used outside the lab."

A woman in an unmarked camouflage field uniform entered the room and said something to Josh.

Josh turned to the others. "I have to step outside and take a call."

Once outside, Josh focused on one of several icons that appeared to be floating in front of his eyes. That symbol linked him to the Oath Group's communication hub in another trailer. "Put the call through," he said.

He was wearing a billion-dollar, body-molding, tailor-made DARPA Warrior Invisibility Suit (DWIS). It could stop a 50-caliber round and spreading out most of the force so he wouldn't be stunned or disabled from the impact. The scientists developing the suit were still trying to figure out how to protect the invisibility layer from damage. Josh told them not to worry. "If they don't know I'm there," he'd said, "they will not be shooting at me."

There was also the carbon nanotube exoskeleton that clung tightly to his body. It protected him from fractures and doubled his specific strength and speed. He could run a mile in five minutes with no effort, but that function devoured energy like a starving wolf.

They powered the suit with flexible batteries that were super thin and conformed to his body's contours and movement. The small, ultra-high-definition cameras embedded in his helmet's outer layer offered a 360-degree visibility field, literally giving him eyes in the back of his head.

There was only one other operational suit like this one. His teammate, one of the younger Oath Group members, was wearing it. They served together with the Army's 1st Special Forces Operational Detachment-Delta, one of the US military's two most elite combat units. SEAL Team Six was the other one.

The icon blinked, telling Josh they had patched the caller through. "Oath One here," he said.

"This is Shadow One," Linda replied from San Francisco. "My contact said Bran retired the day President Obama was sworn in for his first term. When he left, he took some of his people with him. No one knows where they went and what they're up to."

"I can fill in some blanks," Josh replied. "Bran and his people are working for Charles Tweet, who's up to no good. The billionaire is also funding a neo-Nazi militia group in Montana."

"I'll pass that on," she said, and the call ended.

Josh glanced at his power display and noticed the suit's batteries were at 60 percent. Fully charged, they'd last several hours, depending on what he asked the suit to do. When the birds delivered The Oath Group's combat teams to the neo-Nazi's training ranch in northwest Montana, he'd be charging until he dropped into the site. In eighteen hours, at midnight, Operation Paladin would hit the target with eighty-four troops.

The neo-Nazi ranch covered several hundred acres in rugged, forested terrain. The population fluctuated, but the average was seventy, counting women and children. Most of the structures were underground and linked by tunnels. There was a separate, fenced-in compound inside the northern perimeter with a forty-foot-by-sixty-foot concrete building with two levels, one above ground and the other below. The structure was shielded and guarded 24/7. During the flyover, the surveillance drones couldn't discover what was inside. However, they revealed that a narrow trail left the compound and snaked north through the rough terrain. Josh thought they were smuggling something into the States from Canada or the other way around.

Why would a hedge fund billionaire want to do something risky like that?

# CHAPTER 29

DR. JANET TATE'S evening drive into San Francisco was getting old. She worked ten-hour days, five, and sometimes six days a week at the Vet Center. So, it was time to schedule Suki for one appointment a week instead of every night. But today, she was giving her favorite vet a drive home and didn't mind.

His name was Isaac, and he was eighty-six. Soon after joining the Army in 1952, during the Korean Conflict, he served in one of the first Special Forces units, the Eighth Army Rangers. During the Vietnam War, he was with Tiger Force, a long-range reconnaissance patrol unit. After thirty years in the Army, he retired as a sergeant major in 1982.

When he first came to Tate struggling with PTSD, he'd been homeless after his fourth marriage failed. He was a master in Taekwondo and still taught several classes a week at a San Francisco studio. The dojo's owner allowed him to sleep there.

Tate helped him get a place of his own through a collaborative program between HUD and the VA, close to the Victorian where Josh's family lived.

Most of the vets Tate treated always carried a weapon—usually a knife and sometimes pepper spray. She suspected Isaac had a firearm. He always wore loose pants. Although he'd never ridden a horse in his life, he walked bowlegged like a cowboy. She'd checked his medical records, and there was no reason for him to be walking around like that unless he was trying to hide something, like an ankle holster. After all, this was San Francisco, where it was almost impossible to get a carry permit.

During the drive from the East Bay, Isaac had reclined the passenger seat and closed his eyes. This was how he relaxed. Tate knew he never slept unless he was inside his tiny apartment with all of his weapons.

"I appreciate you driving me home," he said. "Can't relax on BART. Never know when a thug will think I'm an easy mark because I'm old."

"Oh, hush. You don't look a day over sixty," Tate replied and meant it. "I'd feel sorry for the thief." Isaac had a thick, tangled crop of unruly salt-and-pepper hair. The curly chaos often tempted her to use a brush to bring some order to it.

Isaac chuckled. "I'm thinking of asking a student of mine who just turned seventy to be my next wife. At my age, I'll be dead before she gets around to divorcing me."

Tate noticed he was watching her. "However," he continued, "If you agreed to be number five, I'd have to give it more thought."

She burst out laughing. When she recovered, she said, "Not a chance. I've already had my share of failed marriages. What I don't understand is why you want to do it again."

His reply was a lascivious grin, and he winked. Then his expression turned serious. "We're being followed." Ignoring what she thought was paranoia caused by his PTSD, she slowed the car as they neared his building. He saw threats everywhere.

"Don't stop," he said. "If you make it to the big house without a problem, I'll walk back. My legs want the exercise." He adjusted his seat to the upright position while keeping his eyes glued on the passenger-side mirror. "They're close enough to give your bumper a hickey," he said. "My gut says trouble's riding our asses."

Tate felt her stomach tighten. She spent a lot of time with combat vets who lived with PTSD. Over time, she'd learned that most of them sensed trouble before it happened. A stop sign loomed ahead, and she put her foot gently on the brake pedal.

"It looks like we'll get to boogie after all," Isaac said in a tone that caused the fine hairs on her neck to prickle. Glancing in her mirrors, she saw the four doors on the white, late model Chevrolet Blazer behind her car fly open. Several shadowy figures tumbled out. She was about to race through the empty intersection when a rusty Dodge Ram 250 with oversized tires cut her off, boxing them in.

"Here, Doc, take this. You're going to need it," Isaac said, sounding almost cheerful.

When she saw the .38 six-shot Classic Smith and Wesson revolver in his left hand, her heart fluttered and her mouth dried out. In his other hand, he held an M1911 .45 Colt automatic. She hadn't expected him to have two firearms.

When she hesitated, he said, "Look, Doc, we got to take the fight to them because we're outgunned. You take the crew from the Dodge. I'll take care of the Blazer." He put the .38 on the center console between them. Then he swung his door open, swiveled out of the car in a fluid motion, and without waiting, started firing at the figures behind them. An instant later, they returned fire, and her car's back window shattered.

Tate ducked and banged her forehead on the steering wheel. Then, ignoring the pain, she grabbed the pistol, pushed her door open, and fell out of the car, scraping her knees. Looking under the door, she saw a man headed her way from the Dodge. He was carrying a shotgun.

"Fire, Doc!" Isaac shouted from the other side of the car. "You won't get a second chance."

She heard a blood-curdling scream burst from her throat as she squeezed the trigger. She knew she'd hit the man when he dropped his weapon, staggered back, and grabbed his stomach.

With five shots left, she crouched, looked over the hood, and saw two figures moving fast toward Isaac. "Behind you!"

She flinched at the sound of three quick shots and worried Isaac had been shot until he replied, "Thanks, Doc."

With police sirens wailing in the distance and growing louder, she jerked to the side when the glass in her door shattered. Then another man rushed from the Dodge. She aimed and fired.

---

Damien Bran heard the firefight erupt in the general direction of where the neo-Nazis he'd recruited were supposed to grab Tate. It was apparent the amateurs had fucked up, but that wasn't a problem. The distraction would keep the police busy and give him more time to get the job done here.

"We go to Plan B," he said to his team. They were in a Ford Transit Cargo Van parked down the street from the house. Damien would watch from the driver's seat when his team blew their way into the garage.

They'd use a ropy cord of C-4 plastic explosives on one panel of the roll-up metal door and blow out a section close to the ground to slip through. If anyone was in the garage, the explosion would stun them.

When he saw his team run in opposite directions away from the roll-up garage door, he closed his eyes and waited for the explosion. He didn't want to lose his night vision from the flash.

---

Rachel and Judith Kavanagh were in the garage waiting by the door that led up to the kitchen on the ground floor. Doctor Tate always arrived around this time, and they liked to greet her. They'd been waiting for the sound of the roll-up metal door to signal her entrance.

When the C-4 detonated, Rachel felt a dull thump in the center of her chest. A wave of pressure shoved her back against the wall. With her ears ringing, she shook her head against the effects of the blast-induced concussion.

Then she remembered the Glock. Josh had insisted she always have the weapon with her, even in the house. She felt stupid, but did it anyway. It hid in a shoulder holster under her long-sleeved, loose blouse.

"Judith, lock the door behind you!" As she was fumbling under her shirt for the Glock, she heard the security guard from the agency Josh had hired open fire from his bullet-resistant booth.

There was always one guard stationed inside the garage, and this one spent most of his time in the small booth installed before they'd arrived in San Francisco. There were no guards upstairs.

The booth was in the far corner of the garage, facing the ramp that led to the roll-up door. There was room for two chairs and a small desk that held the monitors linked to the battery-powered, wireless security cameras around the house's perimeter. There was also a panic button, and it had been activated.

As Rachel freed the Glock, she heard the loud staccato sound of a machine gun return fire. She saw the layered ballistic glass protecting the security guard fracture but not shatter.

Chambering a round, she fired at the first intruder to reach the bottom of the ramp. When she saw the man stumble and stagger away from her, she shifted her aim to another moving target and scored a torso hit. Then she saw the first man climbing to his feet. Damn! she thought. He must be wearing a bullet-proof vest. I need one of those.

She shifted her aim to his head and fired twice. The intruder fell backward, spraying the wall behind him with blood and brains. One of the others opened fire on her. The impacts drove Rachel against the wall. As she slid down, she emptied her clip at the other black-clad figures before her head snapped back when another round creased her skull above her left ear.

Judith escaped and lock the heavy, solid-core, metal-clad door behind her. The rest of the family was already sliding down the fire pole to reach the vault-like armored panic room.

# CHAPTER 30

SHADOW SECURITY'S CEO, Linda Griffen, sat in a hospital waiting room staring at her cell phone. With her stomach in turmoil, she avoided making eye contact with Josh's family. Instead, she glanced gratefully toward Dr. Tate sitting beside Suki, holding her hand and comforting her.

With that thought, Griffen tapped in the number for Josh's encrypted phone, half-hoping he wouldn't answer. Still, once she thumbed in the last number, she put the phone to her ear and waited.

The call was intercepted, transferred with a click, and an unfamiliar, blunt voice answered, "Leave a message. I'll deliver it once he's available."

"I need to talk to him now," she replied, but the call ended before she finished, and there was no offer to leave a recorded message. That twisted her stomach into knots.

With a surge of adrenaline-fused frustration, she wanted to throw her phone on the floor and stomp on it. But, before calling again, she had to calm down and took several slow breaths until she reached ten.

Once she'd regained control, she made the second call to the same number. When no one answered, she leaned back and closed her eyes to think. She held her phone too tight and had to force her sweaty hand to relax before a muscle cramped.

There had to be a reason someone else had answered. No one used that phone but Josh. The Oath Group must be operational, she thought, but what would an elite private military contractor like them do in Montana?

Before calling the second number on the emergency list, Rachel's daughter, she rummaged in her bag for a warm 12-ounce bottle of Goldthread Japanese Matcha to help her relax. After drinking half the bottle, she decided she couldn't put it off any longer.

She hated making calls like this. Josh's Rachel had been in the operating room for hours now. Too bad Griffen couldn't forget that she'd been interested in Josh once, about a decade ago, the one guy she wanted to keep that got away. They'd dated a few times and were intimate, but then he vanished on another one of his classified missions. She couldn't even remember the last time she'd seen him.

"Do you want me to make that call?" Judith Kavanagh asked, sitting beside her. "It would be better if it came from me. She is my granddaughter."

With a flood of relief, Griffen made eye contact and nodded, handing her the phone. "Josh asked me to protect his family, and I failed," she said and hated that her voice sounded pitiful.

"Hush," Judith replied. "We can't control what life throws at us. Josh would understand."

---

In Montana, the DARPA super-stealth helicopters had left Malmstrom Air Force Base and were flying toward a small ranch in an isolated area between Glacier National Park and the Kootenai National Forest.

They had launched once Operation Recover Paladin, and a communication ban with anyone outside the Oath Group had been implemented. Griffen had made her first call seconds after the lockdown.

One exception was Brianna Hemmings, an FBI Special Agent in charge of an elite field unit from the Criminal Investigative Division (CID). They were in a two-story cabin on a guest ranch several miles from the militia's location.

Her team focused on narcotics, human trafficking, and violent crimes. If Josh found any evidence of those crimes, he'd call. After all, it would look suspicious if anyone discovered The Oath Group's involvement. That would turn this raid into a legal nightmare.

Brianna and Josh belonged to the secretive Paul Revere Network. And, of course, her agents didn't know that. That's why she'd left the cabin alone to take a walk along a narrow trail, to listen to the radio chatter between The Oath Group's combat teams.

Radical right-wing militias were often better armed than the police and the FBI. So, the DOD had come up with an alternative, sending Josh and his teams to Montana. Fortunately, the racist pukes on that ranch didn't stand a chance against The Oath Groups better trained and armed Tier 1 operators.

Her nerves were already on edge when she heard a twig snap off to her right among the trees. Without a thought, Brianna's hand went to the butt of her 9mm Glock. Then she left the trail in two swift, silent steps, putting her back against a tree, waiting, hoping for the best.

---

Several miles from the guest ranch where Brianna Hemings was located with her agents, Josh heard static and a hiss in his earpiece. Then the pilot announced, "We are over the drop zone. Stealth has a green light."

Josh and his partner Miller moved to the open door. They were going to fall thirty feet without a rope. With the DARPA Warrior Stealth Suits, it was possible to do that without suffering an injury.

During several reconnaissance missions, Miller had been inside the militia's security fence to map the area. Using drones, they had also scanned the ranch with ground-penetrating radar. That gave them a detailed map that included the tunnels linking most underground dwellings together, like a subterranean spider web.

Together, Josh and Miller stepped out of the hovering bird and dropped like stones. Josh bent his knees slightly and landed feet first. The suit absorbed most of the blow. However, the landing was severe enough that Josh's legs, protected by the suit's exoskeleton, acted like springs, and he bounced like a basketball. When he made the second touchdown, he rolled to the left, and finished on his side. Miller had moved in the opposite direction to avoid a collision.

Brianna and every member of the Oath Group's combat teams heard Josh say, "One has landed."

"Ditto for two," Miller's voice echoed.

Miller's first task was to drop canisters of sleeping gas into all the underground living quarters where the families stayed, then padlock the ground-level entrances. They didn't want any women or children ending up as collateral damage.

Josh's destination was the underground bunker where LG was being held. He wouldn't use the main entrance, which was guarded by two armed men. A twenty-five-foot tunnel linked the torture chamber with Riley Pearl's living quarters, where Josh planned to gain access.

Once Miller finished his first objective, he'd sabotage the industrial-sized hydrogen fuel cells that generated electricity for the ranch.

"First goal completed," Miller reported.

Hearing voices, Josh stopped. He was near the main entrance that led to the underground chamber where LG's implant said he was located.

"Did you hear his screams?" a voice asked.

Josh crept closer until he saw the armed guards. One of them cupped his hands around a lit match and touched an unfiltered cigarette to it. Then, taking a deep drag, he shot a stream of smoke skyward. He continued, "I mean, I'm not a pussy, but what Generalmajor Pearl is doing to that old man is extreme, even for me."

Josh didn't like what he was hearing, and he left the trees and moved closer to the armed neo-Nazis. Since he was invisible, he wasn't worried they'd spot him, but he still stopped several feet away.

The other man said, "Torture's the best way to get people to spill secrets. What freaks me out is the generalmajor never comes out in the daylight."

Josh struggled against an urge to slit their throats, but that wasn't the plan.

The first man took another drag from his cigarette, then said, "So, you think our leader is a vampire?"

"I didn't say that." The second man sounded defensive. "He has a sun allergy. That's why he's so pale."

Josh had seen Riley briefly over a decade ago during the man's general court-martial. He hadn't been sensitive to sunlight then. In fact, he'd been heavily tanned. Maybe being exposed to all that sunlight finally caught up with him. Miller's voice came over the communication bud in his ear: "Second goal will be disabled in five minutes. Moving to third."

Josh was running late. He activated a countdown clock inside his helmet and hurried to the escape hatch leading to Riley's quarters. The concealed opening made it a safe bet few knew about it. If Pearl was a general in the billionaire's militant neo-Nazi organization, he wondered if other groups like this one were in other states. Neo-Nazis were also joining the US Army for combat training.

The entrance to the shaft was in thick brush. To reach it, Josh had to crawl on hands and knees along a narrow track that was more like a tunnel than a path. One display inside his helmet guided him to the spot where he cleared away the dead leaves and brush to reveal the round, domed hatch with an embedded handle.

He wasn't concerned the hatch was locked or linked to an alarm because Miller had checked the last time he'd been inside the camp. He'd also opened the hatch enough to send a drone the size of a horsefly down the shaft to take video footage of the landing space at the bottom.

When Josh pulled on the handle, the hatch swung silently up and out of the way. He leaned forward and stared into the darkness of the concrete shaft. A ladder of metal rungs was embedded along one side. Before going any farther, he used the suit's technology to scan the shaft, ensuring there was no sign of life or any other surprises down there. Satisfied, he levered himself into a sitting position on the lip of the opening.

Before jumping, he thought about Rachel and Mia, the only two women he'd ever loved. Then he thought about what must be waiting for him in Riley's torture chamber, and his face hardened. An instant later, he dropped toward the concrete floor fifteen feet below.

# CHAPTER 31

SOMETHING ISN'T RIGHT, Cheéte thought.

His team hid among the trees in sight of the target's north gate. Centered inside that one-acre fenced compound was the large, windowless, concrete structure his Crow warriors had been tasked to take by force.

Josh wanted to know what was inside that building.

A well-traveled trail left the trees and crossed fifty yards of open space to a small gate. Surveillance had reported the regular inhabitants seldom left the ranch. When they did, they used the south entrance, which was large enough for eighteen-wheelers. The only people who used this gate had to be hikers.

The footpath looked used. It also linked up with a vast trail network in nearby Kootenai National Forest and Glacier National Park. The closest trail led to ninety-mile-long Lake Koocanusa that straddled Canada's British Columbia and Montana.

All a smuggler had to do was say he only wanted to fish, pay a fifty-dollar application fee, and be interviewed to get approval from both countries. Once he had the joint US-Canadian

NEXUS card, it was easy to cross the border by boat without being stopped and inspected.

Cheéte's earbud activated, and he heard "Greenlight," repeated three times. That meant Josh was underground, and Miller had sabotaged the power supply.

There were twelve men in his Crow combat team. Dressed in black from head to toe, their fierce-painted faces were not covered with balaclava masks like the other Oath Group teams.

Once the hydrogen fuel cells failed, the electrified fence lost power. The bright LED spotlights on the top of the tall aluminum poles went dark.

Everyone in Cheéte's team wore night-vision goggles. Pumping his right fist over his head, he signaled the advance, and they started across the open space. There was one sentry on this side of the building, and he turned on a Maglite to scan the perimeter with a bright beam. The man grunted and collapsed an instant later when one of Cheéte's men shot him with a tranquilizer dart. His flashlight hit the ground with a thud and rolled around, spilling its light aimlessly at the surrounding fence and the no-man's-land beyond. The other three neo-Nazi sentries guarded a helicopter sitting in a small parking lot at the other end of the building. Because of the distance, they couldn't hear what was happening here.

The combat rules for this mission were to use drugged darts, pepper spray, or stun guns to pacify the enemy. If that failed, shoot them. For that, his team carried MP5A3 9-mm submachine guns and Beretta M9s as secondary firearms. One of his men had a 40-mm, M32 multiple grenade launcher.

The fastest runners reached the fence first and cut through the wire. A moment later, the rest of the team slipped through and hurried toward the building. Half of Cheéte's men split and took positions at the two northern corners of the sturdy concrete structure. The other five joined Cheéte at the door, and the lock-pick went to work. Lock bumping was relatively quick and quiet. If anyone was on the other side of the door, they'd have to have their ear against it in utter silence to hear anything.

Once the door swung open, Cheéte followed the lock-pick inside. He went left, and lock-pick went right as they cleared a space the size of a six-by-eight prison cell. Across from them was a doorless opening to a flight of stairs that descended into darkness. Cheéte flashed a hand sign, and the next two men entered the building, then glided down the stairs, out of sight. When he heard two clicks through his earbud, he signaled the next pair to go.

Before he and lock-pick followed the first four men, they heard the rattle of distant gunfire somewhere on the ranch, followed by the muted blast of a 40-mm grenade. But as they went down the concrete stairs, the sounds of combat vanished.

Dim battery-powered emergency lights fastened to the ceiling every few yards flickered, casting an eerie glow over the cold, clammy concrete.

Before reaching the bottom, Cheéte heard the soft pops of tranquilizer guns. When he arrived, he found his four warriors gathered around two unconscious men in the hallway. Both wore matching dark suits, white shirts, and red ties.

Six doors were spaced evenly along both sides of the hall. At the far end, Cheéte saw a seventh. He pointed at two of his men and, with hand signals, directed them to discover what was on the other side of that one.

He watched as they soundlessly sprinted the distance and slipped through the unlocked door. When he heard nothing, he knew they hadn't run into resistance.

Pointing at his eyes, Cheéte glanced at the other doors, telling the second pair to watch them. The two unconscious men had been disarmed and hog-tied. They'd been guarding a locked door.

Why guard anything inside a secure building protected by armed sentries and an electrified fence? Maybe that white Airbus helicopter parked in front of the building belonged to someone important inside that room.

Cheéte signaled his lock-pick to pop the bolt. It didn't take long before the door swung open, spilling Richard Wagner's "The Ride of the Valkyries" into the hall, revealing a seriously soundproofed room.

The loud classical music made his ears and teeth ache. "What the fuck!" Cheéte muttered as he glanced into the dim room and saw a round, rotating, king-size bed centered under a mirrored ceiling. On the bed was a large, naked, heavyset man with his back facing up.

As he watched, the bed continued to turn until the figure's profile was parallel to him. To see better, Cheéte knelt, and what he discovered chilled him to his core. He saw a little girl pinned face down on the mattress under the big man's flabby gut. Her body wasn't moving as if she were dead.

Without hesitation, Cheéte grabbed the fat man's ankles with both hands. Then he viciously yanked his heavy, corpulent body off the bed, tossing him to the floor like a rag doll. His lock-pick turned off the music, filling the room with blessed silence.

"Watch him," Cheéte said, and the lock-pick nodded. Then, with emotionless eyes, he placed a boot on the back of the naked man's thick neck and forced his face into the scarlet-colored shag carpet.

The man freed his mouth from the thick carpeting. "How dare you! I'll see you flayed..." His deep baritone voice sputtered when he saw the Crow warrior's fierce, hideous painted face glaring at him.

Cheéte reached for the girl and removed a plastic bag covering her head. The silk sheet under her was stained with blood. He rolled the small body over. Looking like cracked glass, the child's lifeless, bloodshot, vacant eyes stared through him. She wasn't breathing. Before starting CPR, he used his earbud com-unit to signal his team's medic to return from the other side of door seven.

Seconds later, the medic hurried into the room and lifted the girl's limp left hand to check for a pulse. "She's alive," he said.

That's when she gasped and breathed again. Cheéte stopped mouth-to-mouth and chest compressions and moved out of the way, giving the medic room to work. He watched terror fill the girl's eyes when she saw their painted faces, causing Cheéte's anger to soar.

The white girl had long, cinnamon-colored hair and vivid green eyes. Cheéte had a twelve-year-old daughter about the same size. Then, turning, he kicked the big man in the gut and growled, "What the fuck, you sick bastard!"

When the prisoner didn't reply, the medic said, "It's called erotic asphyxiation. He chokes out the girl and gets an extreme sense of power while the victim is dying and struggling to survive. He probably can't get an erection any other way."

"Is she okay?" Cheéte asked, struggling with rage.

"I don't know yet," the medic replied. "If you hadn't reached her when you did, she'd probably be dead by now."

Cheéte kicked the fat man again in the same spot. Squealing, he curled into a fetal position and turned his face to the carpet, hiding his features.

Kneeling, Cheéte jabbed the back of the man's neck with the tip of an index finger. "I want to put a bullet right there," he said.

"I will pay you a lot of money to let me go!" the man begged.

With an expression that twisted his painted face into a more grotesque mask, Cheéte returned to the bed and watched the medic wrap the top sheet around the naked girl. Then he offered her a bottle of water. After a few swallows, she said,

"Spasybi." Her voice sounded raw, and she hung her head between her shoulders and started sobbing.

Cheéte recognized the language as Ukrainian. She'd said, "Thank you."

Apparently, the girl had been sex trafficked from Europe through Canada and smuggled into the United States by boat on Lake Koocanusa. Josh hadn't expected that. Weapons and drugs, yes, but not children. "What did you find on the other side of that door?" he asked the medic.

"A couple of dozen young girls like her and a few boys, all naked and locked in dog cages. There were bales of bhang, bags of cocaine, and firearms too."

Cheéte's eyes had turned dry and hot. He rubbed them with both fists to generate moisture. He knew that between fifteen-and-twenty-thousand slaves were trafficked illegally into the United States annually. Eighty percent ended up in the sex industry, where most died young of disease or when they were no longer worth feeding. In other countries like Russia and India, it was a lot worse.

"Hey, Chief," the medic said. "Calm down. I don't want you to have a stroke."

"If you think I'm angry, wait until Josh discovers what we found."

The medic nodded. "Right, I wouldn't want to be that slob when the colonel gets here. He'll probably cut the pervert's balls off, slice and dice them, and make him eat them raw."

"And that will just be, for starters," Cheéte said. "It won't surprise me if Josh slow roasts this creep over hot coals. He hates traffickers as much as I do. But for Josh, it's personal."

"What did they do to piss him off that bad?" the medic asked.

"It happened in Haiti back in the '90s," Cheéte replied. "It's a long story for another time."

Baldy started blubbering, his soft body shaking like a blob of blanched jelly.

Cheéte nudged him with a boot. The man twitched and squealed in fear.

"Sounds like you know who I'm talking about. That reminds me, I better call him so you two can meet. I want a ringside seat when that happens, but with a sheet of clear plastic between us so I don't get splattered with your blood if my friend skins you alive."

## CHAPTER 32

JOSH LANDED at the bottom of the shaft with a dull thud. The layer of dust that covered the floor billowed into the air, and he waited for it to settle before studying the back of the bookshelf unit.

They had hung the cabinet in the opening on pins that allowed it to swing into the shaft after a hidden spring-loaded button lock disengaged from the other side. As a result, he couldn't open it from the inside.

The gap between the shelf unit and the jamb measured a bit more than an eighth of an inch, enough room for the saw blade on his Swiss Army knife. The cheap plastic locking pin didn't take long to cut.

A moment later, he pushed the bookshelf out of the way, revealing the dark room beyond. His suit automatically compensated, and the night vision worked at the proper level, a great feature. For example, if a flashbang went off, the suit's cameras and audio compensated so he'd never see the flash or hear the bang. The suit also came with thermal imaging. Most electrical devices gave off heat, and many had tiny red or blue LED lights on all the time, providing enough ambient light for the suit's night vision to work.

Before entering the room, he took a moment to scan the titles of books and magazines on the shelves. First, he saw an English translation of Mein Kampf by Adolf Hitler, "The Doctrine of Fascism" by Benito Mussolini, and Soldiers of God: White Supremacists and Their Holy War for America. Then, picking up a magazine from a thick stack, he discovered a white nationalist'sAmerican Renaissance copy.

Josh frowned. There were other books and magazines, but he'd seen enough. Stepping inside the room and to the left with his back to the wall, he examined the green glow of Riley's 250-square-foot underground bachelor pad. He noticed a motion detector near the ceiling in the far corner to his immediate right, but didn't worry. Even if the motion detector was active, the suit did not give off heat.

Along the opposite wall, he saw the kitchen and, to the right of that, a closed king-size Murphy bed. To the left, a large flat-screen TV with a couch and chair plopped in front of it. Next to the bed, there was a shower stall that included a toilet inside the same glassed-in space.

The area offered all the standard conveniences, with several feet of reinforced concrete for a roof and lots of packed earth.

Once he determined the place was empty, he activated his mike and said "greenlight" three times. Then he waited to hear a series of clicks answering his call, letting him know his teams were advancing.

The exit from Riley's quarters into the twenty-five-foot passage leading to LG location stood open, revealing a closed door at the other end. When Josh reached it, he placed his helmet against its metal surface and listened.

A song played on the other side, and it took a moment to recognize it as Cyndi Lauper's "Time After Time." There was also a 1979 science fiction film with the same title. Josh knew the song and the film well because they were among LG's shortlist of favorites. A rush of anger filled his head when he realized Riley was using the music to taunt Josh's mentor and friend.

Breathe, he thought. I have to be calm before I go through that door. He didn't think Riley was aware of his invisible combat suit. It was so secret that no one outside of DARPA, including the President of the United States, knew it existed. This was the first time it was being tested in actual combat, with only two in existence.

Josh hesitated to open the door and slip into the room beyond. A heavy, solid-core, fireproof door like this one didn't open by itself. If Riley saw the door open enough to let Josh slip through, that might alert him. He wanted to have the element of surprise and enough time to study the situation before acting, another luxury the suit provided. Once it was available for Special Operations Forces, he wondered how long it would take the Russians or Chinese to come up with a way to detect one.

Filling his lungs and holding his breath, Josh took hold of the doorknob, ready to risk discovery. But what other choice did he have?

Before he turned the knob, he felt it turn on its own. Yanking his hand back, Josh took a few steps away from the door. He watched as it swung open, revealing a nude, pale, plump man splattered with blood.

Josh hadn't expected that.

"Look," the man said, throwing the words over his shoulder, "I've got to pee. I should've had your father add a bathroom to our research lab. Get over it. Do nothing with our lab rat while I'm gone. I don't want to miss any of the fun." His laughter sounded like a donkey braying. "Did you get the joke?"

"Not funny," a woman's humorless voice replied from inside the torture chamber. "Even if he still had all of his cock, I wouldn't let him stick it in me. I'm going to tell Daddy you're talking to me like I'm a whore again."

"Eva," the man said with a whiny crybaby voice, "come on, darling. Promise not to play with that traitor while I'm taking a pee."

"Hurry!" She snarled the word.

The man closed the door, turned, and Josh saw his face. There was no mistaking that this was Riley Pearl. As the exposed man walked the narrow tunnel's length, Josh moved backward until they were both inside Riley's quarters.

Who is this Eva, Josh thought, and who is her father? Is there anyone else in the torture chamber? One mistake, and I could get LG killed. Then he remembered what Eva had said about LG's cock, and his anger was back with a vengeance. He hated losing control and rushing things. When he let anger decide for him, he always regretted it later.

Josh heard Riley talking to himself as he hurried toward the toilet inside the shower stall. "You're my whore, bitch," he said, "and your daddy can go fuck himself."

Halfway across his one-room flat, Riley stopped and stared at the open bookshelf to the escape shaft. "What the fuck!" he said.

Without thinking, Josh grabbed Riley by his neck and yanked him back. He used his other arm to hit him under the jaw with an upward front elbow strike. The jaw shattered with bone fragments and teeth being driven through the roof of the mouth into the sinuses.

Josh leaped away from the shower of blood, and let the man's dead body drop. When Riley's corpse hit the polished concrete, his naked flesh made a wet smacking sound.

Holy shit! he thought. What a clusterfuck! In the heat of the moment, he'd forgotten the suit quadrupled his strength. Whatever info Riley knew about Tweet's organization had died with him.

He didn't bother checking to make sure the man was dead. Riley's eyeballs had exploded from their sockets.

Josh took off, running down the tunnel toward the half-open door at the other end. When he entered the torture chamber and stopped to scan the room, he saw two people. There was the woman Riley had called Eva and what was left of Lieutenant General Linus Lamont Graves.

The shock of seeing the ravaged nude body of his friend and mentor froze his ability to think logically.

They'd strapped LG with heavy-duty zip ties to a metal rack bolted to one wall, and it spread his arms and legs painfully wide.

Eva was standing close to LG, staring at his mangled face. "All that asshole wants to do is fuck me while torturing you. We snip off one of your finger joints, and while you're screaming, before I have time to cauterize the wound to stop the bleeding, Riley makes me get on the floor and mounts me like I'm a mutt. That's your fault, nigger. Every time we slice another quarter inch off your shrinking sausage, he pushes me against the wall and takes me standing up." She started laughing. "And I love it all. This is such a rush. What do you think about that?" She took a step back and placed both hands on her hips to study LG as if he was a sculpture in the making.

Reaching out, she took hold of LG's chin and forced him to look at her. "Hey, Coon, you've inspired me. Here goes. Listen up now. The sinful artist strips the false god cold. Because he's naked, the demon's sculpture is deformed. There is beauty in broken bones and stripped flesh."

Her body was splattered with blood and gore. She reached behind her for a camera sitting on a stainless-steel table. Picking it up, she used it to snap a picture of the human wreckage hanging from the vertical rack.

Josh couldn't take his eyes off LG. One eye socket was an

empty black hole with scabs and oozing puss. The other one was mostly black and blue, almost swollen shut. Only a thin slit between the lid revealed the remaining eye. Rectangular strips of skin were missing from all over his body, showing the raw connective tissue beneath the missing epidermis. They had also scalped him.

He keyed his radio and said, "If you are a medic and your team doesn't need you, I want you in the torture chamber now." He wasn't worried she'd hear him. The suit made sure of that, and she couldn't have heard Riley dying. The door to the torture chamber had been closed. Josh took a halting step toward his friend, and his boot hit something on the floor, sending it rattling and spinning across the concrete. It was a stainless-steel bowl with what looked like some of LG's bloody body parts in it.

Eva said, "It's about time you got back. Stop calling me Eva. I'm not Hitler's girlfriend, and you are not the Führer. My name is Dorothea Tweet. I expect you to treat me with respect since my daddy pays the bills for this place." She turned and stopped talking when she saw no one was there.

She scanned the room and shrugged. "I must be hearing things." She picked up a bone snipper and moved toward LG, who moaned.

"I'm not waiting for that idiot," she said. She jabbed LG in the stomach with an index finger. "What do you think, you damn Black Lives Matter traitor? Should I take off the rest of your small left toe?"

Consumed by rage, Josh grabbed her from behind by the neck and lifted her off the floor. Surprised, she screamed and thrashed around. He squeezed and fractured her larynx, cutting off the noise she was making. Then, with his other hand on her chin, he twisted her head 180 degrees to the right, snapping her spine. Once she was no longer struggling and hung limp in his grasp, he discarded her.

Reaching LG, he caressed the side of his friend's face, and Josh's voice cracked when he said, "What have they done to you?"

LG struggled to lift his chin off his chest enough to spot the dead woman sprawled on the cold concrete floor. Then he croaked, "Is that you, Josh? Please help me die."

# CHAPTER 33

MIA LIVED A MINIMALIST LIFESTYLE, but she was never alone when she went for her morning runs. Her three bodyguards and her longtime friend and assistant, Giselle, were always with her. They dressed in the same dark-grey, loose-fitting cotton sweats with their faces hidden inside the shadowy hoods, five look-alikes.

Giselle carried the special phone, the one that had been silent for weeks. The longer that phone remained quiet, the more Mia's preferred sense of calm was roiled by mental stress.

Why hadn't Josh called or sent her an e-mail? They'd never been out of touch this long before. When Mia said no to him the second time, he asked her to marry him; she didn't expect him to vanish. She'd taken it for granted that their relationship would stay the same. Josh had witnessed the traffickers raping her and the other girls before he and Cheéte rescued them. Because of that one night when she was fourteen, he knew they were the only two men she trusted.

Just thinking about what had happened back then caused the skin on her arms to break out in goosebumps. The first man Josh had shot was the one on top of her, and she'd seen the trafficker's head explode. Cheéte had fired the second shot. Seconds later, all the traffickers were dead.

Her bodyguards—Shani, Naomi, and Esther—planned every run, so there was never a pattern to the routes they took. Instead, Mia thought of them as the tip of her spear. Since Josh had hired them to protect her, one of them was always with her, even at home.

This morning, they were running the six-and-a-half-kilometer Saint-Jean-Cap-Ferrat Coastal Trail and enjoying its spectacular views.

When Giselle stopped and slipped the hood off her head, Mia asked, "What is it?"

"The phone vibrated."

An electric shock rushed through Mia.

The instant they'd stopped, Shani, Naomi, and Esther had moved into positions around the pair facing out, ready to deal with any threats. Fortunately, that early in the morning, soon after dawn, no one else was on the path. Mia shot a gloved hand out toward Giselle. "Let me see."

Giselle pulled the phone out of a pocket and thumbed in the password, then turned the screen so Mia could see the text. It read, "fifty-seven rescued kittens in Montana. Hot wings waiting at NCE. G's SO ok. NISM. LY4E."

After Mia interpreted Josh's text message, it was all she could do not to smile. Back in Haiti in 1994, she'd been one of those stray kittens. The rest of the text message was for Giselle. Her husband was a member of Josh's Oath Group.

Mia understood why Josh wanted her to move fast. She'd read a recent piece in The Irish Times written by Fintan O'Toole that said, "Babies in cages were no 'mistake' by Trump but test-marketing for barbarism."

The trafficked children Josh had rescued in Montana had to

be undocumented. Suppose Trump's US Immigration and Customs Enforcement (ICE) agents got hold of them. In that case, they'd be sent back to the countries they'd been abducted from and end up dead or kidnapped again.

This was going to be a first for Mia's rescue organization. Instead of finding homes in the United States for the young rescued sex slaves, they were going to be smuggling them out of the United States to a safer country in the European Union.

What was happening in the US was unforgivable. The Statue of Liberty had been a gift from France in 1886. The 105-word sonnet written by Emma Lazarus engraved in bronze and added to the statue in 1901 was no longer valid: "Give me your tired, your poor, your huddled masses yearning to breathe free...."

Mia turned to her bodyguards and said, "We have to drive directly to Nice Côte d'Azur Airport. There is no time to pack." Her man was asking her for help. She would not fail him.

She thought about their history together. Mia had been fourteen, and Josh was nineteen the night he rescued her. It was easy to imagine that moment again. How could she ever forget? She was naked and had been drenched with her dead attacker's blood when Josh came out of the dark looking like a gorilla in his camouflage. She'd scrambled away from him, her legs churning in fear, but when he knelt beside her and pulled off the head piece, revealing his features, that was when her life changed in a heartbeat. Looking into his compassionate gray-blue eyes had pierced her soul, and she fell in love. Before the month ended, she told him how she felt.

The age difference hadn't been a problem for her, but it was for him. In France, where there was no clear legal age of consent as there was in most countries, turning fifteen meant they legally considered you an adult.

In a gentle voice, he'd replied, "I love you, too, but my answer has to be no." When he'd seen her face crumple, he continued,

"I'm not rejecting you. I'm saving you from the regrets you'll feel later. I'm not the kind of guy you want to be in love with. I'm also in love with someone waiting for me in Montana. One day, you'll understand and thank me. If it's okay with you, I want to remain friends."

"What is the name of your lover?" Mia had asked with a calm expression, but her heart had been thudding like a drum.

"It's Rachel," he'd replied.

Still, they became best friends, and she couldn't forget that conversation.

In Haiti, Mia's name had been Sisi Teo. To protect her and the others, Cheéte had said they'd get new names and identities.

Once she'd turned sixteen, the age of consent in Montana, with Giselle coaching her, Mia had ratcheted up the charm in small increments over the years to seduce Josh. He was almost thirty when she finally conquered him. Even then, if his Rachel hadn't married someone else, breaking his heart, she might have failed.

Josh and Mia's love story wasn't the only one born in Haiti the day they rescued her and Giselle from the traffickers. Giselle ended up marrying another Marine in Josh's unit. He was thirty-nine and had already been in the Marines for twenty years the day they met. To stay close to Giselle, he'd retired early and followed her to France, where they were married a few years later. The age difference hadn't bothered him like it did Josh.

Now, as Giselle and Mia, along with Mia's bodyguards, reached the airport a few kilometers outside of Nice, a Lockheed C-130J Super Hercules that belonged to The Oath Group was waiting. Not all of Josh's teams were in Montana. More than half were operating in Iraq and Afghanistan or another third-world country.

The pilot said they'd be stopping twice to refuel, and it would take about fifteen hours to reach Idaho and The Oath Group's potato farm.

This would be Mia and Giselle's first trip to the United States. Since they had French passports with an embedded chip from an internationally approved Electronic System for Travel Authorization (ESTA), they did not need to apply for a visa to enter that country.

Mia turned to her bodyguards and asked, "I do not know what Josh has been doing for the last few weeks. His text didn't provide any details regarding how he rescued these trafficked children. I'd like to be prepared before we reach Idaho. Do you know someone you can call to find out?"

There was a moment of silence before Giselle said, "They don't have to call any of their contacts in the Mossad. My man has been telling me some of what Josh has been doing in Montana and Idaho."

"What are you waiting for?" Mia asked. "Tell me."

Giselle broke eye contact. Her expression caused a void to open inside of Mia, fearing what she might hear. Still, she had to know and said, "Please."

Giselle chewed on her lower lip and looked sad. Then she nodded, made eye contact, and said, "The last thing my husband told me was that Josh went home to his family ranch because a rich man's son had raped his sister. Josh's family was getting death threats. A few days later, Josh married Rachel. That's all I know."

Shani cleared her throat, and everyone turned to stare at her. "I was curious about Josh's silence, too, and made some calls. It's true that his sister was raped and there have been death threats against his family, but Josh didn't return to Montana to marry Rachel. I was told the US Department of Defense hired his Oath Group to assess the threat level from white racist militias in the American Northwest."

Other than the drone of the aircraft's engines, the silence was heavy. A moment later, Mia said, "Thank you." Hearing that Josh had married his childhood sweetheart was a shock. She hadn't seen that coming.

She left the others and found a secluded spot inside the cavernous cargo hold where she could be alone with her thoughts. Josh was the only man she trusted, the only man she'd ever loved. She had to figure out a way to keep him in her life.

# CHAPTER 34

IN NORTHWEST MONTANA, in an underground neo-Nazi torture chamber, Josh watched several former Special Operations Combat Medics (SOCM) working desperately to patch LG together and save his life.

Their prisoner, Charles Tweet, was secured to another stainless-steel table. He was being questioned using DARPA's experimental drugs and equipment. He looked like he was also receiving intensive care, with all the tubes and wires attached to him.

The rest of Josh's people, who hadn't left for Idaho, were getting rid of any evidence that might link his group to the raid. Eight neo-Nazis were dead, and that included Pearl and his girlfriend, the billionaire's daughter. Their bodies would vanish, but the FBI'd list them as fugitives who escaped the raid. Another dozen had been wounded and treated. The survivors would get a dose of the drug that would erase their memories from the last twenty-four hours.

Even though some of Josh's men had been hit, their SPS high-strength ceramic body armor had protected them. The Oath Group had not suffered one casualty. Not even a flesh wound.

The fifty-seven trafficked slaves they'd freed were also on Chinooks in route to the farm in Idaho, where Mia would pick them up and fly them out of the States.

"Fire in the hole," he heard through his earbud. There was a thump, and the ground shook as they destroyed another bunker. Only one structure was going to survive, and it was in the one-acre compound at the north end of the ranch. The top floor of the barn-sized building held at least a ton of pure cocaine waiting to be diluted with a cutting agent. They also equipped the same space as a modern laboratory.

Tweet had already revealed that a ton of cocaine reached the ranch each month, then was cut and shipped out. For every dollar he spent on the illegal drug, he made ten. Underground, where the children had been locked in cages, there were enough illegal firearms and ammo to fight a war. Tweet had been selling those weapons to other right-wing extremist militia groups, earning another tidy profit.

The area where the trafficked slaves had been located now held the ranch's surviving inhabitants. Tweet had been moving about 900 through the ranch annually. He sent most of the girls to massage parlors, where they had to turn thirty-to-fifty tricks a day and were lucky to get four hours of sleep a night. They auctioned the virgin beauties on a darknet website. Those girls also never got a day off as they had to service at least one client a day.

Tweet had revealed that the profits for each slave ranged from thousands to hundreds of thousand of dollars before their usefulness ended. Then he'd said, "After they were no use to me anymore, I had them eliminated." His exact words.

When Josh heard him say that, an Antarctic chill had swept through him. He'd almost torn the man's throat out and ended it there, but Brianne had talked him out of it.

Tweet preferred to traffic young girls between twelve and sixteen, but complained that the lifespan of his "working girls" was too short. Another shipment was due in a few days, and Josh was going to keep one team here to rescue them.

Tweet's share of slaves smuggled into the country was less than five percent of the total, and they earned him close to thirty million a year.

That was the last thing Josh heard before he walked away from the fat, malignant narcissist strapped to the stainless-steel table. If he'd heard anymore, he would've killed the bastard, and nothing would've stopped him.

Brianne's FBI team was in the northern compound, taking inventory of the cocaine, weapons, and ammo. Brianne and Cheéte stood on either side of Josh, dressed like the rest of his men now that the two DARPA warrior suits had served their purpose and were on their way back to Area 51, along with the stealth birds.

"What do you want to do with Tweet?" Brianne asked. Cheéte had told her that the young girl he'd rescued from Tweet had been close to death when he'd found them in that underground room.

The previous year, her agency had reported that about 66,000 American children were likely victims of sex trafficking each year. That was almost four times the number of foreign children smuggled into the country. They were snatched off the streets close to their homes and were often brutalized and raped by the traffickers to get them ready for paying customers.

Though Josh had heard Tweet say he preferred foreign teens because it was easier to control them since most of them didn't speak English and were a long way from home.

Thinking about what he'd heard and seen had given Josh a headache. "As soon as we finish questioning him, he's all yours," Josh said to the FBI agent. "He won't remember anything that happened for the last twenty-four hours, but you'll know all the details of his crimes that will put him away for the rest of his life."

The soon-to-be penniless billionaire was telling them everything: where every young girl he'd raped and murdered was buried and how he'd kept his failing financial empire alive.

Before they were done, Brianne and her FBI team would know where to find the evidence, including most of the bodies that would convict this monster and put him behind bars for a dozen life sentences with no chance of parole. His odds of beating the charges were slim to nothing.

"I hope they send the bastard to the Supermax in Colorado," Josh said.

"Even that prison is too good for him," Brianne replied. "He'll live in safe isolation there. I want him sent to the next level down, a high-security prison. Once he's with the general population, it will be the same as a death sentence once the other inmates discover what he's been doing with little girls like the one Cheéte saved. If he isn't killed, he'll live in fear for the rest of his life."

After a moment of silence, she asked, "What about his missing son? Do you know what happened to him?"

"You don't want to know."

Cheéte added, "He wouldn't tell me either."

"I'm not asking as an FBI agent," Brianne said. "I don't care what happens to anyone in this family. Just curious."

"Well," Josh said, "I heard he fled to North Korea seeking asylum and when he couldn't prove who he was, they arrested him. It seems the damn fool arrived without a passport or ID of any kind, just some incrementing photos of one of their military installations. Then there were witnesses that accused him of raping one of their girls."

Brianne's eyes sparkled, and her lips twitched. "Sounds like poetic justice. If he's convicted, North Korea is one of nine countries with the death penalty for rape."

"There is also no extradition treaty with the US," Josh added.

"We also got all the Tweet family's offshore account numbers from that sick fuck," Cheéte added, nodding at the naked billionaire strapped to the stainless-steel operating table.

"How much?" she asked.

"About 320 million," Josh said, "and that money is going to be used to save more trafficked children."

"Good." Brianne nodded.

Josh's satellite phone chirped, and he answered. "How is LG doing?" a four-star Navy SEAL admiral from SOCOM asked.

"Not good. He wants us to put him down, so he never wakes up. I can't make that decision."

"Understood," the admiral replied. "We'll make that decision, not you. We're on our way and will arrive soon."

The three men on the way to the former neo-Nazi ranch—two four-star generals and the admiral—were all LG's friends and had known him longer than Josh had.

"Thank you, Admiral. He was more of a father to me than my dad." Josh felt tears stinging his eyes, and his voice was husky with emotion. Without saying a word, Cheéte put a hand on Josh's shoulder and squeezed.

"We regret what happened to your wife," the admiral said. "Do you want help to find Damien Bran? We have friends in the CIA who are more than willing to do the job."

"Thank you, sir, but no. I will track Bran down myself, no matter how long it takes. I'll find him, even if it's in Russia or North Korea."

There was a moment of silence before the admiral continued, "We've watched the videos of all their victims you found in that torture chamber. When you catch him, take your time before you send him to hell. Now, let me talk to Agent Hemmings."

Pearl and his girlfriend had filmed everyone they'd tortured. LG wasn't their only victim. In some videos, Bran was helping them. Charles Tweet had appeared in two, but he only watched, his face filled with interest and fascination.

Josh handed the phone to Brianne. She went to a far corner in the underground room for more privacy.

"What are your plans now that this operation is ending?" Cheéte asked Josh.

"Wait for the brass to arrive and stay until they make their decision regarding LG. Then hop on a flight to the farm in Idaho in time to be there before Mia and Giselle arrive from France." He glanced at a digital clock hanging on a wall. "They should land in ten hours."

Josh couldn't take his eyes off the billionaire. He wanted to strap that fat bastard to the rack where LG had been tortured and skin him alive with a dull blade. But his conscience told him that if he did that, he'd be no better than Charles Tweet.

Cheéte said, "We want to know if you're planning any more operations like this one."

"When you say 'we,' are you talking for your team? What we're doing isn't exactly legal."

"They got to catch us first." Cheéte's face was unreadable. It was obvious he was angry and shaken from what he'd witnessed, too.

Josh shook his head while watching Tweet and struggling to control his rage. "Sorry, but there are no plans to target another militia. From what we've learned, this group was one of the worst. Most of my people will leave the country to work for the DOD in the war against terrorism, but I'll be staying to be close to Rachel and spend more time with the son and daughter I just met."

"They're going to have questions about how their mother ended up in a shootout in San Francisco. Are you ready for that?"

Josh shrugged. "I'll deal with it." He turned to his friend. "If you want to join The Oath Group, your team will be welcome, but if you aren't interested, don't ask me any more questions about what we do. The less you know, the better off we'll all be."

Josh took a shuddering breath, and his shoulders sagged. "But first, I have this operation to wrap up, and I'll be talking to Mia about Rachel. There's also Damien Bran. As long as he's alive, he'll always be a threat to my family and those I love. I will not rest until I've removed the Strawman from the chessboard."

Cheéte pursed his lips and fingered his chin. "Tell you what," he said. "I'll talk to my team. If they're interested, I'll let you know. After all, we have children, and some of us have grandchildren. It'd be nice to leave this world knowing we did our best to make it a better place."

"Fair enough," Josh replied. "Let's get out of here and take a walk where the air is fresh. This room has a repulsive odor, and it's giving me a pounding headache."

"Me too," Cheéte said. "Evil has soaked itself into the concrete."

That Evil is not just in this concrete, Josh thought. People that joined these violent militias have turned their ears away from the truth. Thanks to his mother's teachings, he knew Jesus had warned more than once that prior to His Second Coming, 'many false prophets will rise, and shall deceive many.'

# CHAPTER 35

JOSH REACHED the 5,000-acre potato farm in Idaho with minutes to spare before the C-130 arrived with Mia. He stood in front of the hangar as the aft loading ramp opened, revealing five women. Looking like a rock band, they were dressed in dark-gray, baggy sweats with hoodies concealing their features.

Josh knew the first two down the ramp would be Shani and Naomi. Their observant senses were like radar. Mia and Giselle would be next, with Esther bringing up the rear. As they reached the tarmac, everyone but Mia headed to the hangar behind Josh. When Giselle saw her husband waiting inside, she broke into a run.

Without a word, Mia walked into Josh's arms. She was five inches taller than Rachel, and her face fit in the space between his shoulder and chin while Rachel would've been listening to his heartbeat. They held each other in silence, and he thought about the unofficial vows he'd said when he married Rachel. The last phrase echoed in his mind, "I pledge thee my faith."

"Think of it as a commitment ceremony," his mother had said. "We'll take care of the paperwork later."

With a knot forming in his throat, he said, "I have something to tell you."

"I already know."

With those words, she dismantled the rationale behind his defense. Mia made his guilt worse when she touched his face with gentle, loving fingertips. Why is she doing this to me? he thought.

Seeing her radiant caramel-colored complexion, her tawny hair, and her bright-green eyes hypnotized him. That always happened after they'd been apart for too long. And, as usual, he had to force himself to breathe again.

"I can tell you were worried I'd be angry. Why would I? You're a man. It's your nature. You've been with other women as I have been with other men. If our relationship is strong, it will survive this too. The only way you're going to lose me is if you are the one who walks away."

Without thought, his mouth opened, and one sentence fell out. "I wouldn't have had my mother marry me to Rachel if you'd said yes."

She stared at him for a long moment, causing him to squirm inside. Waiting for her reaction was like stepping on a Bouncing Betty. When triggered, those landmines launched into the air and detonated about a yard from the ground, cutting a person in two.

"Have you forgotten my answer to your proposals?" she finally asked.

"You said marriage was slavery."

She nodded. "I'm glad you didn't forget. I was concerned you might have developed a short memory span like too many of your country's people."

"With me," he said, "it's the opposite. I can't forget anything."

Slipping away from him, she turned and hooked an arm through one of his. "Let's take a walk."

Multiple layered rows of red pine used as windbreaks surrounded the farm. That natural wall also offered privacy from prying eyes, so they were relatively safe out in the open. With the surveillance technology The Oath Group used, it was almost impossible to infiltrate the area undiscovered.

The first hundred paces were silent before she said, "I want to meet Rachel."

Josh hadn't expected that. Startled, the blood drained out of his head, pooled in his guts, and thickened into knots. Josh wasn't sure he'd heard her right. "What did you say?"

She stopped and faced him. They were so close, her lips were within kissing distance. "You have loved three women in your life," she said. "Those you did not love don't count. They were only meeting your physical needs."

He'd only loved two women, actually: Rachel and Mia. If there was someone else, he'd know, wouldn't he? "I haven't loved three women," he said.

"You love your mother, regardless of your mixed feelings for her. You love Rachel, and you love me. Is that not correct?"

"I..." The rest of the words he wanted to say ran away before he got them out.

"Listen carefully," Mia said. "I want to meet her. She was your childhood sweetheart and gave birth to two of your children."

The way she'd said that made it sound like he had more children out there. "Do you want to meet them too?" he asked.

"No, I don't want that. They'd probably hate me and never forgive you. After all, they are Americans. If they were French, well..." She shrugged.

There was no reason to argue. She was right. They were standing in the middle of a cultivated field, far from the nearest building. She started walking again, and he joined her with their arms once again linked.

"How did you know about Rachel?" he asked. "And what are you going to gain by seeing her? She's in a coma. Her doctors said because of the trauma to her head and body, she might never wake up."

"Soon after we left France, Giselle spilled the secret about the marriage," she replied. "Then my girls told me about the shooting in San Francisco."

She was talking about her bodyguards. Of course, they'd know. They had connections all over the world through the Mossad.

"With all that flight time, I did some reading and learned that it is challenging to predict recovery because every coma is different. That means she will awake one day. What are you going to do when that happens...abandon her like you did when you joined the Marines?" They'd stopped again, and she pulled her arm free of his and took two steps back.

He wanted to defend himself, that he'd never dumped Rachel, but his mouth had turned Death Valley dry. It wasn't his fault that they had deployed him to one hot spot after another, and she married someone else while he was gone. *Why do the women I love always do this to me?* he thought.

Mia laughed. "I have finally cut off your tongue. That is a first." She stepped closer and punched him lightly in the stomach. "Well?"

"What do you want to do?"

"Keep us a secret. I don't want you to have to make a choice, and I don't think there are many American women capable of accepting the way things are between us." Without another word, she moved closer and hooked arms with him again, then they continued their walk.

---

A few days later, in San Francisco, Josh stood behind Mia at two in the morning as she hovered beside Rachel's hospital bed. Visiting hours had ended long ago, but Josh had called a friend who called a friend, and they had made an exception. At this hour, he hoped they wouldn't run into anyone from his family, like his son and daughter. He hardly knew them and wasn't ready to face them again, not yet anyway.

Seeing Rachel looking so helpless and frail with her shaved head, the stitches, bandages, tubes, and wires rattled Josh as nothing had ever done before, and he shuddered. In his line of work as a Tier 1 Operator, danger and death were a constant risk, but this was different. As confusing as it seemed, he loved her as much as he loved Mia. Losing even one of them would be like having half of his heart cut out. Could he survive? He didn't want to find out.

As if she sensed what he was thinking, Mia reached behind her, took one of his hands, and pulled him forward until he was beside her. Then she put her lips next to his ear and whispered, "Men fall in love with their eyes, and now I know why she captured your heart at such a young age. She must have been a precious jewel as a child. From now on, Rachel will be my secret sister, and I will also love her. However, we can never meet because then I'd steal her happiness. Since I know what that's like, I would not wish that on her. No one else must know about us, not even Giselle."

Since Mia had walked down that C-130 ramp in Idaho, his emotions had been in turmoil. As they left Rachel's room, the hallway seemed clotted with blessed silence. The nurse at her station didn't look up as they walked past her toward the elevator. Once they were inside the sealed box, dropping toward the ground floor, Josh asked, "What about Doctor Tate?"

Mia avoided eye contact and didn't reply.

Shit! Josh thought. He didn't want to lie to Dr. Tate. That

wouldn't work. She'd see right through any attempt to deceive her. There was only one choice. He'd cancel his counseling appointments for the time being.

That idea bothered him, because he counted on Dr. Tate to help keep him centered so he could manage his demons.

Damn, what was he going to do? He'd been between the proverbial rock and a hard place many times before, but this time...What a clusterfuck!

Now that Mia was back in his life, he didn't want to lose her again. They'd been friends before they were lovers, much longer than he'd been with Rachel. Cheéte's suggestion that he could have both of them floated to the surface, a temptation impossible to ignore. Then Dr. Tate's voice joined his mother's, telling him that was wrong.

# CHAPTER 36

ARLINGTON NATIONAL CEMETERY is on Confederate General Robert E. Lee's confiscated estate. In the summer, it was more brown than green. The 624-acre city of the dead was the last resting place of over 400,000 men and women. Many had died in combat. Above, a thin gray haze smeared the humid sky, and in the distance, an invading pale-blue band of color was spreading slowly across the horizon.

An average of twenty-five burials were performed daily here.

For this burial, eight pallbearers marched with military precision to the back of a hearse to remove a flag-draped coffin. They all wore starched dress uniforms representing the Army, the Navy, and the Marines. Two of the pallbearers were four-star Army generals, one a four-star Navy admiral, an Army general with three stars, and another with two. There was also a full-bird colonel and the Sergeant Major of the Army. Josh was wearing his Marine Corps Dress Blue uniform.

Every man carrying the coffin had rows of medals over his left breast. They all had Purple Hearts with oak leaf clusters or small stars, showing they'd been wounded more than once.

Josh shouldered his share of the coffin. It was no burden at all. In fact, it seemed light as a feather. LG had written in his last will and testament that he wanted one eulogy given by Josh. As he took one step after another, Josh thought about what he was going to say. Every time I think I'm important, I'll remember how modest LG was. Even as a three-star general, I saw him treat privates with great respect and cry with them when friends were wounded or died in combat. I don't think I ever saw him discourteous to anyone. If someone deserved a dressing down, he'd talk softly, respectfully. Somehow, that made it worse, and no one who served with LG wanted to disappoint him.

While an Army band played, the pallbearers carried the coffin from the hearse to the bed of an open wagon pulled by three horses wearing empty saddles. The band then led the procession along the road toward LG's ultimate resting place.

As the wagon carrying the coffin reached the ten-foot-long, five-foot-wide plot, thousands of trees scattered across the cemetery were in full foliage. The army of white marble headstones, thirteen inches across and forty-eight inches tall, marched into the distance. That landscape offered too many places for a sniper to hide and send someone else to an early grave.

If Bran the Strawman was out there, Josh's sister Susan was a potential target, and so was he.

Precautions had been taken. The DOD, CIA, and the Oath Group had men spread throughout the area, and high-flying drones were scanning for any signs of a potential threat. While the pallbearers moved the coffin from the hearse to the wagon, a bomb-sniffing dog and its handler checked out the gravesite.

They decided the odds were against Damien Bran attempting to kill Josh and his sister here. It was too risky. Bran was known to only act when the odds were in his favor, but desperate men did dumb things.

During the meeting earlier, the Navy SEAL admiral had his

eyes on Josh when he said, "If I knew I was a dead man running, I'd want to take out my biggest threat."

The Sergeant Major of the Army replied, "I read Bran's uncensored CIA profile, and I don't think he's that foolish. He's probably hiding in a country unfriendly to the US."

"I agree," an Army general said. "That man has developed assets all over the world, and he has many friends who were former Nazis. Precautions, of course, must be taken."

That was why Josh and his sister were sweating more than anyone else. They wore bullet-proof long underwear made of a nano-multilayer grapheme fabric, another short-term loan from DARPA. It was better than Kevlar and absorbed ten times the kinetic energy that steel did.

While Josh was out in the open with the pallbearers, walking beside the wagon, Suki was dressed like all of LG's former wives and standing with them. Clumped together, they were wearing matching black outfits with wide-brimmed hats and dark glasses. The two oldest, along with Suki, even had black lattice veils covering their faces. Behind the women were LG's platoon of children and grandchildren. It would be almost impossible for a sniper to identify his sister in that crowd. No, if anyone was an easy target, it was him, and he hoped the bastard was here and would take the shot.

Then there were dozens of men in military uniforms who had served with LG. Some were retired, and others still on active duty. A few had come with their families—and Mia, also dressed in black with a hat and large, aviator-style dark glasses, was with that group. Her three bodyguards were with her. Mia had met LG years ago, and they'd become friends.

As Josh and the other pallbearers lifted the coffin off the wagon and slowly stepped toward LG's patch of ground, he thought about the last week.

After the trip to San Francisco with Mia, Giselle had returned to France with almost a hundred rescued children. Mia had stayed behind for the funeral.

Over the years, with Josh and LG's help, she'd put together a network of agents who gathered information. Then Mia sent in her twelve-man strike team to hit hard and fast. They never spared the traffickers. The rescued children ended up with new identities and families to live with. Her organization was as secretive as Josh's Oath Group, but not as large.

With almost 46 million people enslaved in 167 countries, including the United States, it was a daunting, never-ending challenge.

Josh stood at attention beside his mentor's grave when the honor guard fired three volleys from their rifles. If Bran was there, this was when he'd take the shot. When it didn't happen, Josh was disappointed.

Then the Army bugler played "Taps" and tears wet Josh's eyes.

When the funeral was over and Mia on a flight back to France, Josh wondered how long Damien would evade him and the army of spooks searching for him. The man was in his eighties, and from his medical records, it was apparent he wasn't that healthy. The bastard might die before they found him, but Josh was counting on the stubborn, misguided fool holding on for another decade or two, at least long enough to find him and make him pay.

Since there was no need to rush, Josh had taken a well-earned month off. He was going to spend some of that time in San Francisco with his mother, grandmothers, and Rachel before returning to Montana to work beside his father on the ranch. It's what Rachel had wanted, so he was going to make it happen.

His mother was paying for an air ambulance from the Air-MedCare Network to transport Rachel from San Francisco to the ranch. One of the five bedrooms was being converted into a hospital room, and private nurses had been hired, so one would be on site at all times.

---

Legacy.com obituary: Green Beret Lt. Gen. Linus Lamont Graves (US Army Retired) Medal of Honor Recipient was born in Lubbock, Texas, in 1945. He graduated as a second lieutenant from the United States Military Academy at West Point in 1968, and served his country for thirty-nine years in many countries, such as Vietnam, Lebanon, Grenada, Panama, Somalia, Serbia, Iraq, and Afghanistan. He retired from active duty in 2007 but continued to serve as a private military contractor until his death in 2018 at seventy-three. Lt. Gen. Graves was buried with full honors at Arlington National Cemetery. His family and friends attended the funeral.

Thank you for reading ***The Patriot Oath***. If you enjoyed this **book** (or even if you didn't) please visit the site where you purchased it and write a brief **review**. Your feedback is important to me and will help other readers decide whether to read the **book** too.

Please join **https://thesoulfulveteran.com/** to receive info about military issues/PTSD and to be notified when ***Never for Glory***, the next novel in the Josh Kavanagh Oath Group series, is released or contact me at **lloydlofthouse@gmail.com.**

Printed in Great Britain
by Amazon

41561897R00155